MW00576658

THE LAST TIME WE MET

THE LAST TIME WE MET

A NOVEL

ANNA E. WAHLGREN

TRANSLATED BY ALICE MENZIES

NEW YORK

This is a work of fiction. All of the names, characters, organizations, places and events portrayed in this novel are either products of the author's imagination or are used fictitiously. Any resemblance to real or actual events, locales, or persons, living or dead, is entirely coincidental.

Published in the United States by Crooked Lane Books, an imprint of The Quick Brown Fox & Company LLC.

Crooked Lane Books and its logo are trademarks of The Quick Brown Fox & Company LLC.

Library of Congress Catalog-in-Publication data available upon request.

ISBN (hardcover): 978-1-63910-534-2
ISBN (ebook): 978-1-63910-535-9

Cover design by Heather VenHuizen

Printed in the United States.

www.crookedlanebooks.com

Crooked Lane Books
34 West 27th St., 10th Floor
New York, NY 10001

First Edition: August 2024

10 9 8 7 6 5 4 3 2 1

For Ronny

Friday, July 3, 2009

THE PERSIAN RUG in William's hallway was hidden beneath a sea of discarded shoes the evening everything came to an end. A muddle of strappy sandals, glossy pumps, and dusty sneakers covering the threadbare black and red pattern. The thinning trail snaked past crumpled handbags and black leather laptop bags that had been dumped against the wall, leading toward the heart of the apartment, where the bass from the stereo in the living room pulsed through the walls.

In the kitchen, the air was hot and stuffy. I was in the corner, squashed in behind the round dining table, with my hands clasped in my lap. A cold, damp nose brushed against my leg, and I pushed the little dog away with my foot and watched him trot off down the hallway. The window was wide open, and the sounds of the street down below came flooding in—sounds that still wake me in the middle of the night even now, until the complete silence of my bedroom embraces me once again. Screeching brakes, people shouting, life going on as though nothing had changed. A warm, soft breeze blew in every now and again, carrying the scent of jasmine and cigarette smoke, but I kept my eyes on the slim figure reaching up toward the ceiling.

Ava was balanced precariously on the seat of her chair, but she kept glancing back at me with a smile. Her blond hair was gathered in a bun, and the few rebellious tendrils that had come loose had curled in the sweat on the back of her neck. When she stood on tiptoe to reach higher, her top rode up on her back, revealing a strip of damp, bare skin. Finn was on the floor beside her, wearing a white T-shirt that was clinging to his back, hands trembling with frustration as he watched her every move, ready to catch her if she fell.

I made a real effort to block out all the noise. The music Tess had turned up high in the room next door, the sound of Ava moving china around in the cupboard. Instead, I focused on the dull thud I'd heard a few minutes earlier, expecting to hear it again. A dull thud followed by a scraping, almost creaking sound.

"It's just the pipes," Finn had said. You know what these old buildings are like.

That's all.

Ava briefly lost her balance, and I held my breath as she teetered. Finn caught her a second later, his awkward hands on her hips.

She looked down at him with a grin.

"Where's William?"

The voice tore me out of my trance, and I saw Finn pull his hand back from Ava so quickly he hit the back of the chair. His eyes darted from me to Charlotte, who had appeared in the doorway. She was leaning against the frame with her arms folded, long nails drumming her skin. Her red hair was loose, her entire being an explosion of color in her patterned dress.

"He's not here," Ava replied in a strained voice, her fingers brushing against the glass on the top shelf and pushing it out of reach. "Finn, could you get these glasses down? I don't know why he keeps them so high up."

Before she'd even finished her sentence, Finn had held out a hand and helped her down from the chair. He shot a brief glance toward Charlotte, who ignored him, and then got up onto the chair to grab the tall glasses. Charlotte rolled her eyes and wandered off down the hallway. Without really knowing what I was doing, I got up and followed her, as though in some kind of fever dream.

Her hips swayed as she walked ahead of me, feet swollen from a night in heels as she crossed William's mosaic of mismatched rugs. My fingertips brushed the framed vinyl sleeves on the walls, old concert tickets tucked in at the edges, and I resisted the urge to turn off and disappear through the doorway again. I noticed the red half-moon on the lock on the bathroom door as Adrian barged past me. He started rummaging for his shoes, the whisky on his breath lingering long after he passed.

"Fresh air," he mumbled without even looking at me. As ever, that meant a cigarette down on the street, his phone clamped to his ear.

Charlotte paused in the middle of the living room. The coffee table was barely visible beneath all the beer bottles, but the desk at the far side of the room was clear, the chair turned toward us, as though someone had just leaped up from it. Tess was sprawled on the sofa, with her kohl-lined eyes closed, her highlighted hair spread out like a fan on the crocheted cushion. She had one hand draped across her stomach and the other on her forehead, and her tattooed ankle and foot were bobbing in time with the music, the only sign of life from her.

Hugging myself with one arm, I gripped the doorframe and picked at flaking paint. Beyond Charlotte's back, I could see the open bedroom door, but I knew there was no one in there.

"Seriously, where *is* William?" Charlotte asked again, louder this time, turning down the volume on the stereo.

Tess lowered her hand from her forehead and propped herself up on one elbow. The strap of her black dress slipped down from her shoulder.

"What do you mean?" she asked in her husky voice. She always sounded like she had been screaming at a concert all night, either that or chain-smoking cigarettes with Adrian.

My grip on the doorframe tightened until I felt a stabbing pain in my nails, but I couldn't let go.

"I can't find William," Charlotte continued, slowly turning around, as though she had known I was following her all along.

"Isn't he in here?"

I flinched at the sound of Ava's voice right behind me and moved forward into the living room to get out of her way. Right then, I heard a soft growl in the hallway, followed by a loud bark.

"There's someone in the bathroom," Finn shouted, picking up the little terrier.

The sound of his knocking seemed to reverberate through the air.

"William?"

"Is he in there?" asked Ava.

"It's locked, but I can't hear anything."

Charlotte marched out of the living room, and Tess got up from the sofa and trailed after her. I backed up until I hit the wall, struggling to keep my breathing calm. All alone in the living room, I stared out at the top of the birch tree beyond the French balcony, blinking to force back the burning sensation in my eyes.

"Get a knife from the kitchen," said Ava.

I heard Finn's heavy footsteps on the floor, the sound of rattling cutlery.

His footsteps drew closer again, and I closed my eyes.

I shook my head, as though the movement could chase away what I already felt, deep in my bones. In the hallway, the dog started barking again. As though he knew too. As though he could smell it.

"William?" Charlotte's voice faltered. "Can someone just open the door?"

"Use the knife to turn the lock," Ava mumbled.

I heard the sound of metal on metal, hinges creaking as the door slowly swung open.

Still in the living room, I clamped my hands over my ears just in time to hear Ava's despairing scream cut through the summer night.

TEN YEARS LATER

NOVEMBER 2019

CHAPTER 1

Now

"SO YOU'RE SAYING that love is worth making sacrifices for?"

The radio studio is practically bathed in darkness, but I like to work with the soft, flickering glow of a scented candle on the desk in front of me. It helps to set the mood. That and a cup of hot strawberry tea, laced with rum, to relax my throat and make my voice deeper. Other than the candle, the only light is from my computer screen and the pale green bulb on the post in front of me, letting me know I'm still live on air. The sky outside has been dark for hours, and I push the microphone away in order to muffle a sigh as the rain starts drumming against the window.

The man on the other end of the line is young. He can't be much older than twenty, and I can just imagine how exhausting the constant struggle to fit in and find validation must be at that age. *Why hasn't he called? Why does he call so often?* For your entire life to revolve around whether or not your feelings are reciprocated, whether someone loves you back.

I can hear the beers in his hoarse voice too. Two, possibly three cans of cheap lager.

"I know it is," I reply, my fingers gripping the mic stand. "Love is the most beautiful thing on earth, and it's something we should cling to."

I pull a face as those last few words leave my mouth, and start looking for the right button on the mixer console to start the next track. It doesn't matter what I say; he's never going to be satisfied, and I've run out of clichés. *Dump her.* That's what I really want to tell him. If you're already having problems two months in, then there's hardly any point going on. But this show is supposed to offer hope; my producer is strict on that point. This is a forum for the lonely to share their experiences. "These people don't have anyone else, which means you're important to them. Remember that," Irene always says, peering at me over the top of her glasses. *Night Talk With Natalie* goes out late every Friday and Saturday night, but I'm still not sure how much hope I can really offer when the whole thing is based on a lie.

For one thing, my name is Sophie, not Natalie.

But the biggest lie of all is that it's a relationship show, and I'm playing the expert.

"Even if it means they'll never accep—" he begins, but I don't have the energy to hear him tell me that his girlfriend's parents don't want to meet him—I suspect they have good reason not to—so I cut him off and end the call, just to be on the safe side.

"Always, Niklas. Always. Promise you'll let us know how it goes," I say as the opening notes of Whitney Houston's "I Wanna Dance With Somebody" finally start playing.

Mic level down, headphones off.

There are fifteen minutes of the first *Night Talk* of the week to go. Whitney, another call, then I can thank the listeners with one last tune. I read the text Malika sent me an hour ago, right after she left the studio. I was excited at first, but after reading the full message I turned my phone screen-down and pushed it away.

> *Join us at Simonsson's once you're done? It's karaoke night! Everyone's here.*

Everyone's there.

Thanks but no thanks, I reply. My only plans tonight are with my pillow. Maybe even a glass of Chablis or the dregs of whatever white wine I have open in the fridge. Okay, two or three glasses, plus some terrible horror film on Netflix. I can never usually get to sleep after I've been on air.

The music fades out, and the post in front of me is now glowing blue, one of the phone lines blinking on the screen. Call waiting. I sip my cold tea and wash it down with a mouthful of mineral water straight from the bottle, take a deep breath, and turn the mic level back up before hitting the button to answer the call.

"Listen up, folks, we've got time for one last question. Welcome to *Night Talk With Natalie.* Who do I have on the line?"

Silence. A second passes. Two. The line is still glowing on the screen.

"Anyone there?"

Three seconds, four. Dead air. Radio's worst enemy. My finger hovers over the mixer, ready to end the call. There's a risk that someone might start panting and groaning if I don't, something I personally find far worse than the uncomfortable pause; that's the downside of broadcasting live late at night. But just as my finger finds the button, a quiet voice breaks the silence.

"I'm here."

A woman. Her voice is soft and low. Delicate almost. I have to crank the volume right up in my headphones to be able to hear her.

"Hi there. Just in the nick of time. We can fit in one last quick question, so how can I help you, my friend?"

I hear her breathing, calm and composed but oddly drawn out somehow. It almost sounds like a sigh.

"I have a problem," she says. "I've got feelings for someone I shouldn't."

"Ah," I say with feigned empathy, an icy shiver passing down my spine and making me button my black cardigan. I lean into the mic with my elbows on the desk, as though the movement will bring me closer to her. There's something eerily familiar about her voice. We all have something that characterizes the way we sound—it could be a huskiness, a brightness or a particular timbre—and her voice seems to wake something inside me, but whatever it is, it's too vague for me to pinpoint. I'm the only person still at the station at this time of night, and the doors are locked, but I still spin around in my chair and peer out through the window to the corridor behind me, just in case. There's no one there, of course.

"Then you've called the right place. But I have to ask, is it really a problem? I mean, so long as you're not related, then surely there's nothing stopping you?"

I laugh and wait for her to join in, but my voice is all I can hear in the painfully quiet ether.

"The problem," she says, her voice now firmer—I lean forward, hands pressed to my headphones so I can catch every syllable—"the problem is that I'm already in a relationship."

There it is, the source of all our problems. The burden society dumps on us when it comes to who we're allowed to love and how we should divvy it up. The reason I stopped even trying.

"I understand," I say, blowing out the candle. A thin column of gray smoke curls up toward the ceiling, and I find myself wondering how much it takes to set off the sprinklers. "Tricky. My only advice is to follow your heart and be truthful and honest with everyone involved. You're the only one who knows what's right for you."

With my right foot, I search the floor beneath the desk for my boots, pushing my toes into the top of one of them when I find it.

"Is that what *you* would do?"

It's now my turn not to speak. I glance up at the clock. I'm already running over. There is no time left for the closing music, yet another sultry ballad from the late eighties or early nineties.

"Be truthful and honest, I mean," the woman clarifies, her voice now making my heart race.

"I don't think I caught your name," I say, staring down at the illuminated call on the screen. "Hello? Are you still there?"

The line goes dead. I hear the sound of my own heavy breathing in the microphone, and for a few seconds I just stare at the screen before eventually remembering that I'm still live on air.

"I'm afraid we seem to have lost our connection there, but thank you so much for ringing in. With a bit of luck, your heart will guide you in the right direction. That was all we had time for tonight, but I hope you'll keep me company again tomorrow evening. Until then, sleep well, my friends."

My hand is shaking as I set the theme tune playing, and lean back in my chair with a sigh. I need to stop hosting this show. If it's not lonely men calling in because they want to meet me, it's women who've lost their grip on reality, wanting to put me in my place or waiting outside when I leave. Things have gotten so bad that I've actually started using the back entrance if I see anyone loitering on the street.

But this . . . this was different.

Somewhere, deep down, I already know whose voice that was. But there's no way. This is a local radio station, and I broadcast using a pseudonym.

How could she have found me?

I hurry to switch everything onto autopilot for the night, then I lower the mic level and shut down the studio before grabbing my handbag and scarf from the floor and my black leather jacket from the hook on the wall. Crouching down, I manage to find my other boot beneath the desk, and I pull it on before backing out into the corridor and making sure I've locked up properly.

A soft rain hits my face as I open the front door and step out onto the street. I've been in Malmö for ten years now, but I'm still not used to its mild winters, which seem to consist entirely of pouring rain and sudden gusts of wind rather than swirling snowflakes. I lean back against the door and squint in both directions as I wait for my eyes to get used to the darkness, trying to make sure there isn't anyone lurking in the shadows. With my hands in my pockets and my scarf wrapped tightly around my neck, I cross the street, smiling as two drunk men without coats whistle and shout something inaudible after me. One of them trips on the edge of the sidewalk, and I laugh and shake my head as I round the corner.

I love it. The sounds of the night—or rather the lack of sounds. The narrow streets lying deserted ahead of me, the way I can zigzag down the middle of the road, quietly singing to myself. I love the way the lights of the city bounce off the dark, wet asphalt, and I cut through Folkets Park—something Mom always makes me promise not to do at night. As I pass Tröls Bar, I briefly enjoy the hustle and bustle of the people inside, even though most of them are hipsters drinking low-alcohol beer. With the rain lashing against my face and the wind picking up, I cross Amiralsgatan and continue in the glow of the streetlamps. The moment I turn the corner by the parking garage, I catch the aroma of fried rice and hearty stock, and the door to Kwang Garden has never felt so light in my hand.

The last few diners have already left; the restaurant is closed. Amid a sea of fairy lights, bamboo, and wind chimes, a young woman in a pair of headphones is busy wiping down tables. The takeout menu is still brightly lit—mapo tofu, dumplings, kung pao chicken—and a slim figure in a white chef's jacket is leaning over the counter beneath it, dark hair poking out from under his hat. When he spots me, he hits the counter, taps his watch, and holds it to his ear.

"This thing must be broken, because it's telling me it's one thirty. I thought we agreed you'd be here at quarter past at the latest. We close at one, you know. *One.* I could be halfway home with some hot girl who'd been patiently waiting for me in the bar all evening."

"Are you telling me you've met someone?" I laugh and unwind my scarf, shove it into my bag.

"No, but I could have. And then you'd starve. Huang started clearing the buffet before I could get to it, so there wasn't much left, but I saved you a bit of beef and some noodles."

I wipe my feet on the mat by the door and shake the rain out of my hair before making my way over to the counter and sitting down on one of the tall stools.

"That sounds great, Alex. You're an angel for taking such good care of me. My mom would be proud."

"So how come I never get to meet her?"

Alex disappears into the kitchen, where the sound of pots and pans clattering against stainless steel worktops echoes through the room. He returns a few minutes later with rosy cheeks and a white plastic bag in one hand. He puts it down on the counter and pushes the card reader toward me. This must be the best deal I've ever done. I turn up just after closing time and buy the leftovers from the buffet for a fraction of the normal price. If I hadn't bumped into Alex in the lift at the studio and helped him carry a stack of takeout cartons to a conference room on the floor above, I would never have even come in here, despite having trudged past the restaurant on a daily basis for two years.

I'd probably be ten pounds lighter too.

"So, what happened?" he asks, studying me as I enter my PIN. "I didn't think you had any listeners."

"I don't," I say, glaring at him. "But someone called in just before I came off air, and I got the sense that . . ."

Just the thought of the voice makes me gaze out at the rain blowing past outside.

"What?"

I tug down the zip on my coat and gather my damp hair at the back of my neck.

"Nothing. The connection dropped and I lost the plot. It was stupid."

"But since no one listens, I guess it doesn't matter." He grins. "I put a tub of fresh wonton soup in there for you too. On me."

I immediately open the bag and reach for the tub to give it back.

"You didn't nee—"

Alex interrupts me with a hand on my arm. "*You* need it. So eat your soup and get some fresh air when you crawl out of bed tomorrow. Who knows, you might even get a bit of color on those pasty cheeks of yours. Go on, go home."

I reluctantly grip the handles of the bag and get up.

"Thanks, Alex."

"See you tomorrow, Sophie. Just make sure you get here before I lock up."

He waves his hand in the air and turns back into the kitchen, and I leave Kwang Garden to walk the short distance to my building next door. Gripping the handrail, I drag myself up the stairs to the second floor, my boots thudding against the tiles. Managing my bag, the food, and my keys proves a bit too much, and I stumble into the apartment and hear the door slam behind me. My phone beeps in my bag, and I dig it out from among the powder compacts, tissues and nasal spray. The screen illuminates the hallway as I read the message from my mom.

> *Listened to your show earlier. Would you like to come and stay next weekend? I've got theater tickets. Have something I need to ask you too.*

For a split second, I worry that she has caught the train down here and checked into a hotel nearby, but then I remember that I showed her how to stream the show from our homepage. I try to picture the two of us sitting in a dark theater, Mom's hunched shoulders and dull eyes. Mom, who never met anyone else after Dad died, because she wanted to honor his memory and what they had together.

Can't, I reply, shoving my phone into the back pocket of my jeans.

Something rustles beneath my feet, and I fumble for the switch on the table lamp, which is perilously close to the edge of the chest of drawers. The soft glow of the low-energy bulb slowly grows brighter, illuminating the parade of picture frames jostling for space beneath the mirror. William on a rocky beach in Portugal, William on a jetty by the lake, William and I with red noses and mirrored ski goggles at the top of a slope.

All there so that I'll never forget.

The mail is sticking out from beneath my feet on the doormat, and I see Luna sitting in front of me with her matted gray fur and her fluffy tail wound around her front paws. I dump my bag on the floor and kick off my boots by the shoe rack, then tuck the mail beneath my arm and carry the food through the dark apartment. Without switching on any more of the lights, I maneuver between the stacks of books and frames I've never gotten around to hanging, still leaning against the walls. Luna hisses at me as I pass, then darts off into the shadows.

I'm an only child. Being alone is my lot in life. Despite that, I never felt lonely growing up. My parents always treated me as an equal. They had guests over several nights a week, teachers from the school where Mom worked or other Frenchmen and their wives that Dad had met since moving to Sweden. That meant lots of Côtes-du-Rhône, sweet desserts, and music. They let me sit at the table with them, juice in my wineglass, and whenever they were invited somewhere, they almost never left me with a sitter; they took me with them instead.

I used to love seeing them together. Mom was so beautiful in her figure-hugging dresses and her dark red lipstick, and Dad always seemed to be glowing like he was the happiest man on earth. I thought he looked like a film star, with his dark hair and tanned skin. I wanted to be just like them when I grew up, and as Mom and I read in their big bed every evening, he would crawl in between us and say that he loved us more than anything else. I would have believed anything he told me back then.

But now William and Dad are both gone, and I barely ever see Mom.

I'm all alone, and I've come to realize that it's best that way.

* * *

I have the cartons lined up on the walnut coffee table in front of me—Szechuan beef, fried noodles, and wonton soup—beside a neat pile of today's post, the top envelope with my dirty boot print on it. As I struggle out of my leather jacket, I move over to the window and peep out through the blind. I turn the tilt wand and take another step toward the glass; cautiously lean forward and scan the street below.

It's deserted, like always. Cars parked bumper to tail along the sidewalk, several so close together that I doubt they'll be able to get out come morning.

I close the blind again and turn on the lamp on the side table, still just about visible behind the stack of rustic interior design magazines and paperbacks. Gripping the chopsticks in my right hand, I grab the carton of spicy beef and start wolfing it down, reaching for the noodles with my left. As I chew, I flick through the stack of mail. Nothing interesting, just promotions from the grocery store, offers from credit card companies, and more bonus deals from the same grocery stores, trying to lure me in with special prices on chicken.

And a handwritten envelope.

I wipe my mouth and grip the envelope with both hands. Whatever is inside is sturdy, a single sheet, and the writing feels familiar. As familiar as the voice earlier, which has already etched itself into my memory. My fingertips trace the name on the front. Sophie Lind.

Lind.

Not Arène, which was Dad's surname, the name I was given at birth and which I used until a year after William's death.

I get up again and move back over to the window, peep through the blind to the street outside. A huge puddle has formed around the blocked drain that spits out more water than it swallows, but the street is still deserted. I slump back onto the sofa and open the envelope without tearing the paper. The same way Mom always opens her Christmas presents, neatly folding the gift wrap to use it again. There's a card inside. A blue and green card, printed on thick paper.

I get up and pace the short distance between the kitchen and the living room as I read the brief text over and over again.

An evening in the company of old friends. Three-course dinner and good drinks.

The words, the address, the name at the bottom of the invite.

I glance down at the envelope on the sofa. My name, my address.

How did she find me?

Ava.

I reread the last line on the card, then raise my arm to study the hairs. They're literally standing on end, and I rub them until they lie flat again.

You'll be missing out if you don't come.

I can't go to her dinner. Not a chance. Still gripping the invite, my hand drops to my side, and I take in the room around me: the clothes dumped on a chair by the table, the withered palm in one corner. Right then, I hear a soft lapping sound. I turn my head and see Luna standing with her front paws on the coffee table, her head in the carton of spicy beef.

"No! Down!"

Luna mews unhappily as I lunge forward to chase her away from the food. I take it through to the kitchen and scrape the rest of the beef into the trash. Only then do I realize that I still have the card beneath my arm, and I read it one last time before tossing it in on top of the meaty mess and slamming the cupboard door.

I quickly march back through to the living room to eat my wonton soup and load Netflix, hoping to chase away the unwelcome thoughts now crowding my mind.

CHAPTER

2

Now

William's death was big news. Not just in the *Gefle Dagblad*, which wrote about him every single day for a week, but also in the tabloids. His parents had supplied the papers with a picture taken outside their cabin one day in autumn, after the maple leaves turned red. William was wearing a black woolen sweater that made his blue eyes pop, and the wind was tugging at his messy curls as he looked straight at the camera, with a smile. If you zoomed in far enough, you could see the reflection of the person taking the picture in his pupils. Someone with dark, shoulder-length hair and a baggy white beanie hat. I can still remember that day.

I stopped using the internet and stayed home out of fear of seeing him staring at me from a front page or a Facebook post.

"Tragic Death at House Party."

"Young man found dead."

"Circumstances unclear."

He would have hated it.

"We're family," William mumbled, his lips against my head, the first time I woke up beside him. It was a bitter winter's morning with frost flowers on the windows, and we were huddled up beneath layer upon layer of blankets in his bed, thick socks on our feet.

We were all gathered around the table in Charlotte's kitchen the night before, drinking mulled wine and swapping gifts, when I suddenly started shivering. It was something they did every year. They each bought a gift, wrapped it beautifully, then put them all in a heap in the middle of the table. I'd spent hours trawling the shops before eventually settling on a pretty candleholder made from engraved glass, and it wasn't until I opened the gift Adrian thrust into my hand that I realized I shouldn't have taken it so seriously. I left not long later with the fluffy handcuffs and blindfold stuffed into my coat pocket. William came with me, refused to let me walk home alone through the snowdrifts—not that I made it home.

His parents were there when we woke the next morning, but he didn't seem to care that they were pottering around only a few feet from his room. The underside of my arm was sweaty from being wrapped around his bare waist, as though someone would snatch him away from me if I let go. The smell of fresh coffee and toast drifted in through the gap beneath the door, and I could have stayed in his bed forever.

"And now you're part of the family too," he whispered, his breath tickling my feverish cheek, nibbling my earlobe.

Even now, I sometimes wake up and miss the heat I felt spreading through me then.

Because I love you.

* * *

The nightshift has just started at the station. The pens I brought with me are stacked neatly on top of my notepad, but I flick the pile and bring it tumbling down. I absent-mindedly brush my cheek with the back of my fingers, and my skin is cold. I felt like I'd risen from the dead when I woke on the sofa this afternoon, one arm draped over my face and the smell of congealed food lingering in my nose. I probably still looked like that when I got to the station at eight.

I skim through the tracks the producer has lined up for me and try to gather my thoughts. The dark circles have taken up permanent residence beneath my eyes, and there probably isn't enough coffee on earth to shake any life into me right now. I open my pot of caffeine pills and pop two, washing them down with a mouthful of Coca-Cola. The music fades into an ad, and the door opens. Malika is standing in the doorway, her sleek black hair pulled back in a high ponytail and her golden skin shimmering on her cheekbones. She has already changed into a pencil skirt and black tights, and she is wearing lipstick. My eyes linger on her perfect eyeliner.

She looks incredible in her knee-high boots, like some sort of female superhero.

Wonder Woman.

"How long do we have?" she asks in her thick Skåne accent, white-tipped nails drumming the doorframe.

I screw the lid back onto the Cola bottle and push it away from me, then pull my cardigan tight around my body with a shrug.

"Three minutes, maybe. Four max."

"You look like shit, by the way, but whatever. Erik was at Simonsson's last night. He's having a party at his new place next weekend. He invited me and said it was cool for you to come too. His friend is going to be there, the one with the green eyes and the tattoo on his arm. Do you know who I mean? There'll be food and drinks and—"

"No, Malika."

I can already feel my skin crawling, and I hold up both hands to make her stop.

"You know I don't like hanging out in a group. Why don't you just come over to my place instead? We can eat that brie and open a bottle of wine. I've got some sauvignon blanc."

Malika can never say no to sauvignon.

"That brie has been in your fridge for two months. You can smell it the minute you open the door."

"Yeah, because you never come over. Please."

Fawning usually always pays off, and she smiles.

"Would it kill you to make an effort to meet someone?" she asks. "You know how hard I've been trying to make sure you don't wither away on your own, right? You'll be forty before you know it."

"Very possible. But you know I never actually asked for your help, don't you?"

"And yet I do it anyway—that's how much I like you."

She blows me a kiss and winks.

I spot the corner of the green card sticking up out of my bag. It was four in the morning when the sound of a scream on the TV woke me, and the first thing I did was rescue the card from the trash. I tried to wipe it clean with a damp cloth, but the brown stains from the Szechuan beef are still visible.

"That reminds me," I say, reaching for the card and waving it in the air in front of her. "I've been invited to a dinner party."

"What's this? Are you telling me I'm not your only friend?"

She clutches her chest in mock surprise and then snatches the card from my hand. It's painful to watch her read the short text with a furrowed brow. As though she can see straight through me, even though she has no idea what any of this is about.

"An evening in the company of old friends."

"Friends since high school, hung out for years afterward. But we haven't seen one another in . . ." *Ten years, four months, and three days.* "A really long time. I moved away ten years ago, when we were twenty-four and still had our whole lives ahead of us."

It suddenly feels like it was just last week that I was twenty, moving out of the little brick house by the cycle path that snaked between the tall pines in order to get my own pokey apartment in town. I remember Charlotte's walk-in closet in the old villa her parents owned, its glass doors and sloping ceiling. The racks of dresses and the shelf full of shoes on the creaking wooden floor. I remember Finn's dog, a little wire-haired thing he got the minute he left home, and which always wanted to sit on your lap. Adrian's booming laugh and his strong hands, Ava's sharp wit and her intellect.

I remember exactly how it felt when William wrapped his arms around my waist and kissed my neck.

"Sounds like there are plenty of juicy details to delve into there. I wish I could tag along and be a fly on the wall, see all these people who shaped the mysterious Sophie. I'm convinced there's so much that you're not showing us, lurking beneath the surface. You're not allowed a plus one, are you? I can be really nice when I put my mind to it."

"I'm not sure I'm even going to go," I say.

"You should."

Malika's words set something in motion inside me. A fluttering in my stomach, which spreads through my body, making my arms and legs tingle. I point to the mic lamp, which turns red as I push the slider, then I pull on my headphones and wave her away.

"Welcome back. Now, let's see, do we have anyone with experience of dealing with mothers-in-law? How do you cope?"

Malika grins, flashing her pearly white teeth. She then backs out of the room and closes the door behind her. I miss her already. She has left the card on the desk in front of me.

* * *

Two hours later, I can barely remember a single word I said to the handful of people who called in, much less what went into my never-ending monologues between tracks. My mind keeps whirring, getting caught up on rain-drenched black curls beneath a streetlamp on a dark night; a pair of bright blue eyes in the cold glow of a TV with the volume turned down low; snuggled up beneath a bobbled fleece blanket. I spend a long time slumped in my chair, with my stockinged feet on the desk, after my show ends, and when I pass Kwang Garden forty-five minutes later, I don't even need to try the door to know that Alex is long gone. Casting a quick glance into the dark restaurant, I make my way over to my door and enter the code.

I find Luna waiting in the hall, peering up at me with her narrow yellow eyes. I'm starting to think she spends all day sitting there when I'm out, just to have the satisfaction of greeting me with bared teeth the minute I get home. Not surprisingly, it was Malika who talked me into getting a cat for company. I'd failed so catastrophically in terms of human relationships that I was on the verge of becoming antisocial, she told me. And so, after months of nagging, I finally gave in to the romantic notion of having a soft, warm body curled up beside me, and Malika took me to see a breeder who had fenced off their porch and kept a litter tray beneath the kitchen table.

I've regretted it every day since.

My handbag hits the floor and I trudge straight inside without stopping to take off my shoes. I throw my coat over the back of a chair in the kitchen and squint in the glare of the refrigerator when I open the door. The open bottle of sauvignon blanc is still in there behind the ketchup, and I unscrew the lid and pour myself a glass. It's Saturday, after all. Cupping the glass in both hands, I wander through the apartment, sipping my wine. Around the sofa and the coffee table, back and forth down the hallway, where I kick off my shoes and head through to the bedroom.

I can't say yes.

What would we even talk about after all this time?

What would I wear?

With the glass in one hand and my head cocked, I rifle through the hangers in my wardrobe. Charlotte would have grabbed the most colorful dress and held it up in front of me as she studied us both in the mirror. She would have pushed my hair out of the way, pressed her cheek to mine, and nodded approvingly.

This one.

I take out a black blouse and close the wardrobe door.

No matter how hard I try, I can't remember the last words I said to Ava. I remember she was standing beside me outside the church and that her hand almost brushed against mine—but only almost. Her hair had never seemed lighter than it did that day, dressed entirely in black. I should have said something when I saw her bloodshot eyes and her trembling hand, but the very last thing I actually remember saying to her were the words I spat out just before I ran down the stairs and out onto the street when I left William's apartment.

It's your fault.

I smooth out the bedspread to avoid having to look at my crumpled sheets, then leave the bedroom with what's left of the wine. In the living room, I slump down onto the sofa and reach for the table lamp beside me, knocking a stack of magazines to the floor in the process. My hand lingers on the switch, and I turn it off again. My glass is empty, and I tip my head back against the cushions and close my eyes. Exhale.

"You'll be missing out if you don't come."

How could Ava have found me?

I'll admit that I've looked for the others. I've read what little is visible on their private Facebook pages, searched in vain for their accounts on Instagram. Spent a long time staring at Tess's profile pictures, in which she never looks straight at the camera. Finn updates his header image from time to time, with photographs of lush forest trails or the sun dipping behind an icy ski slope. Charlotte's profile pictures are all selfies, her made-up face in different colors, taken from different angles. I didn't even have to look for Adrian, because his face is a permanent feature of the finance pages in virtually every paper.

But I've been trying to find Ava's address for several years, trawling the internet without success, and now *she* has managed to send an invite to my unlisted address—after I changed my surname at that. I wouldn't have to stay all evening. I could just show my face and then claim to have a migraine and head home. The thought that Tess might show up, getting to hear her incredible laugh again—that would make it all worth it.

Everyone would be there. Or almost everyone, anyway. And it wouldn't be for my sake; it would be for William's.

I pour the last of the wine into my glass and head back out into the hallway. I dig the card and my phone out of the bottom of my bag and ignore a message from Malika without even opening it. I enter the mobile number from the invite and then write a single line:

Thanks for the invitation, I'll be there.

CHAPTER

3

Now

TEN YEARS WITHOUT seeing one another. Ten years without a single phone call. It's strange, now that I think about it. The way close bonds can break apart in the space of just a few hours, crumbling to dust and being scattered by the wind. Maybe they were never that strong to begin with, or maybe that's just what guilt does to people. Everyone who loved William was gathered in his apartment that evening, but not even that was enough of a reason for him to go on living. We were all within reach, yet none of us could see what was about to happen or do anything to stop it.

How do you go on after something like that?

My train leaves Malmö Central at eleven thirty, and the journey will take me half the day. Much of the route weaves past bare fields that eventually give way to spruce forests beneath heavy skies, and I lean back with my chicken mayo baguette and my earbuds in. The air in the carriage is damp and stuffy from all the wet coats. I'm sitting opposite a man in a pair of smart trousers and a sweater vest, and he is busy flicking through the free magazine that was on the table between us when I changed trains in Stockholm. He boarded in Uppsala and immediately stretched out his legs, kicking me in the shin.

The train ride reminds me of a similar journey north sixteen years ago. Back then, I was crammed between Mom and Dad in the front seat of a rented van. Dad's eyes were on the road up ahead, Mom's gazing out through the side window, but I just stared down at my hands and arms, covered in cuts and bruises I didn't remember getting. Deserted roads in the pouring rain, several stops along the way, eating hotdogs and mashed potato beneath a parasol by the side of the road, not saying a word to one another. Behind us, in the back of the van, our lives were packed into brown cardboard boxes.

"This is your final chance," Dad said without looking at me, gripping the wheel as we passed a sign announcing that Gävle was three miles away. "If you mess this up, we won't help you again. You'll have to solve your problems on your own."

It didn't take much more than a glance for me to remind him precisely what my problems stemmed from, and he immediately regretted opening his mouth.

Mom didn't say a word, as ever.

This was a month before my eighteenth birthday, and just two weeks later I found myself standing in front of the final-year students taking the social sciences program at Borgarskolan. That was the first time I met them, and nothing would ever be the same again.

I tip my head back and study my reflection in the train window, taking in my blunt fringe and black-rimmed glasses. I have a reservation at the Elite Grand Hotel, and if I feel like it, I can just stay in my room until Sunday morning, when I have to check out to catch the train home. My suitcase is on the rack above my head, stuffed with enough clothes to last a week. The black blouse on top, then three dresses of varying colors and lengths. My eyelids feel warm and heavy, and I give in to my weariness and close them for a while. When I do, I see William as clearly as though it were yesterday.

He was the one who approached me. Contrary to what Dad expected, I took his words seriously and kept to myself at school—just to be on the safe side. During break I sat with my back against the metal fence outside, smoking badly rolled cigarettes while I waited for the next class to begin, and at lunch I waited until all the other students were already leaving the canteen before I sat down with my tray in the corner.

But William saw me.

When I closed my locker in the corridor one day, there he was, with his dark, wavy hair and his dimpled chin. It was pretty obvious he had decided I was going to be his, and for a long time I let him think that I wasn't interested. But just like that, I became part of their film evenings in Finn's chilly basement and their parties at Ava's house by the shore when her parents were away. I told Tess and Charlotte that we'd moved to Gävle because Dad had lost his job, and I wished that were the case. I told Ava that we'd moved because Mom was depressed, and in some ways that was true. I told William the truth because I couldn't bear to look him in the eye and lie.

Except when it came to one thing, apparently.

"William," I mumble, my fingers digging into the seat, opening my eyes.

The man in the sweater vest glances up from his magazine and gives me a wry smile before turning the page. I reach for the bottle of mineral water on the table and wash the taste of sleep from my mouth. The sky is already dark, but in the glare of the floodlights I can make out the familiar shapes of the industrial area flanking the railway line. The train has slowed down, and it changes tracks. I can see the Dalapalatset building in the distance, all red bricks and turrets, and a green tin roof; I see the brightly lit path I used to stumble along beneath the railway, the bridge over the river where I sat on the railing, with my legs swinging over the swirling black water below.

I'm here.

* * *

After a sleepless night in what must be the smallest room in the hotel, having gotten up to adjust the thermostat more times than I can remember, I eat an early breakfast and then slump back onto the bed and doze all day. When I wake, my dresses are hanging where I left them on the open bathroom door. A black-and-white polka-dot number I'd feel most comfortable in, an airy turquoise and pink option I know Charlotte would approve of, and a snug red dress Malika gave me for my birthday last year.

After some careful consideration, I pull on a pair of dark jeans and the black blouse, which is still in my suitcase. I gather my hair in a bun and run my fingers through my fringe. Studying myself in the mirror, I try taking off my glasses. Mom used to console me by saying that they were just for reading, that I only had to wear them when I was working or wanted to read a book. But these days the lenses are varifocal, and I realize that there's no way I'll be able to get through the evening without them. With the glasses sitting firmly on my nose, I raise my chin and nod at my reflection before pulling my boots on and calling for a cab.

Because I don't recognize the address, I double-check it several times. The driver doesn't react when I read it to him, but I still feel slightly dubious as we pass the police station and drive under the train tracks, over the Gävle River and out toward Alderholmen. Tess once told me there was nothing out there when they were kids, nothing but an occasional market with a fun fair on the undeveloped land. I see the new Gävle Strand district up ahead, all the stylish buildings that started popping up just before I left, but the taxi swings off to the left and makes its way deeper into the old industrial area around the Gevalia coffee roastery. Through the window, I watch as we drive along a deserted street of old warehouses now housing hairdressers, cafés and secondhand shops.

"I think we might have gone the wrong way," I say, leaning toward the driver's seat. "I said Andra Magasinsgatan. This can't be right."

If he turned off onto the ring road right now, we could be at Mom's house in Stigslund in a few minutes.

"This is right," says the driver, and just as I'm about to open my mouth again he turns sharply to the right and pulls up outside a new apartment block tucked behind the old nineteenth century buildings.

I press my face to the window and tip my head back to follow the facade up to the sixth floor. Polished concrete and huge expanses of glass edged with polished steel; balconies stretching the entire width of the building.

I slowly open the car door and get out onto the pavement. The rain has turned to sleet, catching in my hair and on my thin coat, and I have to blink away the flakes as I look up at the sleek spectacle of a building towering in front of me. This isn't the kind of place I'd imagined Ava living, nothing like her sparse student apartment with its secondhand furniture and fairy lights wound around the curtain rail. She used to spend hours hunched over a sheet of paper, with a slim brush in her hand, painting delicate watercolors of lakes, forests, and flowers. Most of her paintings featured the jetty by her parents' house on the north shore of Gävle Bay, the tangle of raspberry bushes at the edge of the lawn. Always against the light, with dark clouds looming behind the treetops and long shadows creeping across the grass.

Those paintings covered the walls in her living room. I've always imagined her living in a simple house in the countryside or some sort of rustic villa a stone's throw from the Mediterranean, close to the water and with a garden full of sweet peas and lush green leaves.

This is the exact opposite of all that, and it suddenly dawns on me that I have no idea what any of the others have been doing these past ten years. I don't know a thing about their lives, but it's clear that Ava's is far removed from mine, hiding away in a tiny rental in one of the shabbier parts of Malmö.

The car door slides shut behind me, and the taxi immediately speeds off down the slushy road, splashing my jeans.

"Wait!" I shout, trying to hit the lid of the trunk, no longer sure I want to go in.

But he's already gone.

I scan the empty street as the wind whistles around me. There are no more than a handful of parked cars, the buildings dark and eerie. Back in senior high school, and for years afterward, we played a game that involved not being first to arrive anywhere. I almost never lost, partly because I was so bad at keeping time but mostly because Finn was always so damn punctual. I search the slushy ground for signs of footprints and wonder whether it'll be me who loses this evening. The cold air is starting to make my cheeks sting and my fingers throb, and the huge door into the building behind me feels increasingly inviting. I give up and head in.

The lobby is bigger than my entire apartment. Enormous slabs of pale, polished stone on the floor, the sound of my heels echoing between the walls as I shake off the snow and walk through it. The walls are also pale, painted to look like marble, stretching up to the high white ceiling with its gold edging. The place reminds me of Ava's parents' enormous villa by the water, their expensive taste, which makes it even more surprising that she would choose to live here.

On the wall by the elevator, the names of all the residents are listed in a gold frame. I scan through the relatively short list and find Ava's name at the top.

The penthouse.

I press the button, and the doors roll open to reveal the space beyond. Mirrored walls, clean floors. I reluctantly step inside and press the button for the penthouse. The doors close without a sound, and the floor jolts as the elevator starts making its way up. I move from mirror to mirror, studying myself and smoothing my fringe. Over to the other side, where I fish my lipstick out of my bag and touch it up with shaking hands. Whenever I was nervous, William used to grab my hands and blow on them with his hot breath. He looked me deep in the eye, and though I couldn't see his mouth, I could tell from the fine lines on his face that he was smiling. Maybe it was the warmth that made me relax, or maybe it was the look in his eyes that made me forget whatever I was afraid of, but it always worked. The last time he did that was five minutes before we rang the bell at his parents' house, planning to show them the ring he had pushed onto my finger two hours earlier.

I unbutton my coat and have just started using it to fan myself when my cell phone pings.

> *Have a great time tonight! I want all the juicy details on Monday.*

Malika. I don't bother to reply and am just about to drop my phone back into my bag when another message arrives.

> *I want pictures and updates all evening too. Especially if any of them are single.*

My lips curl into a smile as the doors open, and I see a man dressed in black, standing outside. He has a high forehead and a faint hint of stubble on his cheeks, and he's wearing jeans and a blazer. He must be about six foot five, with broad shoulders.

"Sophie?"

It takes me a moment to process that he just said my name.

"Yes?"

"This way, please," he says, turning and striding across the carpeted floor.

I remain glued to the spot in the elevator, still gripping my phone, surrounded by my own reflection as I wonder what is going on and who he could be. I should have expected something like this, I realize. Ava always loved planning surprises for us. She might send us all a message with nothing but an address, and when we arrived she would have prepared a picnic on the rocks by the sea or a moonlit treasure hunt in the forest. It wouldn't surprise me at all if the man tore off his trousers and started dancing the minute I set foot inside the apartment—either that or if he said he needed an assistant to saw in two.

"Are you coming?"

He has paused and is looking back at me over his shoulder. I put my phone away and can't help glancing down at my empty ring finger before I step out of the lift and follow him. He is already by the door, which he is holding open with one hand, gesturing for me to go in with the other.

"Welcome. You're expected."

So formal. So stiff. So unlike Ava.

I hesitate for a moment before stepping inside, and the door immediately closes behind me. I'm standing in the entrance, with a hallway leading deeper into the apartment off to my left. I hear the sound of clicking heels approaching, and before I have time to leave the doormat, Ava rounds the corner from the hallway, more striking and beautiful than ever. Her platinum blond hair is tied up in a perfect ponytail, and she is wearing a strappy cream-colored dress made from some sort of glossy, light material. It's about as far from the faded jeans and V-neck T-shirts I remember her wearing as one could get. She looks like a dream.

She looks just like her mother.

Ava smiles, her lips painted a subtle shade of pale pink, and wraps her arms around me. I feel my body tense in her embrace.

"Sophie," she sighs against my cheek. "Finally. I've been waiting for you. Come in—let me take your coat."

Her voice makes me gasp. I still haven't managed to say a single word, too busy wondering whether she has thought about me the way I've thought about her. I stand perfectly still just inside the door in the surprisingly modest entrance hall, watching Ava as she takes my coat. There is no sign of anyone else here. The woman in front of me isn't the person I remember, and I feel a sudden pang of shame that I'm broadly the same as I was ten years ago. With a gentle push on the wall, a hidden cupboard opens, and Ava carefully drapes my coat onto a hanger. I step forward in the hope of catching a glimpse of the others' coats inside, but Ava closes the door and turns around.

She holds out her hands, her eyes boring into me in a way that makes me shrink back. I really should say something. Anything. Instead, I force my lips into a smile and bend down to unzip my boots.

"No," says Ava, stopping me. "Keep them on unless you brought any slippers. Just wipe them on the mat. Oh, how silly of me—I almost forgot."

Standing on tiptoe in her dainty pumps, she reaches up to the only shelf and takes down a silvery box made from some kind of woven metal. It's full of mobile phones, and she holds it out to me with an encouraging nod.

"I want us to focus on one another and forget about everything else for a while this evening. Don't you agree that our obsession with screens and constantly being connected is just too much? When did you last have a conversation without opening Instagram?"

"You're right."

There. I've said something at last, broken the silence, but the tension in my body refuses to let go. I rummage through my bag for my phone with Malika's messages on it and drop it into the box with the others. I guess this must mean I'm not the only one here after all.

"Perfect. You can have it back later, I promise. Come with me."

Ava sweeps away across the smooth stone floor in her four-inch heels and her thin dress, which is low cut at the back. She walks ahead of me like a mirage, and I still can't quite believe I'm actually here. I breathlessly admire the high ceilings and the dove-gray walls leading off the entrance hall, adorned with a couple of enormous oil paintings. So, Ava has kept painting—though these are very different from the light, bright watercolors she scattered around her in high school. These are all murky colors and hypnotic patterns, painted with thick brushstrokes. I can barely tear my eyes away from them.

Ava keeps glancing back over her shoulder, with a soft smile, as though she is afraid she might lose me along the way. I'm only a few yards away from the entrance hall when I hear the lock click behind us. The man in black has just locked the door from outside. I turn my head to look back, but Ava grabs my arm and pulls me off to the side.

"Here. Come with me first."

She grips my elbow so lightly that I can hardly feel her fingers, but I still can't think about anything else. Her nails are short but neat, painted a glossy shade of beige.

"I want you to myself for a moment."

CHAPTER

4

Now

"Come this way—the kitchen's just through here."

The kitchen, the heart of the home. The place where Mom and I could spend time together without having to say more than a few words to each other. Sweating over trays of oven-roasted vegetables and nodding to each other over pans of reductions. We whisked Italian meringues over bains-marie and burst out laughing when the mixture came out the wrong end of the piping bag. It was a place where Mom could forget that I'd spent the past few years getting blind drunk on the weekends, hanging out with people who, combined, were risking several years in prison. Somewhere I could briefly forget all the secrets I was keeping from her.

I remember Ava's kitchen with the same fondness I remember Mom's. Ava had filled her window sill with a jungle of herbs, their leaves straining upward beneath the net curtain. She was the only person I knew who had a full-size bookcase in her kitchen, yet her table was still always cluttered with books. Fitzgerald, Wilde, Harper Lee. I used to flick through the old novels she bought secondhand, enjoying the scent of the yellowed pages mixing with the aroma of all the cookies she baked and stored in the pastel-colored tins on the shelf above the stove. She loved that apartment so much that she insisted on commuting the hour or so to Uppsala when she started university there.

Or maybe it was just that she couldn't let go of us.

I'm dragged back to the present and the open-plan layout of the new apartment as Ava draws me away from the narrow hallway flanked by cupboard doors. I'm drawn to her like a moth to a flame, just like I was that first day of school. There was something about her eyes that told me she knew something no one else did.

Something about me I didn't even know myself.

Her proud neck, her slim shoulders. I want to put my arm around her and hold her close, apologize for not being there after the funeral, but the words catch in my throat. We walk through a doorway into the kitchen. Ava's shoulders immediately relax, and her fingers leave my elbow. She makes her way over to a large island unit in the middle of the room, where she has a number of different bottles. Something about the sheer volume of alcohol feels wrong. Ava was never a drinker, and whenever she invited us over to her place, there was never a drop of booze on offer. Tess always used to sigh at the sweet drinks with frozen berries in them, the fruit juice. Ava never went anywhere without a bottle of water, and I can only remember seeing her drunk once.

The night that ended with William dying.

I linger in the doorway, my eyes on Ava's shimmering dress. It falls so softly over her modest curves that it could be a part of her skin. My brain still can't quite process seeing her in something so expensive and elegant, and I wish I had worn one of my dresses instead of my jeans. Moving one step at a time, I make my way over to the island and peer around the room. The kitchen is big and open, with pale, glossy cupboards and counters made from black granite. The few baskets and bowls on display are all made from brass, just like the handles on the drawers and cupboard doors. Nothing about the room gives me any sense of who Ava is today. There are no open newspapers, no half-read books, no lush herbs on the counter. No hint of yeast or baking in the air. In fact, I can't smell anything other than cleaning products.

There isn't a single trace of life on the polished surfaces.

Ava's hand hovers above the alcohol, her fingers dancing in the air before she grabs a bottle with a blue label. She carefully fills the only glass on the island and turns to meet me with a satisfied smile.

"Prosecco, right?"

The bubbles spill over my hand as I take the glass from her. I can't claim I was ever really that fond of prosecco in the years after senior high school, but it was sweeter than white wine and cheaper than champagne, and I thought it felt fancy to toast with something fizzy. I often just chose a bottle at random, based on whichever label I liked best, and I rarely drank more than one glass because it always gave me a pounding headache the next day.

"How did you remember?" I take a grateful sip, longing to feel the numbing effects of alcohol in my bloodstream.

"I've had plenty of time to think," she replies, leaning back against the round kitchen table. "You were the only one who liked bubbles."

Ava studies me, taking in my scuffed faux leather boots and my dark jeans, my black blouse. She then puts her arm around me, giving me a brief, firm hug before ruffling my fringe with her fingers.

"I can't believe you're actually here. You're just how I remember you."

Her touch sends a shiver down my spine. I don't know whether to take her words as an insult or a compliment, but I decide to plump for the latter because her smile seems so genuine.

"Come on—sit down! We need to talk."

Ava leads me over to the velvet stools by the island and forces me down onto one of them. She perches on the one beside me and puts her hand on top of mine on the cold granite.

"So, tell me. What are you up to these days?"

I could say that I spend as much time as possible at the radio station so that I don't have to go home to my apartment, that I spend most of my days asleep. I could reveal that I eat almost nothing but takeout and prepared meals and that the only conversing I do in the evenings is with my cat, who doesn't let me get anywhere near her and who coughs up hairballs in my shoes.

"Oh, you know," I say with a shrug, as though she knows what I mean. "Time just marches on. Work, everyday life. Nothing exciting."

"I remember you used to call me early in the morning on the weekend, whenever you couldn't sleep, and we'd drive out to Vårvik and walk along the rocks at sunrise. Do you remember that you and I were always the first to go swimming in spring? Before it was really even warm enough, in May. It didn't matter how cold the water was—you never hesitated."

I do. I remember all those things. How, in another life, she was constantly in my thoughts. In some ways she still is. She laughs, and for a split second the old Ava shines through the polished exterior. Her faint laughter lines remind me of everything I've missed.

Everything I've longed for.

"Do you remember our dinners?" she asks, quieter this time, cocking her head so that the spotlights make her eyes glitter. "At Christos Taverna?"

"Yes," I say, because no matter how hard I try I'll never be able to forget sitting at the table in the corner, the linen-clad seats.

Those dinners were Ava's idea. After we graduated from senior high school, she suggested meeting for dinner every Friday, to make sure we didn't drift apart. I thought it sounded stupid at first—grown adults who were busy with their studies or making headway in the world of work, who had less and less in common with every day that passed—but the others thought it was a great idea, and the fact that we started going to Christos's Greek restaurant every week after just a few months was really nothing more than a coincidence. We took turns picking the restaurant, and one Friday Charlotte wanted us to go to a tapas place none of us could really afford. It also happened to be closed for renovation, and when we turned to leave, with the cold wind biting our cheeks and our breath forming clouds in the air, we saw Christos Taverna on the other side of the street. The shabby restaurant just felt perfect somehow. Like its hotchpotch of chipped and dented furniture, we were a mismatched group of people who, on paper, shouldn't have had anything in common.

"I really miss them, our Friday dinners. Don't you?"

This time I hold my tongue.

"Don't you think it's all so tragic?" she continues, picking at an invisible mark on the island and crossing her legs. "The wedding that never happened, the house the two of you went to look at. Sometimes I lie awake at night, thinking about what life might have been like if everything had gone to plan. How we all would've been, what we'd be doing right now."

I turn away because suddenly I remember exactly what separated Ava and me.

William.

When I close my eyes, I can still see the house, as though it were just yesterday. The sunshine filtering in through the window, golden light painting the parquet floor. The brick fireplace and the room William showed me with his lips against my ear. The room that would have become a nursery one day. Before we left the house and caught up with the estate agent on the driveway, William led me out onto the wooden deck, which was buried beneath a layer of bright maple leaves. He sat down in a flaking wooden chair and pulled me onto his lap. I was straddling his knee and . . .

I open my eyes.

"What about you?" I ask. "What have you been doing all these years? Your apartment is . . . amazing. Things must have gone well for you."

She flashes me a quick smile and then gets up and moves over to the counter.

"My parents found this place for me. I had an apartment in the center of town, with a balcony looking out onto the park. It was fantastic, with old oak floors and original features. The kitchen had a bay window, so I put my dining table there. The light was incredible in the mornings."

"Why'd you move?"

"It was best that way."

Ava picks up a couple of brown paper bags from the floor behind the island and starts lifting plastic containers out of them. The kind that come from a catering company.

"So, what do you do for work? All that behavioral science and psychology you studied—what do you spend your time doing?"

"Ah," she says, pausing with her back to me. "Not much, to be honest. I'm not working right now. Haven't for a few years."

Her words leave me speechless. Ava was always the most driven of us, the one who stayed up all night cramming for exams, lacing her tea with energy drinks in order to stay awake. Her parents had more money than she could ever need, but she refused to take a penny from them. She wanted to forge her own path, create a life of her own, and she was looking forward to working hard and making a difference.

I open my mouth to say something, but she turns around with one of the plastic containers in her hands.

"I ordered food from one of my favorite restaurants, Experiencia. Have you ever been there?"

I shake my head and hold my tongue.

"I heard about your dad," she says, crumpling both bags and pushing them into the trash. "How's your mom?"

It's been five years since Dad died, but I still can't let go of the guilt that we didn't manage to forgive each other before it was too late. A slight tickle in his throat, and just seven months later the cancer had done its thing and he was gone, dead and buried with his secret.

Our secret.

It weighs heavy on me now. I've barely seen Mom since he died, no more than a handful of times, on her birthday and once or twice on mine. I don't want her to come to my apartment in Malmö. She'll never forgive me for the way I behaved toward Dad, and I'll never forgive him for the way he treated her.

"She's fine. Still living in the house."

"Are you staying there tonight?"

"No." The word feels cold and hard in my mouth. "I have a hotel room."

"I wish you could have stayed here with us. Just imagine," she says dreamily, her eyes narrowing, "lying awake half the night, chatting like we used to. Eating a late breakfast. Pancakes with cream, fresh fruit. I could have baked croissants."

She straightens the plastic tubs, which are already in a perfectly neat line, and opens the refrigerator.

"But with things as they are right now, sadly that's not possible."

"Us?"

My question makes her pause with her hand on the fridge door, looking back at me with an open mouth.

"Sorry?"

"You said *us*. Are you married?"

Ava frowns and seems to replay our conversation in her mind.

"Did I?" She laughs to herself and leans into the fridge. "No, it's just me here—no one else. That's for sure."

"How exactly did you find me?"

"What do you mean?"

She straightens up and closes the door with slightly too much force.

"I changed my surname."

"To your mom's maiden name, yes."

"I can't remember ever telling you what she was called before she got married."

"It's a surname, Sophie, hardly classified information. And not especially difficult to find out either. Why are you making such a big deal of it?"

"But my address isn't listed. And neither is my phone number."

Ava is quiet for a moment, her hands by her sides, fidgeting with the seams of her dress. She turns her head toward the other door into the kitchen, as though she just heard someone shout, but everything is as quiet as it was a moment earlier.

"They're waiting for us. Are you ready?"

She grins and reaches out to me as though none of what I just said matters. Who knows? Maybe it doesn't. We're together again this evening, all under the same roof for the first time in ten years, and maybe this is exactly what I need. Maybe it's what I've been waiting for all along.

"Everyone is waiting for you."

I get up from the stool and slowly make my way over to Ava. I take her hand, and she grips it tightly. Hand in hand, we leave the kitchen together.

CHAPTER

5

Now

I'M THE CLEAR winner, the very last to arrive, so why does it feel like a punishment to leave the safety of the kitchen, where Ava and I were alone, and come face to face with the people I've seen in my dreams for the past ten years? The glass in my hand is half empty, and I grip the stem. Beyond the kitchen, the apartment opens out into a spacious, airy dining room with floor-to-ceiling windows dominating the far wall. The views across the old warehouses in the sleepy industrial area around us are stunning. I can see the lights from Brynäs in the distance, glimpses of the dark water dividing the city in two.

The long table on the Persian carpet in the middle of the room has been tastefully set with thick linen napkins and a large vase of flowers. Two silver candelabras cast a warm glow around the space, and there is a silver cloche on every plate. It looks just how I imagine a dinner at a lavish estate would, or at the Nobel Prize ceremony.

"I'll be back in a moment," Ava whispers behind me, and by the time I turn around, she is already gone.

Despite the open-plan layout of the apartment, the dining room is partly separated from the living room by a wall, entirely hidden behind a row of tall china cabinets. My eyes struggle with the contrast between the bright spotlights in the kitchen and the soft candles on the table. All around me, I see dark figures peeling away from the shadows on the walls, and before I have time to think, someone rushes over and wraps their arms around my neck.

"I can't believe it! Sophie?"

Long fingernails dig into my shoulders, and a sharp scent of perfume makes my nose sting. I manage to pull myself out of her grip, and there she is: thick red hair flowing over one shoulder, wearing a long-sleeved emerald velvet dress that hugs her curves.

Charlotte.

"Oh my God, we have so much catching up to do. Where have you been all these years? Do you still live here?"

She trails a hand over my hair, squeezes my arm, and pokes at my earring. The small black pearl.

"No, I moved right after the funeral."

Right after, as in I packed my bags before I'd even changed out of my black dress, still dusty from the gravel outside the church, and booked a train ticket before I even knew where I was going to live.

"Wait, what are you drinking? Is that prosecco?" She takes the glass from my hand and sniffs it with a crinkled nose. "You know it always gives you a headache the next day."

Charlotte takes my glass over to a long sideboard by the wall outside the kitchen and puts it down.

"It's not worth it, and you know it. Come on—you've got to say hello to the others. We were just talking about you. No one thought you'd actually show up."

She hooks her arm through mine and drags me around the dining table, over to the wall of windows, where two male figures are in silhouette against the pale light of the city. One taller than the other, with a navy blue shirt and short hair. For a split second, I want to fight back and pull away, because all I can think is that he looks like William. But then he turns to the side, revealing a profile with a square jaw and a straight nose, and I relax.

"Adrian?" I ask, unable to hide the joy in my voice.

Adrian, with a whisky glass in one hand. His smile is so broad that I can see his white teeth gleaming, and he holds out both arms so that I can walk over and press my cheek to his chest. With our foreign parents, his from Chile and my dad from France, we always felt comfortable around each other. The culture clashes we had experienced brought us together, and I never felt like I needed to explain myself when I was with him. Adrian accepted me as I was, without any questions, and maybe the reason we got on so well was because I did the same to him.

Adrian is also the one I know most about, largely because it's so hard to escape what he has been up to. Two years after I left Gävle, he broke onto the scene as one of Sweden's up and coming stars in the world of finance. He built his business from the ground up, and it proved so successful that he'll never have to worry about how to pay the bills again. The papers love writing about Adrian, and he loves ignoring their questions. They snap pictures of him outside his apartment in central Stockholm or at his summerhouse on Gotland—which is bigger than most actual houses—and he always just grins in his black shades before getting into one of his flashy cars.

I should be proud of him, but no matter how I twist and turn it, I can't help thinking that some part of his success should be William's.

"You *have* to tell us what you're up to these days," he says to me. "Finn is convinced you ended up taking your teaching exams and that you're atoning for old sins at some high school somewhere, but Charlotte thinks you're married with three kids and that you've put your career on hold."

Finn.

I turn my head and study the other figure by the window. Finn winks and raises his chin in a silent greeting. His hair is as thick and wild as ever, but he has it slicked back, and his face looks rounder than I remember it. He is wearing a pale blue shirt, neatly tucked into a pair of black jeans with a black leather belt. These days he looks more like a preened Christopher Nolan than his teenage idol and role model, Quentin Tarantino.

I wonder whether they can see it on me, whether my face is pleading with them.

Don't ask about him.

Don't mention what happened.

"What about you?" I ask, meeting Adrian's brown eyes. His shirt feels silky soft beneath my hands. "What do you think I ended up doing?"

He studies me with a solemn face and lets go of me. Perhaps my eyes are saying something else. But then he smiles and sips from his glass.

"I think you went your own way and that you're right where you want to be. I'd never expect anything else."

"Wimp. But no, you're all wrong."

Without elaborating, I point to another big oil painting on the wall behind Adrian. The dramatic colors are ominous, but I can feel it pulling me in. The others turn around. It reminds me of the other canvases I saw in the hallway, but this time it is a chaotic swirl of blue.

"I guess Ava still paints," I say, my eyes following the thick brushstrokes, which move in a dizzying spiral to a clearer shape higher up. There is something sad about the lines, like waves washing up on an empty beach.

"You think Ava painted that?" Charlotte cocks her head and sucks in her cheeks.

"Ava was always painting," I say. "Her place was full of watercolors. Don't you remember? Though those paintings were never like this."

"I never went over there much. I thought it was kind of weird that she stayed in that pokey little apartment when her parents could have bought her an entire house. Like, who was she trying to kid?"

Charlotte rarely came over to my apartment either, and I never had a problem with that. She had a tendency to touch everything, drifting around the room, picking things up and opening drawers. She might grab a cushion from the sofa and squeeze it before mumbling something and putting it down again, as though nothing I owned was quite good enough. She spent far more time at William's place.

We all did.

"Did you never think that maybe that was exactly why she stayed there?"

Finn's voice is low as he moves over to Charlotte and puts a hand on her shoulder. He squeezes it softly and grazes her hair with his nose.

"Why would anyone choose that?" asks Charlotte, turning away from the painting.

"Because it was a chance for her to actually *choose* something."

Finn kisses her on the cheek, and if I were still drinking my prosecco, I would have spluttered it right now. I stare at the gold ring on Finn's finger, then down at Charlotte's hand, where a large rock glitters in the soft light.

"Hold on a second . . ." I grip Adrian's arm as though I'm looking for moral support. "Are you two married?"

"Nine years this summer," says Charlotte, holding out her hand so that I can get a better look at her ring.

Nine years. That means they must have gotten together pretty much right after William died. Finn shrugs, as though it's as incomprehensible to him as it is to me.

"That's great," I blurt out. I assume that's what they want to hear, but in my mind I'm thinking back to the midsummer we celebrated at William's parents' summerhouse. Barefoot and in short dresses, we tiptoed through the dew-covered grass and clambered up onto a rock down by the water. Me, Tess, and Charlotte. With an itchy blanket over our legs, we laughed at the boys breaking the surface of the otherwise calm lake, and we said all sorts of things we never should have said—things I wish I could take back. One of the things Charlotte said about Finn has always stuck in my mind.

She said that he was the only person she wouldn't miss if we never saw one another again.

I turn to Finn and smirk, but he is looking the other way.

"Yup," says Adrian, starting to make his way over to the table. "We had one more dinner together, at the very least."

"Have you seen each other since?" I ask, hot on his heels. "Over the years, I mean."

I hope they haven't. If I'm the only one who has been alone all this time, it'll make everything feel much worse. It would mean they had talked about me and where I went. I avoid their eyes, focusing on the table instead, on how much time Ava must have put into getting everything just right. A gray linen table cloth without a single crease in sight, a dark purple place mat beneath each setting. Matching napkins pushed into wooden napkin rings, and a small box tied with a silver bow by every plate.

"I wish I could say we had," says Charlotte, moving over to my side. The relief is enormous. "But life has a tendency to get in the way. I'm in TV these days, working on a load of morning and other entertainment shows. You just kind of end up hanging around in those circles instead."

But you weren't in TV back then, I think. At some point you must have made the same decision as me and stopped speaking to the others.

"What happened to Ava?" I ask, quieter this time. "I didn't expect to see her in something so . . ."

"Exclusive?" Adrian grins.

"Yeah. And the food . . . She had bags from a caterer, but Ava always loved cooking. She used to say that was half the fun of having us over—forcing us to pitch in."

I used to come over early to help her in the kitchen as she baked tear-and-share bread and made dips and boiled cream for her desserts. I can't believe she would just give that up, especially now that she has a home where she can cook whatever she wants.

"I guess she changed her mind."

"Are we the only ones here?"

The others exchange a glance before turning toward the wide arch into the living room. My eyes move from face to face before I do the same, and I catch sight of a slim figure hunched over on an L-shaped sofa by the wall on the other side of the door into the kitchen. I must have walked right past her earlier.

"Tess?" I whisper, turning back to the others.

"She was here when we arrived," says Finn. "We said a quick hello and Ava gave us something to drink, and when we turned around, she'd gone over there. We didn't want to bother her."

So, Tess was today's loser. She had been the first to arrive.

"But it's Tess," I say again. I don't know how they could have left her all alone like that. Tess, who always greeted people with a hug and a kiss on the cheek, who had to be told to arrive an hour before everyone else because she was so bad at keeping track of time. Tess, who could turn every setback into a joke that made us all laugh.

"Yeah, it is," says Adrian, moving back over to the windows, to look out at the city.

I'm ashamed. Ashamed that we're chatting and laughing while she's all alone over there.

"Are you coming?" I ask Charlotte, but she shakes her head.

Without waiting for any of the others, I make my way around the dining table toward the living room. Tess is sitting bolt upright. Her hair, which I remember being light blond, with sun-kissed highlights, looks darker now, gathered in a high ponytail. She is wearing a pair of smart black pants, neatly pressed, and a snug white shirt with the sleeves rolled up. So proper, so professional. I feel a strange warmth in my chest, a sense of pride at how well she must have done for herself. As ever, she is barefoot, her toenails painted, and I can make out the tattoo on her ankle. A twisting vine of ivy that would help keep her grounded, she always said. The years have left it slightly blurry, and I can't imagine anything on earth that could have held her back. As I get closer, I realize she is actually wearing a thin pair of stockings, but she is still the only one of us not in shoes. She feels like a strangely stiff shadow of the person I once knew, and it dawns on me that I no longer have any idea who she is.

"Tess?"

She slowly lifts her head. Her face is pale and smooth, lightly made up with muted colors.

"Hi, Sophie."

Her voice is low and monotone, the words something you simply throw out without a second thought. Finn and Charlotte are standing together by the window, watching us. I see Charlotte lean in to whisper something in his ear, and he nods. Adrian has turned his back on the room. Charlotte gives me a slight shake of the head, as though to tell me I should leave her alone. But how can I do that? Tess is one of us.

Or she was, anyway.

"Mind if I sit down?"

Tess glances to both sides before she shuffles along to make room. As I slump onto the cushion, her body tilts toward me and our thighs briefly touch before she moves away.

"How are things?"

I don't know why, but my words come out as a whisper. Something about Tess makes me want to huddle up and get closer to her, as though we both share a secret that the others can never find out. But for whatever reason, I get the sense that she feels the exact opposite. Tess sits up straight and smiles. A soft, light smile that makes her eyes narrow. Cat's eyes, William always used to say.

She raises her pointed chin.

"I'm good."

She looks good, and I'm glad. If I'm really honest, that's not what I expected.

"I've often thought I should—"

"Come and take your seats, everyone. Dinner is ready."

Ava interrupts me from where she is standing at the end of the table, hands gripping the back of the chair. Tess immediately leaps up and smooths her shirt over her stomach.

"No," she says without looking at me.

I blink in confusion. "What was that?"

"I said no. You haven't thought that at all."

With that, she leaves me alone.

My cheeks feel hot. It could be the shock of what she just said, or maybe it's the shame of knowing that she's right. Because I haven't thought about calling Tess, not even once. I made do with checking her profile picture, a photograph of her with the wind in her hair on a rocky beach somewhere. Made do with knowing she was alive. Still on the sofa, I clasp my hands and see Adrian mouth something to me: *What did I tell you?* Ava is darting around the table in her heels, straightening the already straight napkins and moving the vase slightly to one side, turning it a fraction before pushing it back to its original place.

"I've assigned each of you a seat," she shouts. "Your names are on the boxes."

I get up, hesitating briefly before making my way over to the table, where the others are trying to find their names, hands touching arms and shoulders, laughing.

"Sophie, you forgot your prosecco."

Ava has found my glass on the sideboard, and she thrusts it into my hand.

"You still have half of it left. Just let me know if you'd rather have something else."

I nod and smile, unable to tear my eyes away from Tess, who keeps her distance from the others and immediately sits down in one of the chairs.

I start at the end of the table, checking the names. *Adrian.* Charlotte's fingers brush one of the little labels, and she sits down on the other side of the table, next to Finn. I slowly move behind Tess, checking the label beside her.

Sophie.

Tess doesn't even glance in my direction as I pull out the chair and take a seat.

"Ava has decorated so beautifully," I say, but she turns away.

With a sigh, I pick up the small box and hold it to my ear, shake it. Unexpectedly light and obviously empty.

"But there's nothing in—"

Ava has appeared right behind me, and she takes the box from my hand and puts it down in the exact same place on the table.

"Not yet," she whispers into my ear.

She then sits down at the head of the table, the one closest to me, and lets out a deep sigh, a trembling smile on her face.

"There's no rush; we've got all evening. Plus, I've prepared a little surprise for you all."

"I told you," Charlotte almost shouts, nudging Finn with her elbow.

Adrian fumbles with his napkin, still looking out through the high windows. Tess is sitting with her hands in her lap, staring down at her plate. I just lean back in my chair and focus on the fact that one of us is missing.

CHAPTER

6

Seven hours and thirteen minutes before William's death

THE LAST TIME it had been quite so unbearably hot was the summer they'd graduated from senior high school. With rolled-up shirt sleeves, jackets thrown over arms, and the girls carrying their shoes in their hands, they'd rushed down the sun-drenched steps outside Borgarskolan and thrown their student caps into the air as though nothing on earth could stop them. As the sun dipped below the rooftops, they'd left the parties in town and cycled the five or so miles to the shore by Ava's house, Sophie perched on William's pannier rack, with her slim arms wrapped around his waist. When they'd reached the jetty, they'd peeled off the last traces of their champagne-soaked youth and plunged beneath the surface, which brought no more than a slight hint of coolness.

Six years had passed since then, and plenty had changed. Still, the mercury had been hovering around eighty-five for almost a week now, the nights tropical and the sheets sweaty, and William's insomnia was finally starting to take its toll on him.

Just like on graduation day, when his starched shirt had clung to his back, he had been desperate to get out of his sweaty shirt all afternoon. The shirt that office policy said he had to wear. The damp patches beneath his arms grew as the heat rose in the open-plan office, and by the end of the day, the squeaky fan on his desk was doing nothing but pushing hot air around. One by one, William emptied the folders on his laptop, deleting all traces of himself and gathering client information to hand over to one of his colleagues before he walked down the long corridor to the elevators for the last time. With every key he hit, every document that disappeared, the gnawing feeling that it had been a huge mistake to resign grew and grew. Last but not least, he grabbed the framed photograph of Sophie on a blanket in Boulognerskogen Park. The sun had been bright that day, making her squint so much that her nose was crinkled, pulling her face into a grin.

She had already dozed off by the time he'd tiptoed into the bedroom and closed the blinds last night, and she had been gone when he woke that morning. The denim shorts she had dumped on the floor had vanished, and her bag was no longer leaning against the shoe rack, but the scent of her perfume still lingered in the kitchen and hallway.

Everything would be fine; he would make sure of that. For Sophie's sake, everything would work out for the best.

It had to.

* * *

Dropping his shirt to the bath mat and stepping beneath the cold shower had come as a welcome relief, but he was only halfway to Christos Taverna when new sweat patches began growing beneath his arms and on the back of his pale gray T-shirt.

There was a large sign obscuring most of the glass on the door of the restaurant, and William studied it for a moment or two before pulling the handle: "Closed for summer."

But not for them.

It took his eyes a few seconds to get used to the darkness inside and another few to realize he was still wearing his sunglasses. He hoped Adrian would be first to arrive after Finn, so he could talk to him before the others showed up. He was sure there must be a good explanation. If he could just get him up against the wall and tell him what he knew, Adrian would have no choice but to give him answers. The chink of daylight faded as the door swung shut behind him, and the draft carried the aroma of garlic over from the kitchen.

"Close the door—it messes up the air conditioning!"

The bar was to William's front right, but the raspy voice had come from the kitchen, where he could hear pots and pans clattering. With a sigh, the fan above William's head started blowing a cool breeze again.

As expected, most of the tables in the dining area to the left of the door were empty, but not all of them. An elderly couple were sitting by the window, and a lone man with huge arms bulging from a short-sleeved shirt was at the table by the TV on the wall. There was no sign of the others.

Sophie had been ignoring his texts all day, but she had called him in the middle of the afternoon. William had started to ask her about that morning, about her empty side of the bed, but she'd interrupted him. Said she wanted to push back the time they had arranged to meet, that she had something she needed to do first.

But now she wasn't here.

The swinging doors opened, and Christos came waddling out of the kitchen with a wooden spoon in his hand. The arthritis that had long plagued his sixty-year-old knees had now spread to other joints. His white top was drenched in sweat, and his forehead was glistening beneath his dark curls.

"Ah, it's you. Another heat record today," he said, coughing into his elbow. "Remember you heard it here first."

"Hi, Christos."

Christos followed his gaze over to the other diners.

"Regulars. I didn't have the heart to say no. But don't worry—they'll be gone soon. Their food's on the way."

With that, he shuffled back toward the kitchen, pointing to the back corner of the restaurant with his wooden spoon.

"The usual table's ready for you. You're the loser today, William."

His words made William raise his chin and take off his sunglasses. Despite the punishing heat, he felt an icy chill spread through him.

"What did you say?"

Christos paused and shrugged with his hand on the swinging door. "You're first to arrive. You lost."

William shook his head at the stupid game they had been playing for far too long. At his demons, which had multiplied. He heard shouting and cheers from the TV as one of the soccer teams scored a goal, and the man with the big arms muttered to himself and slammed his glass down on the table. William couldn't shake off the feeling that he had actually lost far more than some dumb competition.

Behind him, the door opened, and he felt a hand on his shoulder.

"Beer," Adrian gasped in his ear. "I'll do anything for an ice-cold beer."

His grip tightened, and he pushed William over to the little wooden bar, reeking of cigarette smoke.

"What do you want, William? A Mariestad?"

"Yeah, whatever. Listen, we need to talk, Adrian."

Adrian nipped behind the bar and opened the fridge. He looked the same as ever, his shoulders relaxed. The summer had only just begun, but his arms and neck were already tanned—though his South American heritage meant he was always darker than the others. There was no sign of any dark circles beneath his eyes.

At least one of them had been managing to sleep.

"I'm taking two Mariestads, Christos!" Adrian called over to the swinging doors. "Can you add it to the tab?"

Gripping the necks of the two bottles, he opened them both and thrust one into William's hand.

"What do you want to talk about?"

William turned to the couple by the window. The woman was facing the door, watching their movements as she poked at her food.

"Not here. Let's go over to the table. I've got something I need to show you on my laptop."

Adrian studied him for a moment before nodding and heading over to the table. William adjusted his laptop bag on his shoulder and followed him. Things suddenly seemed nowhere near as easy as they had in his mind.

Where was he supposed to start?

How much should he reveal that he knew?

In a quiet corner at the back of the restaurant, their table had been set with a white tablecloth, the plates and glasses ready and waiting for them. Adrian pulled out one of the chairs, slumped down, and necked a third of his bottle. William sat at the end of the table and took a couple of deep gulps before cradling the bottle with both hands.

"I got a call at the start of the week," he began as Adrian's focus drifted from his face to a point above his head.

"You had a tough week too, huh?"

The smooth voice came from behind William's back. It was Ava, clutching an armful of books. The sunlight from the window illuminated her fair hair, which was messily tied up, a few loose strands framing her flushed face. She dropped her course books to the table with a thud. Dog-eared textbooks about behavioral science, printed articles about psychology. She had her glasses perched on top of her head and a smear of pencil on her chin, probably because she had fallen asleep with her head on her notes, on the train back from Uppsala.

"Am I interrupting something?"

"No, not at all." Adrian leaped up and offered his seat to Ava. "I was just going for a cigarette."

Adrian always smoked when he was nervous. During their final exams in senior high, he had spent every break out in the yard, a glowing cigarette in his trembling hands. William watched him stride out of the restaurant, but then he felt Ava grip his hand, bringing him back to the table.

"Are you all right?" she asked.

He laughed quietly in an attempt to mask how bad things really were.

"I'm fine, just tired. This heat sucks all the energy out of me."

"It's the same with all of us, but it'll be over soon. Did you manage to get any sleep last night?"

William trailed a thumb over the soft skin on the back of her hand, then turned it over to touch the pale scar. Ava pulled away before he managed to get a better look at the Band-Aid on her forearm.

"What are you doing?" she asked.

"You didn't pick up when I called this morning. What'll be over soon?"

"I was talking about the heat wave, William. That's all."

He didn't believe her.

"When you called me last week . . ." he began, though that was as far as he got before he heard the sound of footsteps approaching.

Adrian and Charlotte were making their way over to the table together, Charlotte with a glass of red wine in each hand, wearing a pink, white, and green dress that was fitted in the bodice. Her long red curls hung loose over her shoulders, and her nose and cheeks were peppered with tiny freckles. When she saw them, her face broke into a smile. She hesitantly held out one of the glasses to Ava and kissed her on the cheek before putting an arm around William and hugging him tight.

"Wine?" he asked Ava, nodding to her glass.

"Just one, to help me relax."

"God, finally!" Charlotte exclaimed, taking a big sip from her glass. "I thought this week was never going to end."

"You're not the only one," said Ava, moving her mountain of books over to a chair by the wall.

"Exam?"

"Exams."

"You're going to work yourself to death, woman," Charlotte sighed. "Is five years of studying not enough for you, like the rest of us? And have you never heard of taking a break over the summer?"

"Here was me thinking I'd save time by doing summer courses. I'm giving myself a future." Ava smiled and put her glass down. "You'll see."

"What have I missed? I had to stay until closing, even though they knew I had plans." Tess had appeared behind Charlotte, short of breath, with her bag in one hand and a blotchy red neck. Her blond hair was poker straight, just touching her bare shoulders, and her eyes were bright, her pupils big.

Too big.

"Glad to hear *someone* is planning for the future," Charlotte muttered, sipping her wine.

"You haven't missed anything; we haven't ordered yet." Adrian moved around the table, clearing away a plate and glass from one of the seats. "Someone must've counted wrong; there's one setting too many."

Ava glanced over to William and shook her head. He wished he had the energy to tell Adrian to leave them, but he held his tongue. If he was going to talk to him this evening, there was no time for bickering. Instead, he tried to make eye contact with Tess, but she was looking everywhere but at him.

"Tess," he hissed as she passed just out of reach, spinning away before he could grab her arm.

She rubbed Ava's back, ran her fingers through Adrian's dark hair and wrapped her arm around Charlotte's waist before sitting down, as far away from William as she could, with a satisfied sigh.

"Who's up for shots?" she shouted, tucking her hair behind her ears. "I feel like dancing. There's a new place in Söder, and they're opening up the entire backyard tonight. Fairy lights, fresh air, the stars—what could be better?"

She was high: that much was obvious. And if William had any say in the matter, the only place she would be going was back to her apartment.

"Are you crazy, Tess? You can't dance when it's this hot."

"What's everyone eating?" Tess asked, ignoring Ava. "I think I'll just get a salad."

"We're doing small plates, no?" Charlotte picked up a menu and opened it, though she already knew every dish on it by heart. "And sharing like usual? A few starters and mains, and then we split the bill?"

She grabbed a stack of menus and handed them out around the table.

"But I just want a salad," Tess replied.

"The only thing I know I want is saganaki." Charlotte closed her menu. "I've been dreaming about grilled saganaki since three o'clock, when I realized the coffee machine was broken—again."

"Where's Finn?" asked Ava, craning her neck. "He's usually first."

"Yeah, there was no sign of him when I got here. I was first today."

William swigged his beer, felt the condensation on his palms, and glanced down at his watch. Sophie hadn't arrived yet either. When she'd said she couldn't meet him outside the office, they had arranged to meet here before the others showed up. He lowered his beer and felt Ava's eyes on him from the other side of the table.

"Sorry I'm late."

The low hum of voices around the table died down. William turned his head, and there she was: standing in the middle of the restaurant, one hand on the strap of her bag. She was wearing a white knee-length skirt, so white that it had to be new, making her legs look much more tanned than he knew they were. Her brown hair was wavy and unruly, and just seeing her made his heart race and his mouth turn dry.

"Sophie, come and sit down."

Ava patted the seat beside her, and Charlotte pushed a menu over to the empty space. Sophie rubbed the back of her neck, her eyes darting around the table until they found William and softened. She strode over, sat down, and shuffled forward in her chair. William's hand found hers and gave it a squeeze. He wanted her to know he was there, that he would never do anything to risk what they had. She looked up and kissed him softly on the lips before peering down at the menu.

"Where have you been?" he asked quietly.

"I got held up," she replied without looking at him. "I had to finish an essay and hand it in ahead of the weekend so I can catch up before the autumn term."

There was a good reason—of course there was; he was stupid for thinking otherwise. Leaning back in his chair, William took in the group of people he knew better than anyone else. People who knew him better than he knew himself. He closed his eyes and took a deep breath.

CHAPTER

7

Now

"YOU HAVE NO idea how often I've fantasized about what you've all been up to these past ten years. Let's go around the group!"

Charlotte leans forward, with her elbows on the table, her chin resting on her interlinked fingers. There is something almost eerie about how quickly we've fallen into our old roles: Charlotte loudly steering the conversation, Finn letting her get away with it, Adrian poking fun at her without her catching his sarcasm. Beside me, however, Tess is sitting quietly, not meeting anyone's eye, and I feel an urge to grab her slim shoulders and shake some life into her.

"I'll start," Charlotte continues.

Ava has passed a stainless steel carafe around the table, and everyone now has a glass of full-bodied red wine in front of them, staining their lips. Tess's is untouched, but she keeps turning her water glass in her hand, taking a sip from time to time. The soft lighting from the candles is atmospheric, playing on our skin and our faces. It reminds me of our summers at William's little log cabin, where we gathered around the fire in the evenings, toasting marshmallows and drinking disgusting liqueur from plastic mugs. The cabin wasn't really big enough for us, but we squeezed into the pine bunkbeds and slept on inflatable mattresses on the floor. William loved it when we were all together, everyone he cared about in one place. That often made me feel small and insignificant, as though I would never be enough for him.

We're all together again now, but William is no longer with us.

I turn my wineglass in my hand, lift it to my nose. I haven't drunk red wine since Dad died. He lived for charcuterie and red wine, and he used to love thrusting a glass into my hand and telling me to write down what I could smell.

"Did you detect any unexpected aromas?"

"Would you say it was full-bodied or light?"

Feeling a certain hesitation, I take a sip and let it wash over my tongue. Black pepper, licorice, blackberry.

Shiraz.

"As I said earlier, I work in TV production," Charlotte goes on.

She drags out the last word and chuckles to herself, as though TV is the only profession worth anyone's time. I'm not surprised by her choice of work. Even in senior high school, she made sure she had three solos during the Christmas concert, and after that she took acting classes in the evenings. I tune out Charlotte's nasal voice, her stories about production company parties and directors she has toasted with, poking at the silver cloche over my plate instead, pushing it slightly around until it hits whatever is underneath. So, it's not as empty as the little box seems to be. For a moment or two, I had started to suspect that the entire dinner was just one big joke at our expense, but why would Ava go to all that effort?

It was a mistake to doze off in my room after breakfast, I realize. A few hours' terrible sleep on an overly soft mattress, and I'm now so hungry I might take a bite out of my napkin if Ava doesn't give us the sign to lift our cloches soon.

"And we're married, of course," she says, waving her ring in the air. Everyone takes the bait and starts oohing and aahing over the diamond.

Everyone but me, that is. I'm too busy watching Finn. He looks like he wants to crawl out of his slightly too snug shirt. Finn's chin is resting on his palm, and he has pushed his lower lip out like a grumpy child—like someone who would rather be absolutely anywhere else. His gaze comes to rest somewhere out in the hallway, and he has just closed his eyes when Charlotte elbows him in the side.

"Finn."

"What?"

"I just said that we're married."

"Great."

Charlotte strokes his rosy cheek and straightens the collar of his shirt.

"We live in a house in Solna, a stone's throw from the mall and the station; you couldn't get much closer. I guess that's the compromise we had to make. I would rather have an apartment in central Stockholm, of course," she says, turning to Adrian, "but it's a new build, set over three floors. It feels good to know that no one else has lived there before us. No kids yet, but we're working on that, right, Finn?"

"There are worse jobs," Adrian says with a grin, and Charlotte pretends to be insulted as she kisses Finn on the cheek and ruffles his hair. Everyone but Tess laughs, and Finn looks down at the table.

"We've got enough space when the time comes, in any case. Tell them about your job, Finn." Charlotte raises her glass to her lips. "He's a computer genius—they'd never survive without him. The company practically grinds to a halt whenever he goes on holiday, which unfortunately means he almost never takes any time off—and when he does, they just call every other day. Tell them, Finn."

"I think you've just covered most of it," he says, a crooked smile on his lips.

Despite his rounder cheeks and the lines the years have etched into his face, he still has his boyish looks. I can imagine that the last thing he feels like doing is talking about his job. Finn would much rather talk about traveling, visiting historic places, kayak trips on raging rivers, and classic films he has managed to tick off his long list—things that I doubt he has managed to do much of if he's been married to Charlotte for the past nine years.

"Don't be so shy. Go on—tell them."

"I'd rather hear what Adrian has to say. How's life on the French Riviera? Bought any new Ferraris lately?"

Adrian shrugs and sips his wine. "It's just a house."

"If that's just a house, then ours is a shoebox," Finn snorts.

Adrian laughs and shakes his head, but I catch a glimmer of something dark in his eye.

"It's actually a Pagani, not a Ferrari. And I sold the house in France a year ago."

"But you've still got the place on Gotland, right?" asks Ava.

"Sold that too. I guess I just don't like sea air."

His words grate, as though it wasn't entirely his decision. But why else would he sell?

"That's what you always said, isn't it?" I say. "That you'd make millions. Do you remember what you promised me?"

People make lots of promises when they're young and have hopes and dreams they don't quite believe will ever come true, and to be perfectly honest I've only just remembered it myself.

"I have no idea what you're talking about," he says, his eyes narrowing to dark slits, the way they always do when he is about to laugh.

"I think you do," I say. I love teasing Adrian, and I know he loves teasing me too, because he knows exactly which buttons to press. "Once you made your first million, you said you would replace my rusty old Polo with a new car. I'm still waiting."

"You're not telling me you still drive that tragic thing?"

"God, no, I had it scrapped years ago. You're not telling me you still haven't made a million?"

"I'll buy you a nice car, Sophie."

I laugh, but I can't tell whether he is joking or not. Adrian winks at me, and I blow him a kiss. I then turn the other way, toward Ava. She is sitting quietly at the end of the table, one hand on the tablecloth and a faint smile on her lips. But she isn't looking at the others.

She's looking at Tess.

I straighten my already straight cutlery and sip my wine before slowly turning my head in Tess's direction. She seems so uncomfortable, like someone who has wandered into the wrong lecture but is too scared to let anyone know. But then she smiles the creepiest smile I've ever seen, her eyes completely empty. I can't help but follow her gaze back to Ava, who is now looking at me with a wry smirk. Ava then turns her attention to Adrian, as though she had never looked away from him.

"What about your love life, Adrian? Anyone special waiting for you back home?" she asks.

He shakes his head. "Nope. Just me."

"Come off it," says Charlotte. "We all remember the groups of girls that used to trail Adrian down the corridors at school, don't we? Or all those doe-eyed girls crying over you in nightclubs once we graduated? I'm sure there must be someone waiting for you—though maybe you switch up who you share your bed with?"

"I've got enough on my plate with work."

"But you don't even need to work. You could take a step back and live well for the rest of your life. Start a family, kids."

Charlotte has gone too far now, and Adrian's jaw tenses. Everyone is quiet around the table, and for a brief moment I almost feel sorry for her; Charlotte never thinks before she speaks. But then she opens her mouth again, and the feeling disappears.

"What about you, Tess?" she says. "Tell us what you've been up to since we last saw you. Are you still working in the café? Did you ever find a bigger apartment?"

I glare at Charlotte in an attempt to make her see how inappropriate it is to put Tess on the spot like this, but as ever she pays no attention to anyone else once she gets going. Tess will probably leap up from her chair and stomp off now, just like she did all those times when William had to take her aside to talk to her. She could spend hours in a mood, not saying a single word to any of us, only to be her usual self again the next day, acting like nothing had happened.

But Tess doesn't get up.

She wrings her hands and looks up at Ava as though she has all the answers. Ava gives her an encouraging nod.

"I've been in rehab," Tess says in the same monotonous tone that makes my skin crawl.

It isn't her. It's as though someone else has taken over her body and repressed all the fizzing joy she used to spread around her. After what she just said, I half expect an end to the conversation, blushing cheeks turning the other way, but Ava's glance seems to have unleashed a torrent of words from Tess's thin lips. Her mouth curls into what looks like a smile that doesn't quite reach the rest of her face.

"I didn't take William's death especially well. It was like all the hope I had died with him. You know I was taking a lot of pills back then—I heard you whispering, so don't act surprised. And that—well, it spiraled out of control after everything with William. I just wanted the pain to go away."

Silence settles over the room again.

"Wow, it was so strong of you to get yourself out of that vicious circle and seek help," says Charlotte. "I'm so glad to see that you're doing well now, that you've turned your life around."

"I didn't have much choice after Mom died."

My God.

The entire table turns into a pained group of averted gazes and hands fiddling with cutlery or turning glasses. Charlotte's face transforms into an anxious grimace, and I feel a tug in my chest.

Why did she have to say anything?

"Her partner beat her up. You remember Benke, right?"

Everyone nods. How could we forget?

Benke was already in Tess's life when I first moved to Gävle. A tall, gangly man with hollow eyes and oil-flecked hands. Tess always asked us to wait outside when we arranged to meet at her place. I'm not sure I ever actually set foot inside her mother's apartment or saw her bedroom there. Still, we often heard his deep voice booming down the stairwell when she came out. The minute the door closed behind her, it was as though a weight lifted from her face, and the spark reappeared in her eyes.

Benke was someone who came and went over the years, like a pest you can't quite get rid of.

"Mom had tried to call me, apparently, but I was totally out of it at someone else's place. I guess I must have thrown up on my phone or dropped it or something, because it wasn't working."

"When was this?" I ask, reaching for her cold hand beneath the table.

She squeezes it back.

"Almost a year after William died. She was in a coma for a while, but her brain was too badly damaged for them to be able to do anything for her. I sat by her side every day until they switched off the life support machine, and after that I knew I would die if I didn't sort myself out. I chose to live because she didn't have that choice."

Adrian takes a deep breath and exhales. I'm staring down at the cloche again. If Adrian is going to buy anyone a new car, it should be Tess. Maybe even a house.

"I'm sorry," he says, reaching for her other hand, but she pulls back.

"Condolences, Tess," says Finn. "I had no idea."

"It just made me stronger," she says, fixing her eyes on Charlotte. "It made me realize what I'm worth and that I should stop putting myself in damaging situations. So no, I'm not still working in the café. These days I work at a refuge for women who need help escaping violent partners. I took a course on male violence against women at college, and now I'm renting a house in Valbo."

"That's great, Tess. I really didn't mean to . . . If I'd known that . . ."

Charlotte is grasping for words, desperately looking for support from the rest of us.

"Don't worry about it, Charlotte," says Finn, squeezing her shoulder. "Drop it. No one knew."

"What about you, Sophie?" Adrian grins at me.

I flinch.

"Yeah, come on." Charlotte laughs gratefully, relieved that the focus has shifted from Tess to me. "You never answered the question earlier. Tell us what you do. Are you a teacher? Where do you live?"

"Um, where do I start? I dropped out of teacher training, and these days I work . . ." I pause, my eyes drifting over their curious faces. "I studied communication and ended up getting a job at a radio station."

"Radio? Anything we might have heard?"

"Not unless you're awake in the middle of the night."

"So you actually *talk* on the radio?" Charlotte asks. I can see that she is just waiting for me to reveal my mistake and explain that I actually work in admin or behind reception, so I sit tall and nod with a wry smile.

"I host a relationship show."

Adrian stifles a laugh.

"Something funny?" I ask.

"No, no. It makes perfect sense that someone who . . . Are you serious, Sophie? You give relationship advice?"

"Do you have a boyfriend? A partner, a husband? Anyone special?"

I grit my teeth. This question always manages to hit a sore spot. Charlotte flashes her dazzlingly white teeth and folds her arms.

"You do!" she says, pleased with herself. "Tell us. Who is he?"

"Nope, no boyfriend, though I have dated a bit."

Whenever Malika arranges blind dates without telling me about it, tricking me into a never-ending ambush of cousins and desperate colleagues.

"But I'm happiest on my own."

"You're only thirty-four."

There it is. Ava's voice makes everyone's head turn. I had almost forgotten her at the end of the table, where she is leaning back in her chair, playing with her earring.

"You've got your whole life ahead of you—never forget that."

"She's right—thirty-four is nothing," Charlotte agrees, gripping Finn's hand. "There's someone for you out there somewhere. You'll find him—I'm sure of it. It's not too late yet."

"I didn't say I was looking," I say, because the last thing I want is to end up in a relationship where someone becomes dependent on me and the decisions I make. Charlotte cocks her head and gives me a pitying smile, and I can't bear to look at her, so I turn to Ava instead.

"What about you, Ava?" I ask in an attempt to avoid any questions about why I left and where I went. "What have you been doing all these years? You said you hadn't been working?"

There are more questions I want to ask, simmering just beneath the surface. Like: What happened to wanting to build something from nothing with your own two hands? Or what happened to the down-to-earth girl I loved, who would have given up everything just to be happy? Where did this distance come from, making it feel like there is a gulf between us, even though we're sitting no more than a few feet apart?

"I moved here, to this incredible apartment."

She holds out one hand, and I look around at the expensive decor and the complete lack of personality. She doesn't say it as though it's something she is proud of, but more as a statement about where life took her, and her answer niggles away at me like a stubborn grain of sand in my eye.

"You could say that I've spent the past few years finding myself and the person I want to be."

"What about helping others?" I ask. "The vulnerable. Aren't you planning to go back to what you trained to do? What you used to be so passionate about?"

"You know," she says, raising her glass, "I'm so glad you're all here this evening. I've missed you so much. Let's see if I can actually manage to let you go again."

A knowing smile spreads across her face, and she winks at Tess, who is busy smoothing her already-smooth hair.

"Cheers—to friends!"

We all raise our glasses and smile our broadest smiles. Even Tess, who smiles so much that her sharp cheekbones look like they might pierce her pale skin.

"And cheers to William," Ava adds, lifting her glass to her lips. Charlotte and Finn pause and exchange a glance before turning to me.

Her words hit me harder than expected. I blink a few times, my eyes drifting from Finn to Adrian, who silently mouths, "Are you okay?" I nod and take a sip of my wine, too big a sip, which catches in my throat.

"All right, why don't we tuck in?" says Ava, carefully wiping her mouth before she spreads her napkin in her lap.

"You've set the table so beautifully," says Charlotte, shuffling forward in her chair. "Did you cook everything yourself?"

"No, I bought it. Only the best is good enough for you."

"You're too sweet. I'm starving. I had to swing by the studio before we left Stockholm. We're filming a game show at the minute, and it took much longer than I thought. The assistant messed up the lunch order, so the only thing to eat was a lukewarm salad. Glamorous, huh?"

The clattering of cutlery, glasses, and china spreads through the room, along with the murmur of expectant voices. Adrian lifts his cloche, as does Finn. Both pause with the metal dome in their hands, staring down at their plates.

"Strange choice of starter, I have to say," Adrian mumbles, putting his cloche down.

Beside me, Tess lifts her cloche, and I recognize the smell before I see what it is, immediately lifting my own. In the middle of the plate is a perfectly grilled piece of saganaki with an olive side salad.

"Do you think so?" Ava asks, cutting off a large piece of cheese and spearing it and an olive on her fork. "Delicious."

I'm not sure what concerns me most: Ava serving us saganaki or suddenly liking olives. For the first time all evening, Tess touches me, placing her cold hand on my arm and leaning in to me with a deep sigh.

"Are you all right?"

"Yeah, I'm fine. It's just cheese, right?"

"Not just any old cheese."

"Greek food," says Charlotte, cautiously nibbling a forkful as though she were eating broken glass. "I haven't eaten Greek food in . . ."

She trails off and chews quietly.

"Ten years?" Adrian suggests, putting his fork down.

"So, is this the surprise?" Finn asks, poking at his salad. "Food from Christos Taverna? Is it even still open?"

Ava grins and scans the faces all around her.

"The food isn't from Christos. I've waited years for this, and every detail had to be perfect. Something happened ten years ago, and it tore us apart—something that changed us all forever. My hope for this evening is that we'll be able to find our way back to who we were then. *What* we were."

"We're thirty-four now," Adrian protests. "I don't think any of us wants to go back to who we were ten years ago. I'm pretty happy with where I am right now."

Ava closes her eyes for a few seconds.

"Give it a chance, just for this evening." She turns to me. "And this time no one is going to leave early."

CHAPTER

8

Now

THE CHEESE LEAVES a bitter taste in my mouth, but I had no choice but to eat it. Ava's words are still ringing in my ears as I get up from the table and do a loop of the room, pretending to admire the view. I don't dare touch anything, because everything here looks like it costs more than I earn in a month. Other than the pretty vase of flowers that'll be dead within a few days, there isn't a single plant in the entire apartment.

I pause in front of the large painting again, hugging myself tight.

"And this time no one is going to leave early."

It's probably all in my mind, not at all directed at me, but I can't help feeling like she was talking about that night ten years ago. The night when I left William's apartment and never went back.

Something about this painting speaks to me. There is something fascinating about the thick brushstrokes and the dark colors, the undulating waves flowing toward the bottom of the canvas as though they're trying to escape. Something keeps drawing me in, refusing to let go. Ava must have vented a lot of big emotions on these canvases, things she couldn't express in her more delicate watercolors.

Bottled up, simmering.

I rub my arms and glance back over my shoulder. Ava got up to start clearing the plates away the minute we finished eating, Tess hurrying after her. Flitting in and out of the kitchen like a pale shadow, making sure to stay within reach of Ava at all times. I can hear them talking at the other end of the dining room now. Or rather, Tess is talking; Ava is listening. When I turn around, I see Tess gesticulating wildly. Ava is standing calmly in front of her, one hand on her hip, like she is just waiting for the torrent of words to end. Tess turns away from her and takes a step toward the hallway, but Ava grabs her arm and leans in to whisper something in her ear. It's as though Tess shrinks, and she makes her way back over to the table as Ava's hand leaves her arm. Ava herself disappears into the kitchen.

The interaction between them fascinates me in the same way a couple of strangers having an argument on the street might; I can't tear my eyes away. These aren't two people who haven't spoken in a decade.

The thought comes out of nowhere.

It's almost as though Ava has some sort of hold over Tess.

My half-empty prosecco glass is still on the table beside my wine, and I grab it in passing, pat Adrian on the shoulder, and make my way over to Tess, who is gazing toward Ava in the kitchen.

"Hi."

She flinches and then slowly exhales when she sees that it's me.

"Sorry, did I scare you?"

"I was miles away," she says, glancing over to the hallway.

Close up, her eyes are red and watery. She has been crying.

"I really am sorry I never called after I left, Tess. I wish I'd been there for you."

Every word of that is true. I can't claim I was ever there for her when she turned up outside William's door in the middle of winter, blue and shivering, in nothing but a hoodie and a pair of tracksuit bottoms. I wasn't the person she'd called when her birthdays ended in screaming and broken glasses after she left home. But William would have wanted me there.

He would have been counting on it.

"It doesn't matter anymore."

"Yes, it does. I wish I'd been there for you when your mom died."

Tess gives me a resolute nod and then leaves me alone with my half-empty glass. I knock back the rest of the prosecco and set it down beside a lamp and a silver figurine on a small table by the wall, then take a step forward to close the distance between us. Tess keeps walking, past the dining table, toward the living room. She disappears around the wall separating the two spaces.

As I round the corner, I see her sitting in a blood-red armchair with a high back. She has her legs crossed and her hands on the armrests, her head tipped back. I can see several slim silver rings on her fingers. There are two armchairs, flanking a small glass table. This side of the wall is lined with tall built-in bookshelves. So, I think. This is where Ava has been hiding all her books.

Tess doesn't open her eyes when I sit down in the other armchair. I follow her example and lean back, enjoying the soft cushioning and the velvety fabric beneath my hands.

"My dad died too," I say.

"I know. Were you here?"

"No."

When Mom called to say that he had been admitted to hospital and that I should be there, I'd packed a bag. I even took a cab to the station and stood in the rain on the platform before ultimately catching the bus back home and slumping onto the sofa with drenched hair and my bag on the floor by my feet. Just the thought of seeing Mom clutch his hand as the tears rolled down her cheeks made me feel sick. He didn't deserve her tears.

"Sorry. It must've been tough for you."

Ten years ago, she would have stroked my arm and looked me straight in the eye with that glittering gaze of hers. It was people like us, she always used to say, the ones who'd had to fight along the way, who had most to gain. But today she doesn't even look at me, and I doubt she really means what she's saying.

"It was tough for my mom," I explain. "I'm guessing you and Ava had spoken before this evening?"

Her eyes widen. "What makes you say that?"

"Just a feeling I got," I say. "Am I wrong?"

She closes her eyes again.

"No, you're right. Ava called me. Talked and talked as though it were only yesterday that we last spoke."

Tess snorts.

"So the two of you have spoken a lot since William's funeral?"

"She called me for the first time last week."

I hear the sound of Ava's heels leaving the kitchen, pausing for a moment before continuing into the dining room.

"What did she want?"

I had forgotten how beautiful Tess's eyes are, bright green with pale flecks, framed by the dark mascara on her lashes.

"She wanted me to come today, just like she wanted the rest of you to come."

"But why? Why did she want us to get together right now?"

Tess smiles and struggles up out of the chair. "I guess you'll see. We all will."

"Tess? Sophie?" Ava calls through to us from the dining room.

Tess starts making her way over there, but I stop her with a hand on her shoulder.

"Hold on. What were you and Ava talking about just now? You seemed upset."

"I told her I wanted to go home, and she said no."

Tess disappears around the corner into the dining room, and I'm left staring at the hundreds of books on the shelves. My curiosity takes over, and I move closer, running a hand over the spines and scanning the titles. Lots of them are familiar, the books Ava used to schlep to the library and the restaurant. *The Psychology Book*, *Behavioral Analysis: Step by Step*, plus all the classics she loved so much. Some of the other titles seem a little surprising, however. My fingers pause on the dog-eared spine of a paperback, and I pull it out to study the cover: *Dreams of You*. I take the book down from the shelf and flick through it. Page after page of lust, longing, and passion. The tattered, old paperbacks I carried around in my handbag always made me feel so stupid when I was with Ava. When she sat down with one of her classics, I discreetly shoved my feel-good novels and thrillers back into my bag.

"There you are."

Ava has appeared by my side, and I fumble with the book, eventually managing to push it back into place alongside ten or so near-identical titles, all equally well thumbed. There are several full shelves of romance novels. What was it she used to call them? Fantasies for the braindead?

"Come on—we've been waiting for you."

"I'm coming."

I give the books one last glance before following Ava through to the dining room. She has turned on the ceiling light, and the room is bathed in a soft glow, glittering in the windows and obscuring the view. The space suddenly feels much smaller.

The others are already sitting at the table, laughing and chatting about the New Year's Eve we all got dressed up in glittery dresses and sleek ties, toasting on Ava's balcony at midnight as the snowflakes swirled around our frozen bodies.

"Sophie!" Charlotte cries, waving me over. "Where did you go? I almost thought you'd disappeared on us again."

"I was just around the corner."

"Sit down, sit down—we want to hear more about your job."

They all laugh, but I grit my teeth and take my seat beside Tess.

The sound of metal on glass cuts through the room, and everyone stops talking and turns to Ava, who is standing at the end of the table with a glass in her hand.

"I just wanted to welcome you all again."

Adrian rases his glass in the air. "Cheers to Ava for getting us all together again."

"Cheers!"

There is more clinking as we toast across the table, followed by a short silence as we sip our wine.

"Thank you, Adrian. But I'd also like to explain why I invited you all here today."

Ava takes her seat. Tess didn't join in the toast, nor has she looked any of us in the eye. She is sitting with her chin in one hand and with the other, pulling on the ribbon on the little box in front of her. Her finger moves down to the edge of the lid, and she lifts it a fraction of an inch before letting it drop again, over and over. I have to stop myself from grabbing her hand and holding it still.

"I've had a lot of time to think about everything that happened," Ava continues. "What separated us, what kept us apart. And what I've come up with are details. Details that don't add up. Details that have kept me awake night after night."

Charlotte chuckles softly, still clutching her glass, glancing over to Finn and Adrian.

"What are you talking about, Ava? I thought we were just going to have dinner together."

"We are, Charlotte. We're going to eat dinner and we're going to bring all the details together until the full picture emerges."

"Sorry," says Finn, running a hand through his messy hair, "but I have no idea what you're talking about."

"Everything will become clear soon enough. The details are in your boxes. You might call it a puzzle."

Tess's fingers stop moving, and she pulls her hand back from the box, as though it had just burned her.

"Tess said you wouldn't let her go home," I say.

Tess shoots me a cold look, but Ava simply laughs.

"She just got here. Why would she want to go home?"

"Do you, Tess?" Adrian asks, putting his hand on her arm.

She shrugs and starts poking at her box again. Adrian has always been overprotective as far as Tess is concerned. Where William saw her problems for what they were, Adrian turned a blind eye to the decisions she made and smoothed over everything with a laugh and a hug.

"It doesn't matter. I'll stay."

"You can obviously go home if you want to. Come on."

Adrian gets up and holds out his hand to Tess, and she glances over to Ava before taking it. They walk toward the hall together, and Adrian puts an arm around her shoulder and hugs her.

"Tess," Ava says softly.

Tess turns her head in Ava's direction, but Adrian ushers her down the hallway, out of view. The muted sound of cupboard doors opening and coat hangers screeching on the rail drifts through to us, and Ava leans back in her chair. When we hear a series of thuds, each one louder than the last, everyone turns toward the noise. Banging, pounding, then silence. Adrian marches back into the room, just ahead of Tess. She is wearing a black down jacket with a hood, but has already taken her shoes off again. Her bare feet pad across the floor without a sound, and she pauses an arm's length from Adrian.

"Can you open the door?" he says to Ava.

"The door will be opened once we're done here."

"What are you talking about?" Finn gets up from his chair.

"The door's locked. There's a knob, but the other lock needs a key. And it's not in the hole."

"Locked?" I ask.

This is a twist I didn't see coming. I heard the lock click earlier and realized it was the man outside who had done it, but it never occurred to me that I wouldn't be able to get out if I wanted to. My eyes drift to the wall of glass again. It has transformed into just that: a wall rather than a window. Tiny beads of sweat have begun to build on my forehead, but I wipe them away with my hand and reach for my glass.

"Hold on a second," says Charlotte, holding both hands out in front of her before clamping one over her mouth. "I know what this is! The door, the boxes. Is this an escape room?"

"An escape what?" asks Finn.

"An escape room. You know, there's a company that does this in Stockholm. They lock you in a room and give you an hour to solve the clues and get out. I guess you all saw the man outside when we got here?" She claps her hands in delight and pulls Finn back down into his seat. "Oh, I love this sort of thing. Are these the clues?"

Charlotte picks up her box and weighs it in her hand.

"You could say that," Ava replies, sipping her wine.

"Do we all have to take part?" I ask. "I'm terrible at games. Can I sit this one out?"

I always come in last in the fun activities the station organizes at the summer party. I'm the one who kicks the football into the trees whenever they force me to play, and I'm the one who freezes during charades, who ends up being pushed aside before my turn is even over.

"Everyone has to take part."

"So once we've solved the clues, you'll open the door and we'll be free to go?"

Adrian is standing behind me, gripping the back of my chair. I can feel the heat of his hand on my back. If Adrian is in, I'm in too. He's the kind of person who can solve any problem that gets in his way.

"Exactly," says Ava. "Once we've solved the clues together, you're free to leave if you want to."

"And you'll unlock the door?" I ask.

"Sorry, Tess." Adrian moves back over to his seat. "Seems like we have to play Ava's little game first."

"So who starts? Can I open my box first?" Charlotte shakes her box the way I did earlier, but Ava doesn't stop her the way she stopped me.

"Tess can start," she says.

Tess is still standing where Adrian left her. Her black coat is zipped right up to her chin, and though it must be at least sixty-eight degrees in here, she has her arms wrapped around herself. She takes a step back and shakes her head.

"I don't want to."

"Come on, Tess," says Charlotte. "Just open the box, and we'll solve the clues together. It'll be fun!"

"The quicker we get this over and done with, the quicker you can go home," Finn tells her, placing her box in the middle of her plate, like some delicate little dessert.

Tess stands perfectly still, staring down at the box.

"Should I open it for you?" I suggest, reaching for it.

"No!"

I pull my hand back.

"I'll do it myself."

She slowly makes her way over to the table, tugging down the zip on her coat. She takes her time peeling it off and draping it over the back of her chair, then she picks up the box without taking a seat. Her fingers tremble slightly as she lifts the lid and studies the content.

"What is it?" Charlotte asks, getting up and moving around the table. "Is it a code or a rebus or something? Finn is really good at codes."

"At *coding*."

"Is there a difference?"

Tess drops the lid to the floor and clamps her hand to her mouth. Charlotte reaches her side. She leans in and pokes at the box.

"What is this? I don't understand."

Tess holds up the small object, and Charlotte snatches it from her hand. In that instant, I know exactly what Ava has planned for us this evening.

CHAPTER

9

Five hours and forty-two minutes before William's death

TESS WAS FIRST to take a shot from the round silver tray, closing her eyes as she felt the burn in her throat. Raki. She hated raki. Tequila too. Her choice of drink at the pub was licorice shots, raspberry shots, or hard cider, which simmered away beneath the surface rather than hitting her like a sledgehammer to the head.

But she needed that sledgehammer tonight.

His scent was still clinging to her. She had changed her clothes and taken a long, hot shower, but she could still smell him on her. The minute she opened the door to the apartment, she had heard his wheezing breath from the kitchen and come close to turning straight back around. But then she saw her mom's shoes on the floor, beside his huge boots, and she closed the door behind her. Tess had called to tell her mother the good news at lunch, but she hadn't picked up. She had probably been sleeping. Her mom did that a lot these days.

Favors and return favors. It was as though Mona had been able to sniff it out when they worked together. She had pulled Tess aside behind the counter in the café a few months back and thrust a pack of pills into her hand. They'll help calm you down, she had said, and so Tess had hidden them in the pocket of her apron. Since then, Mona had always been nearby. She swapped shifts so that they would be working together, moved her lunch break so that they could eat together in the sun by the loading bay. If Tess would just do her a favor, then she'd give her the money she needed, and her mom wouldn't have to stay here. She wouldn't have to rely on *him*. But since her mom hadn't picked up, Tess had left work early to swing by her apartment before heading over to Christos. Mona had said she would lock up. Her mom didn't have to stay there; she could pack a bag and stay with Tess until everything was sorted.

But there hadn't been any sign of her mom when she got there, just him. Sitting at the kitchen table with his gross cigarettes and his sweaty cans of beer.

Tess slammed the glass down on the tray and wiped her mouth with the back of her hand. From the other side of the table, she noticed Charlotte watching her. Her freckled shoulders were pink from the sun, her face shiny.

"You want one?"

Charlotte shook her head. "I haven't had shots since school. Maybe you should calm down a bit, though? We haven't even eaten yet."

Tess picked up another glass and knocked it back, her eyes locked on Charlotte. She then lowered it to the tray and flashed her best smile, the bitter taste lingering on her tongue.

"You know me: I'm always calm."

Though she wasn't—not at all. In her head, she was back in the hot kitchen, with his clammy hands on her body, his disgusting breath in her face. It wasn't until her mom appeared from the bedroom with fresh bruises on her collarbone and a nasty shadow beneath her eye that he backed away with a laugh. Her mom had screamed at him, and Tess had gone home. An hour later, she had run down to the restaurant, her skin still stinging after her hot shower.

Tess smiled at Charlotte, who was wearing a pale halter-neck dress. It was low cut, and it was obvious she was wearing it for the attention. Her curly red hair had gone frizzy in the heat. Tess straightened the thin straps on her own shirred black dress and bent down to dig her cell phone out of her bag. Using both thumbs, she typed a quick message and hit "Send."

Is he still there?

Her mother replied less than a minute later.

You don't understand. He swears he'll change. Maybe it's best you don't come over for a while.

She reread those three short sentences, then again one last time before practically throwing her phone into her bag. Oh, she understood. She had understood since elementary school, when there had been another man who'd smoked another brand of cigarettes at their kitchen table. He'd paid for their food whenever he hadn't blown all his money on booze, and whenever her mother was about to kick him out, he would cover the whole of next month's rent.

Money.

Money was king, and that made her sick. It was also the only thing she needed to get her mother to leave town. She had already lined up a job for her at a care home, and as soon as she paid the deposit, her mom could move into the little cottage with a brand-new kitchen. He would never find her there because he wouldn't know where to start looking. Right now, however, his claws were still buried deep in her mother's flesh, and Tess was still short of money. And Mona had already started asking for her cut.

The green blister pack was poking out from beneath her cell phone. Tess should have thrown it out a long time ago, but instead she had hidden it beneath her purse and hairbrush, taking it out to fiddle with it or pop a pill whenever the pressure got to be too much. Charlotte was looking over to where the others were standing, between the bar and the entrance. Adrian nipped outside with a pack of cigarettes in his hand. Tess bent down, pressed out a pill and pushed it into her mouth before straightening up and washing it down with a mouthful of water just as Charlotte turned back around.

Tess got up and moved around the table, putting her arms around Charlotte's shoulders and pressing her cheek to her friend's.

"You look hot tonight, Charlotte."

"It's hard not to in this heat."

"Dressed up for anyone in particular?"

Tess took a seat on the chair beside her and watched as her already-flushed cheeks grew even pinker.

"Oh, shut up. It's tropical out there; this dress was the only thing I could bear to put on. Do you like it? It's new."

Charlotte tugged at the strap behind her neck, hoisting up her prominent bust.

"It's pretty. I love dresses, love letting my legs breathe," Tess replied, flapping the black fabric covering her thighs until she noticed the red marks on the inside of her forearm.

Marks left by his fingers.

With her arms pressed flat against the table, she leaned in to Charlotte.

"Tell me something," she begged her.

"Like what?"

"Anything. Something that makes me forget all about today."

"Tough day working the espresso machine?"

"Something like that."

"Tell you something, huh?" Charlotte tapped her lower lip, her eyes scanning the restaurant. They focused on something, and she leaned back with a wry smile on her red lips. "There's something's going on with Sophie and William."

"Going on?"

Tess turned her head and saw them standing over by the window, but Charlotte grabbed her arm.

"Don't look!"

"What? What's going on?"

"You didn't hear it from me," Charlotte whispered, her head so close to Tess's that their noses were practically touching. "Ava told me that William said Sophie keeps disappearing."

"What do you mean?"

"She doesn't pick up when he calls, and apparently she either leaves the apartment before he wakes up or doesn't go over at all. When he asked her about it, she gave him some excuse that was so unbelievable it's pathetic."

"Did Ava tell you all that?"

Charlotte's head rocked from side to side, and she bit her lip. "Bits of it, but I pieced some of it together myself."

"That doesn't necessarily mean anything. There could be something you don't know about going on, beneath the surface. Something she needs to straighten out."

If there was one thing Tess was sure about, it was William and Sophie. She had never met two people so obsessed with each other before. Just a month ago, William had surprised Sophie with a house viewing, and the ring he'd bought was the prettiest thing Tess had ever seen. It must have cost him a fortune—enough to pay the deposit on a small cottage.

Though now that Tess thought about it, Sophie did look tense. She approached Adrian, who seemed to be avoiding her rather than welcoming her with open arms like he usually did.

"She's definitely got *something* to sort out."

"Charlotte . . .?"

"Yeah?" Charlotte tore her eyes away from William and Sophie and turned to Tess.

"I was at the dentist the other day, an emergency appointment that cost me two hundred and seventy-seven dollars. I haven't paid the rent yet, and it's ages until payday, so I was wondering if—"

"Tess." Charlotte sighed and pushed her chair back, out of reach.

"It would only be for a few weeks."

"I don't lend money. Not to friends. It never ends well. You've got a job now, don't you? You need to learn how to budget. You can't just blow it all on drinking and partying."

"I haven't, but yeah. I understand. I'll work something out."

"It's not that I don't trust you, I just . . ."

Don't trust you.

"Sorry. You really should go back to school, though. Get a better job."

"It's fine, Charlotte. Really. I'm going to the bar."

Tess grabbed her bag from the floor and pulled it onto her shoulder. She gave Charlotte one last glance and then got up and walked over to the bar, which was tucked away behind the wall dividing the restaurant in two. The pill had started to take effect, and her legs felt like spaghetti. She stayed as far from William and the door as she could. Sophie was nowhere to be seen, and he was standing alone by the tinted glass, looking out at Adrian's back and the cloud of cigarette smoke hanging around his head. He didn't notice her as she snuck by and leaned up against the bar beside Ava. Tess's bag tipped over as she put it down, spewing out her cell phone, lip gloss and one of her mom's dog-eared Virginia Andrews books. The corner of the blister pack was peeping out from beneath it. Ava reached for the book, and Tess fumbled to push the pills into a side pocket before dropping her bag to the floor and holding out her hand.

"Why do you read this garbage? It'll warp your view of the world."

"Haven't you ever wanted to get away? Hoped that life might change?"

Ava glanced up at her and turned the book over.

"Seriously, Tess . . . The rich boyfriend and the secret long lost father . . . people getting locked up. Stuff like this just doesn't happen in real life."

Tess snatched the book back and shoved it into her bag.

"No, but it gives me hope that things can change. Come on—come back to the table," she mumbled into Ava's shoulder, hooking an arm around her waist.

If there was anyone who had money to spare, it was Ava, but Tess would never dream of asking her. Ava's parents had more money than she could even imagine, just like the families in her mother's books, living lives full of beautiful clothes and enormous houses. But Ava had never wanted to acknowledge any of that. Asking her for a loan would be like renouncing her friendship.

"I'll be there in a minute."

Ava swirled her red wine and then took a long sip. Tess watched as she raised the glass to her lips, following the dark liquid as it washed over them. Ava never drank red wine, said it made her sleepy. She didn't like how alcohol made her feel in general. Yet here she was, knocking it back like it was water.

"Are you going to come out with me later?"

"You're going out?"

If the alternative was being alone, then Tess never wanted to go home.

"We can go dancing, just you and me. Come on—it'll be fun. We could sleep over at your place afterward. Like the old days."

Ava's eyes were weary as she shook her head. "No, not tonight."

"You work too hard, Ava. You need to rest too, you know. Let your hair down."

Ava let out a dry laugh and turned to William, who had moved closer to the door, as though he was drumming up the courage to go out and keep Adrian company in the oppressive heat.

"What's the deal with William?" asked Tess, drawing Ava's attention back to her.

"What do you mean?"

"Is he all right? Charlotte said—"

Tess stopped herself, glancing over to the wall that was blocking Charlotte and the table from view.

"What did Charlotte say?"

You didn't hear it from me.

"Nothing. Forget I said anything."

Ava drained her glass and set it down with a thud. "See you at the table."

She walked past the door and said something inaudible to William before making her way over to the table. William watched her go, then looked down at his watch and turned to face Tess. Tess immediately turned to the bar and tugged at her bracelet. She could go to the bathroom, lock herself in there for a while, and wait until he had forgotten all about her. But if she was going to do that, she would have to walk right past him.

"Hi, Tess."

He was already behind her.

Tess pushed her bracelet back into place, adjusted her shoulder strap, used the back of her hand to wipe the sweat from her upper lip, and then turned around.

"William, hi. Are you waiting for Adrian?"

"I tried to catch you earlier, but it kind of seemed like you were avoiding me."

"Why would I do that?"

"You tell me."

Tess laughed and tried to move past him.

"I was just going to the bathroom. Time of the month."

Her words didn't deter William, who stopped her with a hand on her arm.

"What have you taken, Tess?"

"What are you talking about?"

"I can see it in your eyes. What is it? Ecstasy?"

"Seriously? Is that what you think of me?"

She tried to shake him off, but his hand was firm.

"I saw the two of you."

Tess paused, still facing away from him. She knew exactly what he was talking about. They had arranged to meet outside the café after closing a few days ago, but he had arrived early. She and Mona had been in the alley out back, and Mona had just handed her the cash when Tess turned her head and saw him standing on the street.

"What are you mixed up in? Are you hooked on something? Are you selling it?"

"No!"

"So why did you ask to borrow money last week? Five thousand, remember? Why did you need that much cash?"

"It's for my mom; she's too proud to ask for help. If I can save up a deposit for the new place, she can take the job there and—"

"Your *mom*? She applied for a new job?"

"No, she didn't, but I spoke to—"

"Just stop, Tess. I don't want to hear it." William closed his eyes and held his hands in the air. "I'm not lending you any money. If you decide to be honest with me, maybe we can talk about it then."

"But I am being honest! I need it for my mom."

"So what did Mona give you after she handed over the money?"

The pills. How could she explain the fucking pills that were calling to her from the bottom of her bag? Why hadn't she just thrown them out?

"Let me know when you're prepared to be open with me, and then I'll give you the money."

By then it'll be too late.

"Sure."

His grip eased, and she pulled away from him and stormed through to the bathroom.

"I'm just trying to look out for you, Tess," he called after her.

The others had dumped their bags by the wall leading to the customer toilet on the far side of their table. Sophie's black leather handbag, Charlotte's Gucci number with a chain strap, William's black laptop bag. Sophie, Charlotte, and Ava were all at the table. They were chatting and laughing, leaning in to drink from their glasses. The doorway was no more than a couple of yards from Tess. She glanced back over her shoulder and heard William shouting to Christos behind the bar, then she dropped to her knees and started tugging at the zippers on his bag. His computer was in the main compartment, the smaller pocket full of papers. She found his wallet in the little side pocket.

Tess raised her head and peered over to the others. From where she was crouching, all she could see was the back of Sophie's head and the others' feet, stretched out beneath the table. She ignored the coin compartment and opened the card section instead, taking out his bank card and shoving it into the inside pocket of her own bag.

She never would have gone through the others' bags. It was the sight of William's that put the thought into her head, purely because she knew he was the only one who would forgive her when he found out.

CHAPTER

10

Now

I BARELY HAD TIME to see what it was when Tess opened the box. It was only in her hand for a few seconds before Charlotte took it and turned to Adrian, with her back to me. Despite all that, I recognized it immediately, even though I've seen so many others just like it over the years that it could belong to anyone. The color, the crack in one corner. I would have known William's bank card anywhere. I can still remember how it felt to trace a finger over the split in the plastic, which happened when he shoved the card into his back pocket when we went to see *The Girl With the Dragon Tattoo* at the cinema, an enormous bucket of buttery popcorn between us, spilling onto our laps.

"I don't understand," Charlotte says, turning the card over in her hand before passing it to Adrian. "Is this meant to be a clue? What are we supposed to do with it?"

It's been ten years since I last saw this card. The day before the final dinner at Christos, William and I went to the park. We stretched out on a blanket beneath the maples, and neither of us said a word because we didn't know where to start. I came so close to telling him everything, but instead

I crept over to his rucksack and found his wallet in the small pocket. I said I was going to get us something to drink, but I actually just went and cried behind the trunk of an oak nearby. On my way back, I stopped off at the café by the mini golf course and bought two bottles of sugar-free soda.

I'm sure I put the card back in his wallet that day, but at the restaurant the next evening, when William asked me to go and grab it to pay our share of the bill, it wasn't there.

"This is William's." Adrian holds out the card in front of him. "Where did you get hold of William's bank card, Ava?"

I turn to her, waiting for an explanation. William could have dropped it after going to the bar? Or maybe he was at Ava's the night before while I sat alone at his kitchen table with two plates of gluten-free spaghetti Bolognese that I eventually scraped into the garbage?

"Tess had it," says Ava.

Tess.

She is still frozen to the spot, with the empty box in her hand. Her eyes are fixed on Ava, her mouth open.

"What do you mean?" I ask. "Did she bring it with her this evening? Tess, did you find the card at Christos's place?"

"Tess had it in her bag the night William died."

Silence fills the room, and I don't know what to say, where to look. Tess slowly leans forward and lowers the box to her plate. Adrian drops the card to the table and then rubs his hand back and forth across his short hair.

"And how did you know it was in Tess's bag?"

"Someone had knocked it over in the hallway at his apartment, and his card and some other stuff had fallen out. I put everything else back in, but I was planning to give the card to William. I just didn't get around to it."

Tess has backed out of my field of vision, but I can hear her breathing.

"Did you take William's card?" I ask, desperately hoping she has a better explanation.

After everything he did for her, I don't want to believe that it's true.

"I borrowed it. I was going to give it back the next day and repay him as soon as I could."

I nod. "You could have just asked, you know."

William would have agreed to almost anything as far as Tess was concerned. Sometimes, when I tiptoed into his apartment late at night, I found her tucked up beneath a thick blanket on the sofa. William would be sitting in the desk chair in the corner, with a finger to his lips as I came into the room. Other times, his phone rang in the middle of the night, and I would hear her bright voice on the other end of the line before he kissed me on the cheek and got out of bed to pull on his jeans.

"I did, but he wouldn't listen. He didn't believe me."

I don't believe her.

"So you just took it?" I say, catching sight of myself in the windows. Jaw tense, my eyes big and black, Tess's fair hair behind me.

I've spent ten years thinking that I was the one who lost his card. When he asked me to get it from his bag at the restaurant and I realized it wasn't there, I spent the whole evening searching pockets and compartments whenever he wasn't looking. Later, after we got back to his apartment, I lied straight to his face when he asked me where it was, and all because I didn't want the evening to end in a fight.

"Seriously, what sort of escape room is this?" Charlotte has moved over to her own place at the table and is staring down at the little box with a look of disgust. "The clues aren't supposed to be personal. They're usually hidden behind pictures or whatever, following some sort of theme. I haven't—"

"Charlotte," Finn cuts her off, pulling her down into her seat, "I don't think it's meant to be an escape room."

"So what is it then? Why is the door locked, Ava?"

"Yes, Ava," says Adrian. "Why exactly have you locked the door? And what can we look forward to finding in the other boxes? Do we even want to know?"

Ava laughs, turning her wineglass. She doesn't have a box of her own, I notice. It's just the five of us whose sins have been wrapped up with a bow.

"William," she says. "It's all about William."

An uncomfortable silence follows, the only sound coming from us squirming awkwardly in our chairs. Of course it's about William. Everything has been about William since that day I first set foot in their classroom, before I even knew he existed.

"Fine." Adrian breaks the silence. "William. So what do you want us to do?"

Ava's eyes glitter in the glow of the ceiling light. Her lips are wet and slightly parted as she takes a couple of deep breaths.

"If no one talks about it, it never happened. It doesn't exist. We need to talk about it. I want us to work out why he died."

I can't tear my eyes away from Ava's lips. Pale, not too full, with that familiar Cupid's bow.

Why William died.

"William killed himself," I say. My voice sounds like a stranger's. It's cold and hard, and it matches exactly how I feel right now.

"Did he?" Ava's icy gaze bores into mine, knocking the air out of me the way it always has.

"You know he did," says Finn. "You found him in the bath. We were all there. The door was locked."

"And you all buy the idea that he just locked himself in there and drowned himself in the tub, do you?"

"Please, Ava, do we really have to dredge all this up again?" says Adrian. "It was ten years ago. What's the point in rehashing the whole thing now?"

"*Again?* Have we ever actually talked about it? The morning after they carried William out of that bathroom, my phone rang. My parents came and picked me up, and they drove me to the police station, where I spent half an hour being questioned in a hot, stuffy room. I bumped into Charlotte on the way out—do you remember that? You barely even said hello. You just nodded to me before you went in."

I remember what it was like. I must have been the last to get to the station, because by the time I left—with the officers who had interviewed me standing side by side in the doorway, watching me go—the sun had already started to set. They gave me watery vending machine coffee and told me to sit in a chair by the window. I didn't have much to tell them—nothing but fragmented memories from the evening before. The food we ate, the music we listened to, how the warm breeze had tugged at our hair as we walked back to William's place together. That was why it felt so much harder when the officers started throwing things the others had said right back in my face.

Was William in debt?

Was he seeing someone else behind my back?

Had he broken the law before?

Once the door swung shut behind me, I'd started walking. I walked and walked until the sun really had set, and that was when I decided to leave Gävle and never come back.

"I was tired and broken," Charlotte says now. "I knew I wouldn't be able to look you in the eye without falling apart."

"Don't you think I was broken too?"

For once, Charlotte seems to have the good sense to keep quiet.

"You all stopped answering your phones after the funeral, and then Sophie moved away, but none of that matters now. The point is that we never actually talked about it, all of us together. We were there; we're the only ones who might have been able to work out what really happened."

"What are you trying to say?"

Adrian looks how I imagine he must look mid-negotiation in a conference room, his jaw tense and his eyes hard. He is leaning back with his arms folded, his short nails drumming against his shirt sleeve. It's obvious he doesn't like what he has heard, and that worries me.

"That William didn't kill himself. That one of us did it." It's Ava who utters those words, not me, but I feel a sudden rush of heat in my cheeks. She is so clearly one step ahead of the rest of us. I look around the table, waiting for the others to react. Even Tess seems to be holding her breath.

But then Adrian laughs, breaking the silence. A brief burst, followed by a longer one.

"Seriously, one of us? *Killed* William?"

Ava doesn't reply.

I want to reach out and squeeze her hand, whisper that she shouldn't say any more.

"And the boxes?" Adrian asks.

"The boxes contain the reasons I'm confident I'm right."

"In that case," he says. "I think it's probably time I said thanks for the food and got going. I have a big meeting on Monday, and this is the last thing I need right now. It was good to see you all—you're just as hot as I remember you. Phone please, Ava."

Adrian holds out his hand, but Ava doesn't move a muscle.

"Now, Ava. I'm leaving."

"You can have it later."

"Fine, whatever. Keep it. I'll buy a new one."

He gets up and walks through to the hallway. We hear the same sounds as earlier, bouncing off the walls, louder and harder this time. The cupboard doors, the hangers, the front door. He tugs at the handle and then starts hitting it with his open hand.

"You can open the door now! I'm leaving."

I half expect to hear the key turn in the lock and for Adrian to start joking with the burly man on the other side as he makes his way over to the elevator. In fact, I'm just seconds away from getting up and joining him. But there is a moment of complete silence before Adrian starts pounding on the door again, with his fist this time.

"Hello? Can you hear me? Open the door!"

"He's not going to open it."

Ava says it so casually, as though she was announcing that dinner is served.

The pounding stops, and Adrian comes sloping back through to the dining room a minute or two later, with one hand in his pocket. In the other, he is holding a pack of cigarettes.

"You're really not going to let me go, are you?"

"Like I said, you can go once we're done here."

"You do realize it's illegal to keep us here against our will, right?"

"Can't you just sit down and eat? I know you're going to enjoy the food."

He snorts and undoes the top button of his shirt, pushes a cigarette between his lips and walks through to the living room. I hear him open another door, and an icy wind blows across my shins before it swings shut behind him.

The balcony.

Snow swirls around the figure moving from one end of the balcony to the other. He leans forward, waving his hand, and I hear him shout something. Adrian then straightens up, and a moment later I see the glow of a cigarette illuminate his face. I watch the bright tip follow his hand as he lowers it from his mouth to hip level, pacing back and forth.

"He'll be back soon enough," says Ava, pouring more wine into her glass. "Once he realizes I'm right."

CHAPTER 11

Now

"IF YOU'LL EXCUSE me for a moment, I need to go and prepare the entrées."

Ava gets up at last, smoothing her dress. We've been sitting in uncomfortable silence for the last five minutes, humming and nodding and stealing glances at Adrian out on the balcony, wishing he would come back inside.

"Sure."

Charlotte keeps fidgeting with a lock of hair, the way she always does when she's stressed. Or the way she used to in high school, at least, when she'd pushed back one exam too many and had several retakes to sit. She winds her red hair around her index finger over and over until it looks like a corkscrew and several long strands have come loose and caught on her dress.

"No worries," I say. "Just let us know if you need any help."

Take as long as you want, because there's no chance in hell I'm going to open the box you've left in front of me.

Ava's eyes linger on me for a few seconds too long, and then she pushes her chair back beneath the table. Charlotte purses her lips and smiles, and I try my best to do the same. The minute Ava leaves the room, we all slump forward with our elbows on cutlery and plates, heads together.

"What the hell is this?" I hiss, nudging my box.

"I don't know," says Charlotte. "I was sure it was a game. What should we do? Do you think we should leave?"

"How do you plan to do that?"

We all turn to Finn.

"The door's locked," he says. "You heard what Adrian said."

"There's no key," Tess mumbles.

She has finished her wine, and she reaches for the carafe to pour herself another. Her fingers drum the foot of her glass.

"Then we'll find it. This is crazy. Our phones too. She took them into the kitchen."

I glance back over my shoulder, and the others follow my line of sight to the doorway.

"I didn't mean any harm," says Tess, staring down at her plate.

"I know."

No matter how hard I try, I can't quite manage to hide the hard note in my voice.

"I never actually used it. The card was gone by the time the ambulance arrived, and I grabbed my bag. But I would've paid every dollar back if I had."

"Forget it, Tess. It doesn't matter anymore."

"Why did you even take it in the first place?"

Charlotte. When will she learn?

"Because you wouldn't lend me any money when I asked."

Red blotches blossom across Charlotte's cheeks, and she sits back. She glances over to Finn and tosses her head. What Tess just said doesn't surprise me at all. When William finished university and I was his plus one to the graduation party, I convinced Charlotte to let me wear her new black dress from Alexander McQueen. It wouldn't suit my figure, she said, because my hips were wider than hers. I ended up having a bit too much fun and stumbled down a step, spilling red wine onto her dress. She demanded I pay half of what the dress was worth, plus cover the dry-cleaning costs, even though the stains were barely visible.

That was the last time I ever asked Charlotte to borrow anything.

"I meant why did you need the money."

"I had a friend who knew someone working at a care home in Norrland. They would have given Mom a job if she'd moved up there. There weren't any rental places available unless you'd been in the housing queue for years, but I managed to find a cabin someone had insulated to a livable standard. It was only a few hundred yards from a lake with a jetty, and there was a greenhouse and a veranda. She would have loved it; she tried to grow begonias and tomatoes on her little balcony, but the cold always killed everything. All I needed was the first month's rent, plus the deposit. That's why I wanted the money. It would have meant Mom could get away from Benke."

Charlotte doesn't speak. None of us do, and I wish Ava had never found William's card, because if she hadn't then Tess's mom might still be alive today. I hardly dare think it, but William might be too.

"So this is what you want, is it?" Tess continues, pulling her full wineglass toward her. "Honesty."

She snorts and takes several big sips, spilling a few drops as she sets the glass back down on the white tablecloth.

"Then honesty is what you'll get. I can't wait to see what's in your boxes."

The cold breeze sweeps over my legs again, and I hear a door slam. Adrian's footsteps are heavy as he crosses the living room and comes into the dining room, and I have to stop myself from getting up to welcome him back with a reassuring hug. He slumps down onto his chair, spreading a waft of cigarette smoke and cool air across the table. Adrian brushes a few snowflakes from his shoulder and rubs his head. With the top button of his shirt undone, a little more of his chest is visible, and I notice a shadow on his dark skin.

A purplish bruise on his collarbone, stretching up toward his throat.

"Where's Ava?" he asks.

"What happened, Adrian?" My hand instinctively reaches up to my own collarbone.

He stares at me for a moment before doing up the button.

"Did someone do that to you?"

"It's nothing. Where's Ava?"

"She went to—"

"I'm here."

Just like that, she's back by my side. She tilts her slim wrist to check her rose-gold watch.

"The food will be ready soon."

"Are you really saying that one of us is a murderer?"

Ava's hand drops to her side, and she keeps her eyes fixed on Adrian as she slowly sits down and pulls her chair closer to the table.

"That's exactly what I'm saying. Come on—surely you must have had the same thought at some point?"

Every time I blink, I'm right back in the doorway between William's living room and hall. I see the door opening, Ava screaming. It all happens in slow motion, without a single sound. A long, drawn-out series of events leading up to the moment when everything ground to a halt.

I see Ava on the floor with her hands in her blond hair, Finn leaning against the wall as he throws up onto William's rug. At some point in that frozen moment, someone must have called for an ambulance. Somewhere between

Charlotte grabbing my shoulders and shaking me, her puffy red face right in front of mine, and Tess trying to drag me away from the doorway, the paramedics came up the stairs with a stretcher. A stretcher that they carried out of the bathroom with William on it. His hair was damp and curly, his T-shirt clinging to his skin. His pale hand hung limply over the edge, and he was still wearing his ring.

I pushed past the woman holding one end of the stretcher, making her lose her grip; I shoved Adrian out of the way as he was heading back up to the apartment, still holding his cigarettes in one hand. I rushed down the stairs, flung the door open, and ran until my legs gave way beneath me.

"One of us in this room?"

Adrian is breathing heavily, leaning back in his chair, with his arm on the backrest. I can see it in his eye, that he has been going over her words as he paced back and forth outside, trying to get a grip on the situation. He's ready to sink her with a crushing argument now, because that's just what he does.

That's how he earned his millions, and someone always has to pay.

"You're going to have to explain what makes you think that one of us would even *consider* hurting a hair on William's head. What do you know that we don't?"

"It wasn't necessarily planned. That's not how people work—you know that. Everyone has certain needs. Those needs will differ from person to person, but if we start to feel like whatever we need is out of reach, that can lead to real frustration. Enough to spur anyone into action if the conditions are right."

Adrian grins. "That's the books talking, Ava. Don't try your psychology crap on us. What do *you* think?"

"I don't think anything. I know that William would never have killed himself, because he had plans. Right, Sophie?"

Hearing my name makes me lift my head and take a deep breath. Why is she dragging me into this?

"What?"

"He told me that night at Christos. The two of you were planning to leave town, to move away from us. So why would he kill himself?"

Ten years have passed, but I still feel my cheeks grow hot. Had he really already told Ava? He must have been at her place the night before, when his phone was off.

"William was planning to leave?"

I'm torn between Ava and Adrian, see him turn to me with a look of confusion on his face. If Ava knew, then I'm surprised William hadn't told Adrian. Surely he, if anyone, needed to know, given they had money invested together.

"Whoa," says Tess, raising an eyebrow. "This changes things, don't you think, Charlotte?"

She sips her wine and smiles at Charlotte, whose eyes have narrowed.

"Why didn't you say anything?"

"It wasn't definite," I say. "It was William's idea; he was probably just waiting for the right moment, and I—"

"Wait a minute," says Charlotte. "So you're saying we met and ate dinner, the way we always did on Fridays; that we were having such a good time that we all went on to William's place, and then someone drowned him in the bath without anyone else noticing? Why would they do that?"

"That's if he did drown."

"Hold on a sec. Back up." Adrian presses his hands to his face and takes a deep breath. "This is too many surprises to process in one go. *If* he drowned? He was floating in the fucking tub."

"He was in the bath, yes. But we don't know whether that's what killed him."

"Seriously, Ava." Charlotte's voice is soft and warm, as though she were talking to a child. "How can you think any of us would be able to hurt William? We were practically family; we'd been friends for years. We were a part of one another's lives, and we loved one another."

"Stop!"

The bright voice cuts through the room, and everyone stops talking and stares at Tess, who has just brought her hand down on the table. Ava checks the time again.

"A *family* doesn't treat its members like that."

"What are you talking about?"

Tess gets up. "Could we stop pretending, just for one evening? It feels like the past ten years have really warped your memories of what things were actually like."

She moves over to the window and leans against the wall beside the large painting. I see her back rising and falling in time with her shallow breaths, and Charlotte raises an eyebrow and plays with her napkin.

"Did I say something wrong?"

"Just leave her," says Finn, squeezing her hand.

"Is she on something?" Charlotte hisses. I try to give her foot a nudge but manage to kick her in the shin instead.

"Ow!"

"What are you trying to achieve here, Ava?" asks Finn.

"I just want us to work out what really happened and for the person responsible for William's death to pay for it."

I try to replay that day in my mind. I remember that I woke before sunrise and tiptoed out of William's bedroom with my clothes in my arms, that my top clung to my skin as I rode the baking-hot bus, and that I called him to say I wasn't going to meet him outside his office. I also remember the greasy food and the tasteless wine, the silent walk back to his apartment afterward. But at no point can I find any memories of what the others were doing, what they were talking about, how they treated William.

Because the only thing I could think about that evening was what I was about to do.

From the hallway, we hear a familiar rattling sound. The lock. The sound is followed by a soft sigh as the door swings open. Charlotte turns to me, and I turn to Adrian.

"Sorry, Adrian," says Ava. "One more surprise."

Adrian immediately gets to his feet and clicks his fingers.

"Come on, Tess. Let's go."

She looks up at him, but she doesn't have time to process what he just said before he grabs her wrist and drags her toward the hallway. Finn gets up, and I do the same. Charlotte whispers to me:

"Now?"

"Now," I tell her.

CHAPTER

12

Now

We don't make it very far, and I don't even try to look through to the kitchen, where I imagine there must be a basket of cell phones waiting for us—one of them full of impatient texts from Malika: *What're they like? What are you eating?* When we reach the end of the table, behind Ava's back, I hook my arm through Charlotte's. We pass the little table with the lamp and my empty glass, and it's oddly comfortable to feel her warmth against my arm, unexpectedly natural to have her so close. If we can just grab our coats and get into the elevator, we could head to a restaurant somewhere nearby and order a bottle of Riesling. She would tie her red hair in a messy bun on top of her head and launch into one of her never-ending stories, and all I would have to do is listen and nod. I can already smell the fresh snow and exhaust fumes awaiting us outside, and now that I know I'll never have to come back here, I allow myself a glance back over my shoulder, taking in all the details I didn't manage to appreciate earlier.

But we don't get much farther than my empty glass on the little table before we hear the door close and the lock click. The man outside can't have had time to do anything but open the door and pull it shut again.

I have a sinking feeling at the thought of being stuck here for an unspecified amount of time, and Charlotte's arm grows heavy and immobile on mine.

"Hey, hang on a sec!" Adrian shouts, and then I hear a low murmur of voices. There is someone other than him and Tess in the hallway. Another man. Maybe the guy from outside came in before he closed the door. From where we're standing, I can only see the near end of the narrow hallway, shadows dancing over the two paintings on the wall. Charlotte and I exchange a glance and try to listen.

"Did someone come in?"

"Maybe it's the man in black," I say, pulling her toward the hallway right as Adrian reappears. He shakes his head.

"Come on, let's go back," he says, flapping his hands at us, as though we were a couple of wayward sheep. "The door's locked. We might as well sit down again."

"But who was it? Why did the door open?"

"Just come back to the table and have a glass of wine."

Tess slowly follows him in, pausing after every other step to glance back at the hallway. Her face seems more relaxed now, her eyes more alert. She says something in the direction of the hall, her voice so low that I can't make it out, and then she walks over to the table with a newfound energy. She was talking to whoever is hiding in the shadows, I realize. All I want is to follow Adrian, to stick close to him, but for some reason I can't move. The warmth of Charlotte's arm disappears, and she leaves me.

"Come on, Sophie," she says as she walks toward the table and pulls out her chair.

But I can't. I hear the footsteps echoing between the walls, drawing closer, and I instinctively back up into the little table, knocking over my empty glass. It breaks on contact with the stone floor, scattering shards of glass around my feet as I manage to save the lamp from the same fate.

"Sorry, Ava," I shout. "I'll clean it up."

But Ava is already out of her seat. I glance over to the others, who are watching me from the dining table; then I turn my attention back to the doorway, where he steps forward and pauses. My eyes take in his brown leather boots, his legs. His blond hair, which used to reach somewhere between his ears and his shoulders, is now short, shaved on the sides and longer on top. Last time I saw him, he had a slight five o'clock shadow, but today it's more of a neat beard covering his chin and jawline, framing his mouth and his full lower lip. Dark jeans and a black T-shirt.

Jacob.

"Hi, Sophie. It's been a minute."

He is more heavily built now, but not overweight. His arms and shoulders look broader, stronger. This is a body that has been used. Either that or he works out a lot. It definitely doesn't look like a body that spends its days in front of a computer, and I can't stop my thoughts from running wild.

What does he do?

Where does he live?

Why is he here?

I decide not to look away, but when he flashes that smile of his, the one that brings out the dimple on his cheek, that's exactly what I do. My eyes focus on his forearms and the fair hair covering his skin, and I feel my cheeks grow hot.

"Hi, Jacob."

He laughs, then looks down at the broken glass around my feet.

"Graceful as ever, I see. Though you missed the lamp."

The familiar sarcasm in his voice, the coolness.

"Nah," I reply, straightening the shade. "I was about to smash it too, but then I changed my mind."

"So, what have you been up to since you fled town?"

"I didn't flee," I reply.

"No? That's what it felt like."

Ava steps over the shards of glass and gives Jacob a hug. "Right on time," she says, holding him at arm's length for a moment. "You look good. Why has it been so long?"

She squeezes his upper arms, and I bend down to pick up the pieces of glass, watching them from the corner of my eye.

"Do you have a phone with you, Jacob?" asks Adrian.

"I gave it to the guy outside. He said it was a screen-free party."

Adrian sighs.

"I'll get that," says Ava, pushing me aside. "Sit down, Sophie. You too, Jacob. I'll fetch you a plate."

Crouching in her tall heels, she gathers the sharp pieces in her hand. She holds up the largest of them, studying it in the light before putting it on top of the others and carrying them out into the kitchen. The glass was probably expensive crystal, shattered in the blink of an eye. I make my way over to Finn by the window, as far away as I can get without actually leaving the room. My fingers wander nervously over my face, rubbing my lower lip, my jawline, scratching my scalp.

"What's *he* doing here?" Finn whispers, his eyes following Jacob as he makes his way into the dining room. That's probably what we're all thinking.

"No idea."

* * *

Jacob was never a part of the group—not really. While the rest of us had been friends since senior high school, sharing memories of long, bright nights on Ava's jetty and exams we'd flunked, he didn't come into the picture until he and William became classmates during the final year of their economics degree. William was drawn to something in Jacob, but I found him irritating from the moment we first met in a dark pool hall.

That evening, as I stood with my arm around William's waist, and Jacob suddenly sauntered over with a beer, I realized that William didn't want to be alone with me. Jacob drifted around and between us, watching us as though he was assessing our relationship. As though he had immediately spotted something William hadn't noticed yet.

"You've got to use your fingers," he shouted as I took a shot, making me miss the ball entirely.

"Lean in closer, focus on the follow-through."

I hated him from the get-go, wanted to run away, but I gritted my teeth until Jacob eventually put down his cue and said goodbye. It was a relief once he left. A relief that transitioned into something else when I noticed that William seemed disappointed in me.

He turned up for dinner at Christos a week later, and I quickly understood that it wouldn't be a one-off. The others' faces lit up, thrilled to have new blood at the table, but I tried to ignore him as best I could. He seemed to blend seamlessly with the group at first, flattering Tess and Charlotte, showing an interest in Finn's stories about ski trips to the French Alps. But as the weeks passed, he grew quiet and withdrawn. He was often the last to arrive and the first to leave, and he would slump back in his chair by the wall and watch the others. It was like I was hypnotized by him. I couldn't stop wondering what he was thinking, what he saw in us that I didn't. And when his eyes came to rest on my face, I was convinced he could see straight through me and the crumbling facade I'd built up. He had an uncanny ability to get under my skin; nothing passed him by. And maybe I had some sense, even then, that something was about to change.

* * *

My shoulder brushes against Finn's as we stand side by side, watching Jacob smile and nod to the others.

"Jacob?" Charlotte moves over to him. "Is that really you? I didn't think you'd come."

She holds out a hand, and at first I think she's about to hug him, the way she did me, but she doesn't. Charlotte takes his hand and shakes it. Jacob grins.

"I didn't expect to see you either, to be honest. It's brave of you to come. I changed my mind at the last minute, which was pretty bad form, but Ava was kind enough to let me say yes so late in the day."

"Why wouldn't *I* have come?" Charlotte seems confused, but Jacob has already turned his attention elsewhere.

"You shouldn't have come," Adrian tells him from the other end of the room.

He strides toward Jacob.

"What's he doing?" I whisper to Finn, tugging on his arm.

"Just wait," Finn replies, giving me a reassuring pat on the hand.

"Oh yeah?" says Jacob. "Why's that?"

Adrian holds out an arm and drags Jacob into a hug, the kind that ends with them thumping each other on the back. I let go of Finn, relieved. I was holding my breath, I realize. The last time they'd had any physical contact was amid a sea of boxes and serrano ham at the party Adrian threw to celebrate moving into his fancy new apartment. The day Jacob's fist had met his face. That had been one week before William died.

Adrian leans sideways to peer through to the kitchen before he replies.

"Ava's gone way too far this time. The door's locked from the outside, and she . . ." He hesitates and looks over to me, then to the table, where four little boxes remain unopened. "She's got it into her head that William's death wasn't a suicide and that one of us had something to do with it."

"With his death?"

I feel a chill spread from my chest to my arms.

"Yeah. It's probably best just to play along and enjoy dinner."

"And the company, right? Interesting. Did it take her ten years to come to that conclusion?"

Jacob looks up and meets my eye, a smile playing on his lips. I turn away. He moves closer to the table and picks up the box with my name on it, trailing a thumb over the tag before setting it down. With his hand on the back of the chair, he continues past Tess's seat, pausing by Adrian's to pick up William's bank card. He studies it for a moment, then the open box by Tess's name tag.

"And all this?" he asks, waving a hand toward the table.

"That's her evidence."

Jacob nods and lets the card drop to the tablecloth.

"So I've walked right into the middle of a murder mystery party?"

"She's serving *Greek* food," says Charlotte. "Saganaki, olives. Who knows what we'll get for the next course."

"Moussaka?"

He laughs, moving around the end of the table toward me. I straighten up and turn in the opposite direction, away from him. For a split second, our eyes meet over the length of the table. I pause by my seat and reach for my glass of red wine. Jacob is now by Finn's side, and he gives him a thump on the back and takes his hand.

"How's it going, man? Everything good?"

"Yeah, can't complain."

"The short hair suits you," says Charlotte, who has paused a few feet away.

"Thanks. Had it cut specially for this evening," Jacob replies, running a hand over the stubby hair at the base of his skull.

He really does look good. The short hair makes him seem more grown up, and it doesn't hide his sharp jawline.

"What about you, Sophie?" he asks.

I blink, realize I've been staring at him. I can't get over just how well he matches the vision of him I've had in my head all these years, despite the fact that so much about him is different.

"What?"

"How are you?"

"Good, thanks."

"Glad to hear it."

Ava reappears with a clean plate, glass, and cutlery. She clears a space between Finn and Adrian's seats and leaves another small box by Jacob's place before filling his glass.

"All right, everyone. Sit down. I'll get the food."

I'm not the only one who hesitates. We all stay glued to the spot until eventually Jacob takes a seat. One by one we follow his lead, slumping down into our assigned places.

"It's cool to see you all again," he says, raising his glass in a toast. "I've always wondered what happened to you."

"I think we all have," Charlotte replies, reciprocating his toast. "We haven't seen one another since the funeral. Isn't that weird?"

"Right, the funeral," Jacob says, pausing to sip his wine. "I never got in, of course. I bought a black suit and I went to the church, but they stopped me at the door."

I swallow and glance over to Adrian, because I'm sure Jacob thinks he must be the reason he wasn't allowed in. I have a clear memory of watching Jacob close his car door beneath the birches at the far end of the parking lot, walking down the gravel path in a pair of black sunglasses, one hand in his pocket. I also remember slipping inside the church before he saw me.

"It was William's parents," says Charlotte. "I'm really sorry, but they wanted to limit the funeral to close family and friends."

"Oh yeah?"

"Did they tell you that?" Tess asks Charlotte. "Did they say that was why Jacob wasn't allowed in?"

"Go easy on the wine, Tess," Adrian says with a laugh.

"I am, Adrian. Maybe you should be more worried about yourself and the effect drinking has on you. Is that your second glass already?"

His laugh gives way to a stiff smile.

"Ava's clearly done well for herself," Jacob says, changing the subject.

He looks around the room, and his brow creases when he notices the large painting behind him.

"Or her parents have, anyway," says Charlotte. "It's not exactly hard to live like this if someone else is paying."

"You're not envious are you, Charlotte?" Tess asks. "Or is it jealous? I can never remember the difference."

Charlotte laughs, though she clearly isn't sure whether it was meant as a joke. Everything has changed since Jacob arrived, and not just because of the little boxes on the table.

We all know that Jacob's arrival in the group marked the moment it slowly began to fall apart.

C H A P T E R

13

Five hours and twenty-three minutes before William's death

THERE WAS SOMETHING about William that drew Jacob to him from first glance. In a sea of try-hard students, all painfully aware of how other people saw them, William seemed to exist in some sort of vacuum. A bubble that shielded him from everyone else, allowing him to move effortlessly through life. Relaxed, easygoing, and inclusive toward everyone who came into contact with him, greedily brushing up against his sphere.

When he wasn't surrounded by other people, William threw himself into the course literature. He could often be found on one of the window ledges in the long corridor, chewing on his pen as he read with a furrowed brow. His determination woke something in Jacob, a curiosity that made him move from the back row of the lecture theater to the middle. From there, he shifted to the third row from the front and, ultimately, the second row. Diagonally behind William. It didn't take long before they bumped into each other on their way out, and when they eventually started talking, he discovered—as he had suspected—that they had a lot in common. Within just a couple of weeks, his chats with William had become the highlight of his day, and he couldn't get out of the apartment quickly enough in the mornings, keen to hear his thoughts after their lectures.

* * *

It was too hot to work out, at least eighty-five degrees outside and probably not much cooler in the gym. The AC unit on the roof was faulty, pumping cold air into the building in winter and hot air in summer, when you really needed the chill. Despite that, Jacob decided to stick to his new Friday routine and switched off his computer an hour early, enabling him to fit in three circuits of every machine in the company gym. He was dripping with sweat before he had even finished the first. The weights were heavier than usual, the ache in his muscles stronger, but he took his time and increased the number of reps. He had nowhere else to be, after all.

Twenty past six.

He hadn't checked the time, but he could feel it as the cold water flooded over him in the shower. By now, Charlotte and Tess would have washed and dried their hair, pulled on their carefully selected dresses or tops, and leaned in to the mirror to add the finishing touches to their makeup. By now, Finn would have arrived at the restaurant, sitting down with a beer that would be empty before the others turned up. Jacob joined him sometimes, whenever he wanted to have a conversation with someone who didn't spend his time gossiping about other people.

William would be there too.

Once Jacob had noticed William's dark, almost black hair in the lecture theater two years ago, he started seeing him everywhere. A few feet ahead of him in the lunch line; at one of the tables in the library; running down the steps outside the building, with an armful of books, and a rucksack on one shoulder. He hadn't expected William's friends to be part of the bargain, but he liked it.

Liked being part of a group.

Having a reason to get out of the apartment.

Jacob learned a lot just by watching people. When he hung back and kept quiet, they lowered their guard and forgot he was there, and that gave him a glimpse of their true selves. Smiles fading, body language changing. An angry glance when they thought no one was looking could say more than a thousand words. Above all, they taught him how to hide his own worries.

As he pulled on his jeans and a fresh T-shirt in the changing room, he still had time to catch a bus to the other side of town and come strolling in just in time for the appetizers. Instead, he walked slowly home along the shady side of the street, the warm breeze on his skin. He entered the door code and dragged himself up to the second floor, then unlocked the door and pushed it open with his foot. A day's worth of hot, stale air hit him. Midway between the living room and the kitchen, he paused in front of the threadbare plush sofa and the cheap polyester pillows, the remote controls and the forgotten mug of coffee on the little table. Out of sheer habit, he scanned the room for signs of disaster. Broken glass, blood on the floor, an unmoving body.

Have you ever thought about trying to find him a place in a care facility?

The room seemed to shrink around him, suffocating him. His eyes drifted over the worn parquet floor and the long-pile rug, searching for something. Something other than the black sweater tossed onto the armrest or the sock kicked under the table. Anything that could convince him it was real and not all in his head.

He should have been there this evening.

He should have been sitting beside William, so that he heard it from him. That way there would be no room for misunderstanding. He should have faced up to Adrian to show him that he wasn't someone who could be scared into silence. But they had decided it would be for the best this way, for all involved.

Whatever that meant.

Jacob strode across the living room and opened the balcony doors before going through to the kitchen to do the same with the kitchen window. That was when he saw it on the counter, in the middle of all the dirty plates and half-empty mugs. A large black and white teacup with the faint impression of a pale pink lip on the rim.

He left it where it was.

"Is she here?"

Jacob turned around and met Stefan's confused eye. He was wearing a pair of gray sweatpants and a T-shirt with the famous Rolling Stones tongue and lips emblazoned on the chest.

"I thought you were asleep, Dad."

"Why isn't she here? She said she'd come back."

"I'm sure she will, soon. But you . . ." Jacob hesitated. "Come on. I'll put the TV on for you. I need to head out for a bit, but I'll be back."

"Why do you have to go?" Stefan protested, pulling his arm back as Jacob led him over to the sofa and helped him down.

"I'll be back before the news is over. We'll have time for a game of contract whist."

"Do whatever the hell you want—I don't give a damn. Why are you even here all the time?"

"I live here, Dad. You remember that I moved back, don't you?"

Jacob knew he shouldn't leave his dad alone, not when he had been at work all day, at the new job he never would have taken if the home help hadn't told him it would be just fine. But he also couldn't stand to be shut up in the cramped apartment, pretending everything was okay.

Because nothing was okay.

Without another word, he did a lap of the apartment, turning on all of the small night lights so that Stefan would be able to get around once darkness had fallen. He then closed the balcony door and double-checked that the stove guard was still plugged in.

In the hallway, Jacob paused in front of the mirror. He ran a hand over his short stubble and through his hair, still damp after his shower.

Five past seven.

It shouldn't be too late. He could call a cab and get there before they'd even finished their first drinks. Instead, he grabbed his keys and cell phone and left the apartment. He walked back the same way he had come earlier, this time with the sun in his eyes and his feet burning in his shoes. The back of his neck was sweaty by the time he turned off into the seating area outside Brända Bocken in Stortorget and slumped down onto a chair beneath one of the umbrellas. He ordered an ice-cold beer and drummed his fingers against the table as he downed it much faster than he had meant to. Still nothing on his phone. No messages, no calls.

I'll let you know once it's done.

Jacob checked the time. The music from the bar pulsed through the air, and three young women at the next table laughed loudly and glanced over to him. With his head tipped back against a pillar, he took a deep breath.

Quarter to eight.

The cab arrived five minutes after he made the call. The drive over to Christos Taverna took less than three minutes on the empty streets, and he spent a long time just staring at the door before he opened it and went in.

It's probably best you don't come.

There was no doubt that William was a generous man. He willingly shared his time and knowledge, and he never expected anything in return. That was why Jacob had been surprised when William had first introduced him to his friends, who were the complete opposite. With the exception of Sophie, who had joined the odd group the year before they graduated, they'd been hanging out since the start of senior high. She was different from the others, with eyes that gave away exactly what she was thinking and moods she occasionally struggled to control. He could see why William had fallen for her.

But the others . . .

It was hard to ignore the way they all pulled at William, and Jacob couldn't help but see the cracks that grew deeper the more he poked at them. Because the more he dug, the more shit he ended up with under his nails.

His feet were moving too quickly for him to change his mind as he marched between the tables, but he stopped dead as soon as he spotted them. The sound of cutlery on china filled the otherwise empty restaurant. They were laughing and reaching for their glasses, and the aroma of cooked meat made his stomach turn. Ava seemed unusually laid-back in her sleeveless top, her platinum blond hair loose around her face. Charlotte was beside her, with her long red hair tied in a high ponytail. Tess was wearing a thin black dress, and she was already drunk, singing along with the music and helping herself to food from one of the plates, silver bracelets clinking. Adrian was hunched over the table and had rolled up the sleeves of his black shirt. He was listening to William, and it was obvious that he didn't like what he was hearing.

For a brief moment, Jacob was convinced she wasn't there, that it was the reason he hadn't heard from her. But then he saw Sophie sitting with her back to him, between the two conversations, turning her glass of water around and around, with her head bowed. Her wavy, dark brown hair was loose over her shoulders, and it was so plain to see just how completely she faded into the background in their company.

Finn was nowhere to be seen. He wasn't at the table, and Jacob turned his head to look back toward the bar. He was sure there hadn't been anyone there when he came in.

"Jacob!"

Charlotte started waving, and their conversations died down as the others turned around to stare at him. Adrian moved to get up from his seat, but William reached out and put a hand on his arm.

Sophie was the last one to turn around, slowly looking up at him.

"What are you doing here?" Adrian hissed.

Jacob was powerless to stop the grin that spread across his face.

"Stop it, Adrian." Ava glared at him before turning back to Jacob with a smile. "You two really need to put this thing behind you. It's starting to get so boring."

"Come on." Charlotte patted the seat beside her, as though he were their trained dog. "Sit. The food just arrived."

Jacob hesitated. He had promised not to come, after all, and he was someone who always kept his promises. But then the moment passed, and he sat down in the seat Charlotte and Ava had cleared for him on one side of the table. Ava reached for a plate and cutlery from the space beside Adrian.

"Finn isn't here yet, so you can just take his plate."

Jacob ignored Adrian, who was staring at him with gritted teeth, and tried to catch William's eye instead. He wanted to see whether his friend was looking at him the same way he usually did or whether someone had already taken him aside and whispered something that made him pull back. But William smiled his usual disarming smile, and all Jacob could do was return it with a grin of his own.

William still had no idea.

"Do you want some saganaki?"

Charlotte nudged Jacob with her elbow, waving the plate under his nose. The smell made his stomach turn again, and he shook his head and got back up.

"I'm just going to get something to drink."

He could already feel the beer from earlier as he walked over to the bar. Christos was just heading through the swing doors into the kitchen, but he stopped in his tracks.

"Jacob, you came! What can I get you? An IPA?"

"That'd be great, thanks."

With one hand pressed to the base of his spine, Christos leaned forward and reached into the fridge. He popped the cap off the bottle and then held it out to Jacob. The cold glass fogged up immediately.

"We can settle up later, like usual."

With that, Christos disappeared into the kitchen, and Jacob took a swig from the bottle. He felt a gentle hand on his back, but when he turned around, he saw a head of blond hair rather than dark curls.

It was Ava, with a soft smile on her face and a pitying look in her eyes.

"I don't think anyone was expecting you to come. Adrian cleared your plate away as soon as we got here. I'm sorry about that."

"Don't worry about it. I wasn't actually planning to come."

"Well, I'm glad you did. What made you change your mind?"

He took another swig from his bottle and moved a few steps away from the bar so that he could see their table on the other side of the wall.

"I needed to make sure of something."

"And?"

He met her blue eyes. "It's lucky I did."

Ava studied him for a moment, then glanced over to the table. William had put an arm around Sophie, and her head was resting against his shoulder. Adrian had moved around the table and was now sitting on Sophie's other side. He leaned in to her and whispered something in her ear before turning around and looking straight at Jacob. Sophie's face cracked into a smile, and she elbowed Adrian.

"Adrian said the whole thing was about William," Ava said quietly. "When you hit him."

It was about self-preservation.

Wasn't that what everything they did was about?

If Adrian opened his mouth, it would all be over, but Jacob seriously doubted he would ever do that. If he did, it would mean Jacob no longer had any reason to keep quiet about what he had seen. Heated voices in a cramped stairwell, a hand gripping Adrian's throat before the person noticed Jacob and laughed, boxing Adrian's shoulder as though it was all just a joke before going on their way. Adrian's terrified eyes when he spotted Jacob in the doorway.

"Isn't everything about William? Isn't that why we come here every Friday?"

Her silence spoke volumes.

"I just hope that whatever it was is over now, so you can get along this evening," she said after a moment. "For everyone's sake."

"Me too," he replied, though he knew this was only the beginning.

"Are you coming?"

"Yeah, in a minute."

Jacob gripped the neck of his bottle and regretted that he had come. For two years, he'd had William's back. He had warned him about what was going on, been his eyes when he wasn't there.

But in the end Jacob would be responsible for the worst betrayal of all.

CHAPTER 14

Now

I WAS THE ONE who had Jacob barred from William's funeral, and I did it at the very last minute so he wouldn't know what was going on. It wasn't something I planned, and I regretted it as soon as the words left my mouth, but as I stood there in the church, fingering the lapel of my black blazer, I just couldn't bear the thought of him being there. Of feeling his eyes on the back of my neck as he sat on the pew behind me, of being able to smell his aftershave.

William's mom noticed that I was anxious. I was pacing the aisle, gripping the red rose so hard that one of the thorns they'd forgotten to remove dug into my palm and caused a trickle of blood to run down my wrist. She took me aside, held my hand, and started talking about how it was a difficult day for everyone but that we'd get through it together, and that was when I spat it out.

I said that Jacob had attacked Adrian and that I was afraid of him.

That was all it took for them to close the doors of the church and for William's uncle and cousin to wait outside, keeping an eye on everyone who arrived and deciding who came in. I snuck out onto the steps to get some fresh air and stood with my back to the wall. I was relieved that he might not even come, but then I saw his car pull up at the far end of the parking lot, and he got out and looked around. The late summer sun made his hair shimmer like gold as he walked beneath the trees. That was the first time I'd ever seen him in a suit, I thought as I crept back inside and listened to them tell him to turn around and go home.

He didn't even argue.

* * *

Herb-crusted lamb and roasted potatoes. That's what Ava serves for our entrée, and everyone eats without hesitating, even though the food is only lukewarm. The conversation is flowing again, chat about jobs and mortgages and taxes. We drink the wine, laugh loudly, and wipe our mouths with the thick linen napkins. Everyone is trying to act like the little boxes don't exist, though from time to time someone inevitably glances down at theirs with a slightly paler face than they'd had when they'd arrived.

I'm painfully aware of Jacob's presence diagonally opposite me. I can see him clearly from the corner of my eye whenever I reach for my glass or nod to Charlotte, and it feels like I'm being watched. But every time I glance up, he looks away.

"You work in film and TV," Ava says without warning, pointing to Charlotte. "Did you know that Jacob is a photographer?"

"No, I didn't. Weren't you an economist?"

"Yeah, but I quit that four years ago. I decided to take a break and try to work out what I wanted from life."

He had already been interested in photography ten years ago, often turning up with his DSLR camera hanging over one shoulder. I would hear the shutter clicking whenever I turned toward him. He always got mad when I tried to look away, so I often used to indulge him.

"Smart," says Finn, spearing a potato on his fork. Charlotte glances over to him.

"Do you do commercial stuff? For magazines?" she asks.

Jacob shakes his head. "Nature photography. I never really shared your interest in superficial stuff like that. I travel quite a lot too."

His words surprise me. I can't quite get them to square with the vision I have of Jacob's humdrum life. Still, I'm pleased to see his face light up as he talks to Finn, telling him that he managed to get away from Gävle, to see the world.

"Oh yeah?" Finn replies. "Where have you been?"

"Iceland. I've been to Norway to shoot eagles and other birds too. And I went to Australia a few years back."

"I've always wanted to go there. Did you drive along the Great Ocean Road?"

"Yeah, I did. It was amazing. I visited the Karijini National Park too. I've got a website with some of my portfolio on it, if you're interested."

He starts patting down his pockets until he remembers what happened to our cell phones, and with that his smile and dimple are back again.

"I'll show you later, once I've got my phone back. You really should go."

Charlotte laughs.

"It's not quite that simple, though, is it? Just packing your bags and flying halfway around the world whenever you feel like it. We have responsibilities at home."

"I guess it depends on what your priorities are," Finn says without looking at her.

"Damn straight," Tess says with a deep sigh. "What are your priorities, Adrian? What's most important to you?"

Adrian meets my eye, and I shake my head. It's not worth getting into an argument with Tess when she's in this sort of mood. He holds his tongue and looks away.

"What's the appeal of taking pictures of nature?" asks Ava. "Why not people?"

She is leaning forward with her chin in her hand.

"You can really immerse yourself in it, stop thinking about anything else; all that matters is what's happening right there and then. Nature is honest too. No games, no acting. What you see is what you get."

Jacob fixes his eyes on me, and I stand up.

"I need to use the bathroom, Ava. Is it . . .?"

I look around and don't remember having seen one on the way in. Ava puts down her napkin and starts to get up, but I wave my hand to stop her.

"No, you stay there. Finish your meal. I can find it. Just tell me where to go."

Her icy eyes study me for a long moment before she sits back down.

"At the end of the hallway past the living room. Just keep going—it's the door at the very end."

I'm halfway into the living room before she even finishes speaking.

"Thanks," I call back.

I pause with my back to the wall once I round the corner, curious to hear what they might talk about when I'm no longer in the room, but their conversation is about TV shows and streaming services.

The living room is pretty spacious. In addition to the wall of bookshelves and the blood-red armchairs, there is a sunken seating area one step down. This part of the room has a pale wooden floor, but I notice that there is a white carpet in the lower section. The windows are big, although they don't quite reach the ceiling like they do in the dining room, and the door to the balcony is right in the middle. There is a three-seater sofa in the sunken area, flanked by a couple of two-seaters, all upholstered in a pale beige fabric. The coffee table between them is made of glass and metal, and I notice another oil painting hanging on the wall behind them. Red this time. I turn my head to the right and see the hallway Ava mentioned, a few yards long and with three doors: one at the far end and another on each side. Another two paintings have been hung on the walls there. One is all oranges and yellows; the other, shades of green. The six canvases I've seen so far—these two, plus the two in the hallway leading to the front door and the ones in the dining room and living room—are all the same size, and I notice what looks like a series of lines beneath the paint at the bottom edge of the yellow one. A sketch? I take a step forward and pick at the paint with my nail. There is something there, beneath all the layers of color.

I hear the sound of chairs scraping the floor, and I make my way over to the bathroom, locking the door behind me and leaning back against it. With a sigh, I see that it has been decorated in the same style as the rest of the apartment. Tiles in warm sandy tones, a glass shower cubicle with two showerheads—one ceiling mounted and another on the wall—plus a Jacuzzi bath in the corner. I can just imagine Ava in a sea of bubbles, a glass of champagne in one hand. I picture her getting out of the tub, with rosy skin, wrapping herself in a thick white towel. In front of me, there is a wide handbasin beneath a huge mirror. I cross the room, passing a wooden shelf full of fluffy hand towels, and turn on the cold tap to splash my cheeks. Hunched over the basin, I meet my own eye and shake my head. I should never have come this evening. How could I seriously think that we would have anything in common after so long apart?

As I straighten up, I notice that there is a gap beneath the mirror, and I hook a finger into it. The gap gets wider.

The mirror is a cabinet.

I hesitate for a moment, trying to convince myself that I'm not someone who snoops through another person's bathroom cabinet, but that quickly passes and I open the door.

The recessed cabinet has three shelves, and I glance back at the locked door before fully opening it. There's nothing to be ashamed of; given half a chance, anyone would do the same. If a person has something to hide, they would keep it somewhere else—everyone knows that.

Ava's apartment might be void of any personal touches, but these shelves are packed. There are a number of expensive face creams and serums on the top shelf. Pots, tubes, and glass ampoules containing some sort of oil. I turn them and reach for a tub of something. Nothing seems to be open. On the middle shelf, there is a simple pot of unperfumed moisturizer, half used and lumpy, beside several packs of supplements: vitamin D, omega-3, nail and skin complex. On the bottom shelf, I can see a hairbrush, a comb, and a few hair ties and clips. No makeup other than a single lipstick and a powder compact. But then again, Ava has never needed it.

I'm just about to close the door when I notice it. A lockable compartment, possibly for keeping medication away from kids. It practically blends in with the back of the cabinet, stretching from the lower corner to the bottom of the middle shelf. I pull on the edge of it, but it's locked. Of course it is.

Disappointed, I close the cabinet and reach for a few sheets of toilet tissue to dry my face. Once I'm done, I step on the pedal to open the trash can. The bag inside is almost empty, but not quite. At the very bottom, there is a plastic pot with a label on it. I stare down at it for a moment, with the tissue still in my hand, then I bend down and take it out.

Risperdal.

It's a prescription medication bottle, and the name of the drug sounds familiar, but I can't for the life of me remember what it is. If Ava hadn't taken my phone I would have been able to google it right now. I drop the toilet tissue into the trash can and use both hands to turn the little bottle over and read the printed sticker from the pharmacy. *Take one pill twice daily.* Ava's name and date of birth are printed in the top corner. I shake the bottle, but it's empty.

Why is Ava on medication?

I drop it back into the trash can, where it hits the toilet tissue with a soft thud. I stare at it for a moment, then take my foot off the pedal. With the sleeve of my blouse, I wipe my fingerprints from the mirror. Then I back up toward the door and cast one last glance at myself before turning out the light and heading back out into the hallway.

Their voices sound louder and livelier now, but I'm in no rush to get back. Instead, I pause by the door to my right. It's slightly ajar, and with a bit of help it swings open to reveal an office with views out onto the old warehouses down below. The room is tastefully decorated, with a pale carpet and matching dark wood furniture. The shelves are full of folders and neat rows of books, and by the big window there is a desk with drawers on both sides. Four slim drawers, plus a wide one in the middle, all ideal places to keep sentimental memories like faded cinema tickets or hastily written notes.

Beside the desk, there is a tall filing cabinet, and on top of the writing pad I notice a sheet of paper and a pen, plus a piece of the same silvery ribbon as on our boxes. I take a step forward to get a better look, but all I have time to see is my own name at the top before I feel a hand on my shoulder.

"Did you get lost?"

I turn around and see Ava standing behind me.

Beautiful, wonderful Ava.

"Your home is amazing. I saw the office as I came out of the bathroom and noticed the view beyond the desk. How long have you lived here?"

Ava leans in so close that I can feel the heat of her body on my cheek. With a firm grip on the door handle, she closes the door, forcing me back out into the hallway.

"Far too long. I still have everything from my old place in storage. Maybe I'll move back to that area at some point."

She slowly takes her hand from the handle, and I half expect to feel her soft fingers tuck the hair back behind my ear.

But they don't.

"Maybe?" I say. "I don't understand why you moved away if that's where you want to be. Why didn't you bring all your stuff here?"

"I know you don't," she says with a slight smile, her fingers brushing my arm.

With that, silence settles over us. Alone in the hallway, away from the others, I can hear my blood pounding in my ears. I feel torn. On the one hand, I want to drag her over to the sofa in the living room, curl up beside her, and ask her about the most irrelevant things. On the other hand, I want to keep my distance because everything will come crashing down if I let her in. And yet something is keeping me here, just like something kept me coming back to her then, despite everything she'd done.

"I was admiring your paintings earlier," I say, gesturing to the wall behind me. "They're incredible. So different from the things you used to paint. So much deeper and more powerful. You know, I still have one of your paintings of the jetty by your parents' house. It's on the wall in my bedroom."

"Really?"

No.

I do still have it, but it's leaning against the wall at the back of my wardrobe, hidden beneath a ski jacket and with a crack in the glass. Ava's face lights up, and she turns to the paintings on the wall.

"So you noticed them?"

"They're pretty hard to miss."

"There are six in total. I've been working on them for years, but I think I'm almost done now. Soon, anyway. I'm always finding new angles to consider."

She cocks her head and reaches out to straighten the yellow painting.

"This one is my favorite," she says, stroking the thick paint.

"When did William tell you we were thinking about leaving?" I hear myself asking, paying close attention to every shift on her face.

Her reaction isn't the one I expected. No blushing cheeks, no wide eyes trying to avoid mine. Instead, she looks amused, like I just said something without stopping to think first and should be able to see just how absurd my question was.

"Let's go back and join the others," she says, turning away from me.

CHAPTER 15

Now

WHEN DID I work it out?

Was it when Ava's messages made William leave the living room for the kitchen, keeping his phone pressed against his leg to stop me from being able to read the text on the screen? Or was it when I could no longer manage my usual crisp bread with cheese in the morning, and my tea grew cold before I'd even had a sip?

For weeks, as the snow melted on the ground and the buds opened up on the cherry trees, it was like I was in a vacuum where neither food nor sleep existed—just Ava. The birthmark on the back of her neck, only visible when she had her fair hair tied up; the way her hand pressed against the base of my spine when she hugged me. Her nails, clawing gently at the skin on my forearms before she finally let me go.

Mom never seemed to think there was anything wrong with Dad's absences while I was growing up. On those long evenings when he was supposedly stuck in a meeting or working late—hunched over God knows who—she would vacuum the entire house and bake pies, spreading the essays she was marking across the kitchen table. The pies always cooled down just in time for Dad to get home, trudging in with his tie all crooked.

"It's about taking care of each other," she always said with a weary smile once he had left her to do the washing up and gone to bed. He was exhausted after a busy day at the office.

She would then pass me a slice of apple pie and slump down on the other side of the table to watch me eat.

"One day you'll have someone to take care of you."

I desperately wanted her to be right and me to be wrong. I suppose that was why I clung on to William's heart so tightly, despite the fact that my own was telling me something else.

* * *

Ava has always been slim, but there is not even a single ounce of fat on her. I don't remember ever seeing her work out, but I do recall that she always wanted something sweet to eat after dinner. And yet she was still so slender. She often went walking in the park, even when it was raining, and on warm summer evenings she sometimes spent hours on her yoga mat down by the water's edge beyond the mini golf course. It was as though she couldn't stand her own company in a confined space.

As she turns away from me now, her shoulder blades look so hard and angular, protruding from her back. I push a potato through the sauce and watch as she moves around the table, clearing the plates. She's pale too, though she was never the biggest fan of sunbathing, and it is November. Could she have some sort of heart problem? During our last term of school, her dad had suffered a stroke and spent two weeks in the hospital. It could be something hereditary.

Maybe it's cancer.

"Are you done with that potato?"

Ava is standing right beside me with a stack of plates on one arm, and she raises her pale brow. I lower my fork and put the plate onto the top of the pile. As she lifts her other arm to hold it steady, I notice something just beneath her shoulder. A couple of small red dots.

"Thank you," she says with a smile, continuing around to the other side of the table.

"Let me help you, Ava." Charlotte starts gathering up the serving platters and dishes. "Do you want everything cleared away?"

"You can leave the glasses."

Adrian gets up and pulls his pack of cigarettes from his shirt pocket. He pushes one of them between his lips and then holds the pack up in the air and nods to the balcony, but I shake my head. The minute he is gone, I lean in to Tess and whisper in her ear.

"Do you know what Risperdal is?"

Her head snaps in my direction. "Risperdal?"

"Shh," I hiss, checking to see where Ava is. "Not so loud."

On the other side of the table, Finn watches Charlotte walk away, before getting up and heading for the hallway. Ava is already on her way into the kitchen, with Charlotte hot on her heels. Charlotte is holding the dirty dishes out in front of her to avoid getting any food on her dress, and her arms are shaking with the effort. As soon as they're out of earshot, I turn back to Tess.

"Do you know?"

"My granny was on Risperdal when she lived at the care home."

"Your granny?"

"She had Alzheimer's."

Alzheimer's.

That was why the name of the drug seemed so familiar: I've seen it in another bathroom cabinet in another apartment, a long time ago. I glance over to Jacob on the other side of the table, then lean in to Tess again.

"So it's an Alzheimer's medication?"

Jesus Christ, this is even worse than I thought. I crane my neck after Ava again. It would explain the change in her, though. The fact that she seems to have completely forgotten all her hopes and dreams, her beliefs. Changed her style. But she's only thirty-four. Do people really develop Alzheimer's at such a young age?

"No," says Tess. "She took something else for that. They put her on Risperdal as it progressed, when she got aggressive. It helped to calm her down and make her easier to deal with."

I'm not sure her answer is really all that reassuring.

"Why are you asking about Risperdal?"

I try to laugh it off and straighten up in my chair. "Oh, it's just something I heard. I didn't recognize the name, so I was wondering. It's not illegal, then?"

"No, I'm pretty sure it's not. But I do know why you thought *I* would know."

My cheeks are burning.

"Do you think Charlotte seems nervous?" Tess asks.

"Charlotte?"

From the kitchen, I can hear her low voice, the sound of china clinking.

"Do you think she's wondering what's in her box?"

"I guess we all are. Should she be nervous?"

Tess fixes her dull eyes on me and sips her wine. "Where's the bathroom? I've needed to pee since I got here, but I didn't dare ask."

"End of the hallway. Watch you don't get lost out there."

She gives me a wry smile and gets up. I watch as she walks away, and when I turn back, I realize that Jacob and I are now alone at the table. He has moved over to Charlotte's seat, directly opposite me. His new beard—which suits him more than I want to admit—is thick and neat, and the familiar dimple in his cheek appears as he smiles. That isn't all that catches my eye. He has a scar I don't remember on his forehead, just beneath his hairline, and the fine lines around his eyes are deeper than they were ten years ago.

"So, you moved," he says. "Were you really that eager to get away?"

Adrian was right: Jacob shouldn't have come this evening. I had sort of been hoping he wouldn't. I open and close my mouth, take a deep breath, and smile. There is nothing I can say that wouldn't take all evening to explain, but he still wouldn't understand.

"I think I'll go and help Ava with the washing up," I say, getting to my feet. "She has a lot to deal with."

"So do you."

We stare at each other for what feels like a long time. His smile is gone, and he is looking up at me with a furrowed brow, the way he always used to when something was bothering him. I reach for the last serving dish and balance a few small bowls and spoons on top before making my way into the kitchen. I'm just a few steps from the doorway when I hear my name.

"When are you going to give it to Sophie?" Charlotte's voice is low, barely audible over the sound of the faucet. "I still don't know how you knew. Did I tell you that evening? I can hardly remember anything after we found William. Sometimes it feels like I wasn't there at all."

"She can have it soon. Is it here?"

Charlotte is busy rinsing a dish, Ava picking up the shards of my broken glass from the counter by the wall. She holds one of them up and presses her finger to the sharp edge.

"It's in my bag. I didn't know where to put it. Finn wouldn't leave me alone before we set off. He kept following me everywhere, almost like he knew something was up. I don't like this, Ava. What are you going to do?"

If I close my eyes, I'm carried thirteen years back in time, but the roles are reversed. Twenty-one years of age, on an empty street behind Central Hotel, Charlotte offering money she doesn't have to a huge man in dark clothing, to drive us over to the other side of town.

"You don't have to like it, Charlotte. You just need to give it to me."

The dish I'm holding wobbles, and I realize the spoon is about to fall to the floor too late to do anything about it. Their heads turn in my direction, and they both pause what they were doing. Charlotte turns off the faucet and dries her hands on a checked tea towel. Ava puts down the piece of glass and pushes the whole pile over to the corner.

"I grabbed the last few dishes," I say, bending down to pick up the spoon. As I'm crouching, I squeeze my eyes shut and hesitate briefly before straightening up again. "Where should I put them?"

"You're so sweet. Just put them on the counter over there. Wouldn't you rather sit down and take it easy?"

"I don't mind helping. Is there anything else I can do?"

Ava glances at Charlotte and then turns back to me.

"Now that you mention it, yes. I was just about to show Charlotte something. Would you mind loading the dishwasher? You don't need to start it or anything."

"Sure, I can do that. Do you want me to—"

"Thanks, Sophie. You're an angel."

Ava takes Charlotte by the arm and leads her out of the kitchen. I watch them walk away and then look down at the mountain of plates and dishes with a sigh. If I can just shove them into the dishwasher, then I can follow them and find out what Ava is planning to show her. Maybe it has something to do with the medication I found.

I start pressing the cupboard doors without handles and pulling on the ones that do, until eventually one of them opens to reveal an enormous dishwasher. One by one, I rinse the dirty plates, shaking off the leftovers, to load them into the machine.

"Why are you avoiding me?"

The sound of Jacob's voice right behind me makes me jump and drop one of the plates. For the second time that evening, a piece of Ava's tableware—no doubt just as expensive as the first—shatters, and this time it splatters food right across the floor.

"No . . ." I whimper, grabbing the tea towel Charlotte used to dry her hands, fully expecting to see Ava come rushing into the room with her hand on her bony hip.

With the tea towel draped over my shoulder, I crouch down and start picking up the pieces of china. Jacob squats down beside me to help.

"Just leave it—I'll do it."

Once I've picked up the last piece, he puts his on top of mine and I lift them all onto the counter.

"Thanks," I say, bending down again to wipe up the sauce, which stains the tea towel orange. It's beyond saving.

It's strange to feel his presence just behind me. Strange and familiar. It was as though William didn't even notice that suddenly there were three of us. When we walked hand in hand to a bar after the last lecture of the day, Jacob would be waiting for us when we arrived. And when I started squirming at the sight of him, William would stroke my cheek and tell me that he was the one who had called Jacob. That he didn't want him to be alone. I smiled and nodded then, because that's what he was like. My William.

He didn't leave anyone out.

I have no idea when my irritation first transformed into appreciation. Maybe it was that evening at the Italian restaurant, when Jacob corrected William as he ordered my meal; he knew that I tried to avoid gluten. Or maybe it was the day William forgot I was giving a talk as part of my Swedish course, but Jacob remembered and snuck in, taking a seat at the very back of the lecture theater. He spent forty-five minutes grinning and started a round of applause before leaving, and by the time I came out, he was gone.

Without really noticing it, he became a natural part of our everyday lives. *My* everyday life. And that was what saved me when William started to drift away. Right until the moment it started putting strange ideas into my head, anyway.

I open the cupboard beneath the sink and toss the tea towel into the trash. Ava can afford to buy a new one. When I turn around, he is leaning back against the island, with his hands on the worktop. His nails are short and neat, his ring finger bare.

"You didn't answer the question," he says.

"Don't be stupid. I'm not avoiding you."

"It definitely feels like you are. It's felt that way for ten years, now that I think about it."

He didn't deserve what I'd done. None of them did.

But there was no other way.

I rinse my hands under the hot tap and search for something else to dry them on. Jacob grabs the roll of paper towels and tears off a sheet, which he holds out to me. I reluctantly take it, and I feel his thumb stroke my palm before I dry my hands and trash the paper.

"I've been avoiding everyone," I say. "It was best that way."

"Best for who?"

For you, I want to say.

"I'm going to go and check whether Ava needs help with anything else."

And see where she has taken Charlotte. Charlotte said she had something in her bag. If they haven't made it back to the table yet, I could open it and find out what they were talking about. Just have a look. I start making my way toward the door, but his warm hand grips my arm.

"I only want to talk, Sophie."

"What is there to talk about?"

He laughs.

"Everything. Life, death."

The twinkle in his eye fades, and he purses his lips. His hand slowly lets go of my arm, and he backs up until he is leaning against the island again.

"Sophie!"

Ava is shouting for me from the dining room, and my heart starts racing.

"Sorry. I have to go."

He lets me walk away without another word, and when I turn back to see him watching me, he is gone.

CHAPTER

16

Now

I SPOT CHARLOTTE'S BAG on the floor by her chair the minute I reach the bright dining room, but unfortunately she is standing right beside it, her arms wrapped tight around herself. She is chewing on her lower lip, and she keeps blinking, making her long lashes flutter. I try to catch her eye, but she looks away. Ava is standing by her seat at the end of the table. She seems calm and relaxed, and she raises her chin when she spots me. Finn is back too. He is chatting to Adrian, who is leaning back with his hands behind his head. Tess comes through from the lounge, pausing at the sight of our uncomfortable triangle of silence.

"Why don't you open your box now?" says Ava, taking a step toward me.

There is a slight smile playing on her lips, and her eyes look big and bright. I instinctively glance over to Tess, who shrugs and turns to Charlotte, who softly shakes her head. I slowly make my way over to the table and pick up the little box, which isn't where I left it. Someone has moved it to the middle of my placemat, just like Tess's box was in the middle of her plate earlier. I peer back over my shoulder and see Jacob leaning against the kitchen doorframe.

"You want me to open it now?"

"Yes, why not?"

Finn and Adrian have stopped talking.

Everyone is looking at me.

"Just play along"—that was what Adrian said earlier. I guess that's what I'm doing as I pick up the box. It's no longer empty, and I tilt it from side to side and feel a small, hard object rattling around inside. I laugh and hold the box up in the air so that everyone can see it, indulging Ava's little game.

"Fine, I'll open it. Are you ready?"

"We're ready," Ava says softly, but I feel anything but.

"Go for it," says Adrian, meeting my eye.

Before I have time to change my mind, I lift the lid and toss it to the table. I stare down into the box for a moment, then put it down and back away. My right hand reflexively reaches for my left, rubbing the skin on my ring finger. I never thought I would see it again; I'd *banked* on never seeing it. But here it is. As shiny as the day it vanished.

"Where did you get this?"

At first, Ava doesn't speak. She just moves closer, until she's right behind my back.

"You tell me," she whispers into my ear. "What happened?"

"Sophie, you don't have to say anything if you don't want to," Charlotte speaks up from the other side of the table. "It's yours. Just take it."

"How did it end up here?"

"Charlotte brought it," Ava replies, still hovering behind me.

"*You* brought it?"

The object in her bag. This must have been it. Has Charlotte really had it for the past ten years?

"Ava asked me to bring it. I don't know how she knew I had it, but I figured she just wanted to give it back to you. I didn't know she was—"

"What's in the box?"

Adrian gets up and moves over to my other side. He reaches out and takes the little ring from the box. I had said I would be happy with something plain and simple, but William insisted on buying a diamond, one he said was as pure and clear as me. The polished rock sparkles in the light as Adrian holds it up in the air.

"Your engagement ring?"

For some reason I was reluctant to tell the others after William pushed the ring onto my finger. He was so excited that it left me feeling exhausted. Cupping my face in his hands, kissing me on the lips, hugging me and lifting me so high that it knocked the wind out of me.

I can still remember the moment we got to the café, where the others were already sitting with their espressos and their pastries, how quiet they all were when he held out my hand to show them the ring and its glittering stone. Charlotte's smile stiffened into a grimace, and she stared down at the ring for a long time before eventually forcing herself to look up at William. Ava just smiled softly, her eyes fixed on the latte she kept stirring and stirring. Adrian was first to get up, thumping William on the back and hugging me.

"Why did Charlotte have your ring?" Finn asks, glancing up at his wife, who looks like she is on the verge of falling apart. "Was this what you were running around with before we left the house?"

"Did you *steal* her ring?" Adrian blurts out.

"No! I found it when I was looking for William. I went into his bedroom, and it was right there on the nightstand. And then we opened the bathroom door, and I never got a chance to talk to you, Sophie. You know that. I brought it to the funeral, but you kept your distance, and I didn't want to bother you when you were already so upset. And then you left Gävle."

"Why didn't you say anything?" Finn asks. He sounds disappointed. "Why didn't you tell me?"

"I kept it because I thought Sophie would ask for it, that she would wonder where it had gone. How was I supposed to know we wouldn't speak again? That's why I was so happy when I saw you here this evening, because I could finally give it back."

She is beaming, and I can see that she's hoping I will smooth things over.

"You must have really missed it."

Adrian presses the ring into my hand, and I shudder when I feel the sharp edges of the diamond against my palm.

"Why did you take it off?" Tess asks quietly. "Why wasn't it on your finger?"

"What?"

She is sitting in her chair, and I look down at her and meet her cold eyes.

"Why was it in William's room?" she asks.

I stare at the ring in my hand.

"I don't know. I guess I must have dropped it."

"Dropped it? Did you often drop your ring?"

"Yeah. I don't know. I can't remember."

"Tell me again why *you*'ve had it for the last ten years?" Tess continues, turning to Charlotte. "What you just said doesn't really make sense."

"I've already explained."

Tess laughs. "But why did you go into William's bedroom? Why were you even looking for him that evening?"

"What are you getting at, Tess? Just come out and say it."

"Ah, I'm not sure you want me to do that. It's probably better if it comes from you."

Tess laughs again, sipping her wine as she gives Finn a wink with one of her narrow, catlike eyes. The top button on her shirt has come open, and I can see the black bra she is wearing underneath.

"You're drunk," Charlotte snorts.

"And you're so fucking fake!" Tess's voice breaks, and a number of red blotches have begun to spread across her throat and chest.

"What are you talking about, Tess?" I ask. "Charlotte?"

I look at both of them, but Charlotte doesn't say a word, and Tess simply shakes her head, making her blond ponytail whip against her shoulders.

"Why were you late for dinner that evening?" asks Ava, finally taking her seat. "We were all wondering where you were. William said you'd changed your plans and that you didn't meet him. Where were you?"

"Where was I? How am I meant to remember that? I probably couldn't find anything to wear, or maybe I just lost track of time, like usual."

"But you called him and said you needed to change plans ages before you were actually supposed to meet. What came up?"

"Ava, I honestly have no idea. It was ten years ago."

I'm lying. I know exactly what came up.

"What about that morning? William said you were gone when he woke up. Surely you didn't have any lectures that day? It was the middle of summer."

"I was taking a summer course to catch up. Honestly, this feels like another police interrogation. What is this?"

"Relax, Sophie. We're all friends here. We're just trying to remember, to make sense of that evening from start to finish. If we work together, we can fill in the gaps."

"Stop, Ava." Jacob's voice thunders across the room. "That's enough."

Ava stops talking at last, and I drop the ring back into the box and push the lid on top.

"Thank you for bringing it, Charlotte. I just need some air."

Six heads watch as I turn, with a shaky smile on my face, and walk toward the balcony.

CHAPTER

17

Four hours and nine minutes before William's death

CHARLOTTE DIDN'T NORMALLY look forward to their Friday dinners anymore. They had Greek food every single week, and all that cheese had started to give her stomach issues. She had been begging them to go somewhere else for months now—or at least try someplace new every other week—but the others were determined for everything to stay the same—force of habit and all that. They liked the shabby old restaurant with its dusty brick walls and sun-bleached plastic plants. Charlotte thought it smelled musty and that the food was overdone and greasy. She was also so sick of fried potatoes that she was willing to eat nothing but salad going forward. But for once she had actually been looking forward to this week's dinner since her alarm had gone off on Monday morning.

Because this week wasn't like all the rest.

* * *

Her parents had met during their first year of university, with her mom studying to become a nurse; and her father, a civil engineer. The way they told it, it all sounded so perfect:

their eyes met across a crowded corridor, and just like that they both knew they had found the one. Three years after that first yearning moment, Charlotte was born. Her mom had been twenty-two at the time.

Charlotte was now twenty-four.

She crossed one leg over the other and tugged her dress down over her thighs. William was still sitting at the far end of the table. Ava had gone to the bathroom; Adrian was smoking another cigarette; and Tess kept drifting between the bar and the table, as though she couldn't quite work out where she wanted to be.

But William only had eyes for Sophie, who was standing in the sunlight by the window, doing something on her phone. She had been on it almost constantly since she'd gotten to the restaurant. If it wasn't in her hand, then it was on the table beside her.

Charlotte had first met William during the happiest period of her life. The boy from the house behind the yard. At seven, they had played soccer matches together on the other side of the cycle path; at nine, they had cycled through the woods, with insect bites all over their legs. She had fallen into her mother's arms with filthy clothing and grazed knees every evening. William was the last person she saw through the window before she crawled into bed, and he was the first person she thought about when she woke.

But then, the summer before Charlotte turned thirteen, his family had moved.

It had been a few years before she next saw him, on the first day of senior high school. His hair was longer, the curls wilder, but his smile and the dimple in his chin were the same as ever. He had grown, and his shoulders were broader as he walked around with his hands in the pockets of his ripped jeans. Charlotte remembered wondering if this was what she had been waiting for, her version of the moment when her mother had realized her father was the one. But

William hadn't recognized her. After she reluctantly let her unruly red curls down, it took four hours before he finally paused and studied her.

"Charlotte?" he asked, and she had seen in his eyes that, to him, she was still just the girl with the grazed knees.

* * *

Charlotte had spent years searching for it, but it wasn't until a few months back that she had finally spotted the crack in Sophie and William's relationship. Everyone could see that they weren't meant for each other; no one understood why they had ever become a couple in the first place, but then again we all make mistakes when we're young. It was just that Charlotte hadn't expected his mistake to go on for quite so long, nor that it would make her suffer quite so much.

Sophie had played her part well. Since William had first introduced her to the group, no one had ever questioned her background. Still, there were no limits to what you could find if you really put your mind to it. And tonight, the time had finally come for Charlotte to share what she knew with William, before it was too late and he got his heart broken.

"You can have whatever you want in life." That was what her mom used to whisper in her ear when she was younger. *"You just need to make up your mind."* By the window, Sophie sighed at her phone and made her way over to the bar. Charlotte got up and carried the half-empty plate of fried calamari around to the other side of the table, where she took a seat beside William.

"There are a few left. Help yourself before someone else takes them."

He turned his head, and his face lit up the way it always did when he saw her, something that usually gave her a pleasant tingle in the pit of her stomach.

"What did I do to deserve someone like you in my life?" he said. "You're always looking out for me."

"Who else is going to?"

She smiled, and he lowered his head to his hand without taking any of the greasy rings.

"Are you all right, William? I don't like seeing you so tired and run down. Is there anything I can do to help?"

She put a hesitant hand on his shoulder, moved it slightly, and gave it a light squeeze. William laughed and shook his head.

"I'm fine, I've just got a lot on my mind. But things are looking up."

He was right about that. Tess had paused between the bar and the table, her eyes on Charlotte. Charlotte took her hand from William's shoulder, then leaned in to him and lowered her head conspiratorially.

"There's something I need to tell you. About Sophie."

"Sophie?"

"How much do you really know about her?"

He laughed again, but his smile faded. "What do you mean?"

Charlotte glanced back over her shoulder, to where Tess was standing, lowering her voice when she saw that Tess had moved closer.

"I've found out a few things about her life before she moved here, and I actually—"

"Ah, is there still some calamari left?"

Sophie had appeared out of nowhere, and she sat down on the other side of William, grabbed a piece of squid, and took a big bite. He immediately turned away from Charlotte and kissed her on the cheek, and Charlotte slumped back in her chair.

"God, I love calamari," Sophie mumbled between chews. "So long as I don't think too hard about what I'm actually eating. Hey, don't you think we should give Finn a call to see where he is?"

She wiped her fingers on a napkin and then leaned forward to meet Charlotte's eye.

"Finn will be just fine," said Charlotte. "I'm sure he'll be here any minute now."

"Nice dress, by the way," Sophie replied. "Is it new?"

Her words sent an irritating wave of heat across Charlotte's cheeks, making her skin tingle. Charlotte sat tall, reflexively reaching up to her hair to stroke the blow-dried lengths that had taken on a life of their own in the humid air. She had bought her first straighteners just one month into senior high school, thereby taking control of her unruly hair that she had previously tamed with a tight bun at the nape of her neck. She had started plundering her mom's makeup bag too, lining her eyes with kohl and mascara and asking for gift cards for her birthdays and Christmas in an attempt to slowly swap out her sweatshirts and jeans for more fitted clothing so that William couldn't fail to notice the woman she had become.

"I guess I've just never worn it around you."

"Are you meeting someone later?"

Sophie grinned and reached for another piece of calamari. Charlotte pulled the plate toward William and elbowed him in the side.

"I thought we were going over to William's place after dinner," she replied, because that was what she had been hoping for when she spent half an hour drying her hair after work.

And in the best of worlds, Sophie wouldn't join them.

"Oh yeah?" Sophie turned to William.

"Wasn't my idea," he said. "Ava suggested it and Adrian agreed, and that was that. It's okay, isn't it?"

Sophie shrugged. "Yeah, sure. I just thought we'd have some time together later."

"I know, but Christos is closing for the summer, so we probably won't see each other for a couple weeks. It'll be fun, I promise."

"Did you have other plans?" Charlotte asked, earning herself an icy look from Sophie, who then smirked.

"Nope, it'll be good. I'm just a bit tired, that's all."

"Perfect," said William. "I need to use the bathroom. Will you save me a bit of calamari?"

"You can have two."

And as though that had been her idea from the start, Sophie pushed the last two pieces over to his plate. William kissed the top of her head before getting up and leaving them at the table. Sophie turned and looked the other way, toward Jacob, who was sitting at a table for two by the wall. Charlotte couldn't believe he'd had the balls to turn up after his fight with Adrian, but he had barely said a word to any of them since he'd arrived. He just kept turning the bottle of beer in his hands, staring at Sophie with gritted teeth.

"He's great, isn't he?"

Sophie turned back. "Who?"

"William, obviously. Who did you think I meant? You're lucky to have him."

"I know."

Sophie looked down and texted something on her phone. A few seconds later, there was a pinging sound somewhere nearby. Over by the wall. On Jacob's table. He picked up his own cell phone and looked down at the screen before turning to the window.

"I'll be back in a sec—I'm just going to get another drink," said Charlotte.

The minute she got up and pushed in her chair, Sophie stole another glance at Jacob. Charlotte started making her way over to the bar on the other side of the wall, but she turned off toward the bathroom at the last minute. When she reached the narrow hallway with the tiled floor leading to the only toilet, she started pacing impatiently. A few minutes later, the door opened, and William came out. He smiled, and before he had time to say anything, Charlotte grabbed his arm and dragged him away.

"I really need to talk to you."

The moment of truth had arrived. Her heart was beating so hard beneath her thin dress that she was afraid he might be able to hear it.

"Hey, relax. I'm listening. What's up?"

He would thank her. He would realize she was only doing this because she cared, right? Charlotte had always cared about him, even when he stopped caring about her.

"Sophie is lying to you."

She paused for a moment, and William waited patiently for her to continue.

"Go on," he said when she failed to speak, because when Charlotte looked into his eyes, she realized she was no longer sure it would go down the way she had thought.

"I stumbled across one of her old friends on Facebook."

That was the understatement of the century. She had scoured Sophie's embarrassingly short friend list, and when that failed, she had started going through her friends' friends instead, until eventually she found someone who had grown up in the same town as her: a black-haired girl with too much eyeliner and a tackily low-cut top. Charlotte had sent her a tentative message and then didn't hear anything for several days. But her answer had been worth the wait.

"Apparently she didn't actually move here because her dad got a new job. They moved because Sophie was arrested. For breaking and entering and criminal damage."

"Charlotte," William sighed, rubbing his forehead. She saw his eyes scanning the room for Sophie. "We all did stupid stuff when we were younger. You borrowed your parents' car when you didn't even have a driver's license, and then you left it in a ditch without even mentioning it to them. Sophie has already told me that she got in with a bad crowd, that she had a tough time."

Had he even heard what she'd said?

"A tough time? She *lied* to us, William. She lied to everyone."

"Probably because she was embarrassed. Besides, she didn't lie to me. She told me exactly why they moved, and the fact that she was arrested was the least of it."

Charlotte was speechless, and she felt her cheeks and throat grow hot.

"How can you be sure that what she told you was true? She's told us all different versions. What else do you think she could have lied about?"

William's smile faltered. "What's this really about, Charlotte?"

What it was really about was that night during their second year of senior high school, a walk with William down misty streets. A change in the air, something electric that brought them closer and closer until William paused beneath the old oak and kissed her with his hands in her hair. About the two dates they'd gone on, or maybe it was three. And how, after the last, he had squeezed her hand and said that he thought of her as a friend.

All he had needed was time, and she had been prepared to give him that. But then Sophie had joined their school that autumn, and the moment she'd stepped into their lives was the moment he'd taken a step out of Charlotte's.

Charlotte stood tall and instinctively backed away from him.

"Nothing, William. I just thought you would want to know, but I guess I was wrong."

"You know I've never been a fan of gossip. I love Sophie. I'm planning to spend the rest of my life with her."

His words cut straight through her, leaving her bruised and bloody. All the old wounds that had finally started to heal were now bleeding heavily, a torrent of shame.

"Then I hope you're happy and that she wants the same thing."

"What is that supposed to mean?"

She shouldn't say it. This was a step too far, even for her, but the words were burning to get out and eventually proved impossible to hold back.

You just need to make up your mind.

"Sophie and Jacob . . ."

"Yeah?"

He was listening to her now. Oh, he saw her now. William's beautiful dark eyes widened, and for a split second she relished being able to hurt him the way he had hurt her.

She took another step away from him, unsteady on her heels, then gave a low laugh and glanced back over her shoulder.

"Forget it," she said. "It's just gossip."

With that, she turned away, eyes burning with stubborn tears, leaving him alone in the narrow hallway. Charlotte had planted a seed of doubt inside him, and that might just be enough.

CHAPTER

18

Now

AVA'S BALCONY STRETCHES the entire width of the building, one of the ones I saw earlier, when my cab pulled up outside. That already feels like a lifetime ago, even though it's just been a few hours. I can make out Adrian's footsteps beneath the fresh snow that has fallen, and I walk as far as I can before leaning out over the railing. The wind is so strong that for a moment I worry it might actually blow me over the edge.

On the other side of the glass, beyond the living room, my engagement ring is lying on the dining table, as shiny and gleaming as I remember it. I should be thinking about William and everything I've lost, but the only thing on my mind is Dad and the betrayal that shaped my whole life.

I probably noticed it long before I ever actually understood. You could see it in the way he moved, hear it in his voice. Dad showered Mom with hugs and kisses, and he brought her roses every Friday, but I could see it in his eyes.

His thoughts were elsewhere.

It was a complete fluke that I caught him at it when I was thirteen or fourteen. I got home around twelve one day, and I remember that I thought it was weird that the door was unlocked, that I paused when I saw Dad's shoes beside a pair of black heels in the hallway. I should have turned around right then and there, but instead I went in and stood at the foot of the stairs, with my hand on the rail. I could hear them upstairs. Heavy breathing, low voices. I knew they weren't my mother's shoes—she was so tall she always wore loafers, didn't want to be taller than Dad when they went out together—and yet I couldn't bring myself to leave before I knew for sure, so I went up the sweeping staircase and crossed the carpeted floor. I hesitated outside the door to Mom and Dad's room, gripped the handle for a moment before I opened it, and there he was: in bed with the blond woman from a few doors down.

He made me swear not to tell Mom, said that the truth would kill her. I didn't want to be the reason she was unhappy, did I? The whole thing was a huge mistake; it had never happened before and it wouldn't happen again.

But it did.

It always did.

That's how much a ring is worth. Ava might not have taken it, but she'd known exactly where it was. I'm sure she could see it all on my face back then, the dirt I could never quite wash off. The darkness in my eyes every time I looked in the mirror. I think Ava knew where things were heading before anything even happened, because I was a speeding train about to veer off the tracks, and there was nothing that could have stopped me from destroying what mattered most. It all started the day William first said he loved me.

* * *

There's always a before and an after. A point in time forever frozen in a haunting *what if*?

"Are you seriously telling me you've never noticed the way Charlotte rolls her eyes the minute Tess says anything?"

Jacob asked a few months before that last evening at Christos.

He was leaning against the bar with his back to the dining area. I was sitting on a barstool with half a glass of prosecco, and I could already feel the tension headache building in my forehead.

"Or how Finn will mention something that happened years ago at least once every time you get together?"

Before Jacob brought it up, I had never even thought about them: the cracks. But with every minute that passed, his words sank deeper and deeper, coloring my thoughts.

"When I first met Adrian almost two years ago, I thought he was super laid-back," he continued. "But now . . ."

He turned so that his back was against the bar, and nodded in the direction of the table, where Adrian had just raised his voice and walked away.

"It's because they've known each other so long," I laughed, though the sound caught in my throat. "So long that they know each other inside out. We're a family. Families bicker."

"If that's friendship, I really don't need any enemies."

For the rest of that evening, I couldn't help but notice William's tense face when he and Adrian moved over to one corner to talk about something he didn't want to share with me. I couldn't ignore William touching Ava's arm or the way he seemed to be drawn to her the minute she looked at him, and before dessert was even served, I got up and said I was going home.

They stopped talking and looked at each other, then at me, accepted what I'd said, and continued their conversation.

As I walked away with tears burning in my eyes, I wasn't sure where I was going. I wasn't even sure I wanted to go home, but then I heard his voice behind me. And when I stopped and turned around, there he was.

Jacob.

We walked side by side in silence. Down the esplanade by the theater, across Stortorget. Along the gravel trails in Boulognerskogen Park and back over the river to Söder until suddenly we were outside Jacob's building. I noticed a different name on the door, the way he seemed to shrink and steel himself before he unlocked and opened it for me. I moved slowly, with him right behind me, surprised by the old furniture and the mess in the lounge. He watched me closely, analyzing every reaction. The stale air, the overflowing shelves of DVDs on the shabby bookcase. At the sound of heavy footsteps in the bedroom, he tensed briefly before going out into the hallway to meet a middle-aged man in a threadbare T-shirt and underpants.

"Who the hell's she?" the man asked, but Jacob just shook his head and tried to usher him back into the bedroom. "What do you want?"

Muttering to himself, the man allowed Jacob to lead him back to bed. Jacob reappeared a few minutes later.

"My dad. Frontotemporal dementia," he said quietly, gesturing for me to take a seat at the kitchen table. "He's been doing better since I moved in."

"How long has it been?" I asked, watching as he slumped down into the chair opposite me and rubbed his face.

"Just over two years. I took a break from my studies to be here for him. That's why I didn't meet William until the last year of the course. But then my dad started having outbursts. The apathy came after that, and the personality changes . . . It was easiest just to move in, which meant I could go back to university and keep an eye on Dad."

He let out a joyless laugh and leaned forward over the table.

"Jacob . . ."

Those evenings when Jacob had turned up late to dinner, if he turned up at all. The way he sometimes got lost in thought and excused himself before the rest of us had even finished eating. For some reason he had chosen to give me a glimpse of his life. Who knows? Maybe he wanted to show me that he needed me as much as I needed him.

"You don't love him," he said another evening as we walked home from the restaurant.

It was spring, but it was still bitterly cold. The delicate buds made the bird cherry look pale green as we walked beneath the streetlamps along the edge of the park. His words took me by surprise, leaving me speechless—possibly because he was right. I didn't love William, not in the way he deserved to be loved. I loved him in the only way I knew how: through secrets and betrayal.

* * *

A wayward snowflake lands on my outstretched hand, but it immediately melts on my palm. I lean farther out over the railing and spot a couple walking by on the street down below, completely oblivious to what is going on above their heads.

"Hello!"

I shout and wave my arms, but thanks to the whistling wind and their hats and scarves, they don't hear a thing. I try to imagine what my night might have been like if I'd actually managed to get the driver to stop earlier, if I had gotten back into the warm cab and returned to the lumpy mattress and rough bedspread in my room. Expensive rental films on the hotel TV, a small bottle of white wine from the minibar. After yet another sleepless night, I would have caught the train home, blissfully unaware of where my ring was.

"I wouldn't do that if I were you."

The railing is still digging into my stomach as I turn my head toward the door. The tiny snowflakes make my eyes sting, and I can just about make out a smile behind the cloud of hot breath rising from Jacob's mouth.

"Do what?"

"Jump. That's never been your style."

"How would you know what my style is now? I'd probably say that jumping from a balcony is the exact direction my personal trajectory has taken."

"Things really that bad?"

"They definitely could have been better."

"Ava shouldn't have done that."

I shake my head and grip the railing with both hands as I look out across the old factory buildings and their tall chimneys, turning my attention to the water.

"She's just trying to provoke a reaction from us," I say. "And you know as well as I do that she won't stop until she's got what she wants."

"Which is?"

"For us to spill all our secrets. Isn't that what she's after?"

Jacob's smile fades. "Can we talk now?"

I look around the deserted balcony. To my right, there is nothing but a glass wall with a dizzying view out over the ground down below. The door is to my left, but Jacob is between me and it, shivering in his thin T-shirt. There are a couple of black covers over what I assume must be furniture stacked against the wall, leaving no space for me to get past him.

"Doesn't look like I have much choice," I reply, rubbing my arms, which have started to ache in the cold air. "What do you want to talk about?"

"We could talk about you."

That's the last thing I want to talk about.

"How are you?"

I laugh and back away from the railing.

"How am I? Great, thanks. My fiancé died while I was in the room next door ten years ago, and I haven't managed a single normal relationship since. I've buried myself in my work instead. You?"

Jacob takes a couple of steps toward me and I take as many back, bumping up against the glass wall. He rubs his neck and cocks his head.

"Thanks for asking. I fell in love about ten years ago, and then I had my heart broken when the person I cared about most left town without a single word. I had to quit my well-paid job as an economist because I couldn't sleep and couldn't focus, and now I travel the world with my camera in an attempt to escape the loss of the only thing I've ever really wanted."

I take a deep breath. He takes another couple of steps. Neither of us speaks. The only sound I can hear is the distant hum of traffic in the city center, the howling of sirens somewhere in the distance. It isn't fair.

He isn't being fair.

"William died," I mumble, blinking back the tears.

"I know he did. I was there."

"It wasn't meant to end like this, and William wasn't meant to die."

Jacob holds out his arms, but I shake my head and dry my eyes with my hand.

"I'm here for you, Sophie. Whenever you need me. I always have been."

I should have been there for him too. There is a certain sadness to his face that I can't bear to see because I know it's my fault.

"Ava knows," I say.

"You don't know that."

"She knows, which means the others will find out too. Do you know what they're going to say?"

"So let them say it. Who cares?"

He reaches out and grabs my hands, lifts them slowly to his mouth and blows on my frozen fingers with his hot breath, not taking his eyes off me for a second. When I close my own eyes I see William, and I pull my hands back.

"Don't do that."

"Sophie, what's—"

"Never do that," I say, barging past him to make my way inside.

CHAPTER

19

Now

SAFELY ON THE other side of the glass doors, I pause and look over to the seating area, with my glasses in my hand. I use the hem of my blouse to dry the lenses. All I want is to curl up on the sofa and wait for this evening to be over.

"This was the year after we graduated from senior high," I hear Ava say as she moves away from the long sideboard with something dark in her arms. "Do you remember the house we rented on Öland?"

"Is this really the time to be looking at old photos?" Adrian asks her.

"The rain came through the bedroom ceiling," Finn mumbles.

"Right!" Charlotte blurts out. "I had my clothes in a sports bag, and everything got damp and smelled like off milk."

I put my glasses back on and peer over to the hallway leading to the bathroom and the office. Ava sets the open album down on the table, and the others remain where they are, looking at each other with solemn faces.

"Why don't we refresh our memories of that last summer?" says Ava. "There should be an album from our last year of school somewhere too. I'm sure I must have some pictures from Christos's place. Look how thin you were here, Charlotte. My God, did you ever eat?"

I quickly cross the soft rug and make my way over to the hallway. When I reach the yellow painting, I pause. My eye is drawn to the line beneath the paint again, and I run a thumb over the surface and feel where the paint has come loose. Without stopping to think, I scratch at it with my nail and a section of paint flakes away. They aren't just lines, I realize. They're letters. The first one is definitely an S, and the second looks like a C.

SC. What does that mean?

I hear Ava's heels clicking across the floor again.

"Here's another one, with pictures of Jacob too."

"Where *is* Jacob?"

"On the balcony with Sophie," Finn replies. "I think the whole ring thing really hit her hard."

I give up on the paintings and move on. The door to Ava's office is still closed, and as I turn the handle, I fully expect to feel resistance from the lock, to have to turn back and look at pictures of me and William, him with his arm around me and his nose in my hair. But the door swings open without a sound. I glance back and hear Charlotte moaning about her frizzy hair, then I take a step forward and pull the door shut behind me.

So, this is where she sits and looks out at the city. Maybe this is where she sketches out her ideas before she gets started with the brushes and paints. I walk over to the desk and pick up the sheet of paper I saw earlier. It's a list—a list of our names. Ava's writing is a little tricky to read, but it looks as though she has written *ring* and a question mark beside my name, which makes sense. Whatever is after Adrian's name is completely illegible, and by Finn's name the only word is *printout.* I skip over Charlotte, see *bank card* by Tess's name, and then turn my attention to Jacob's.

Ava hasn't written anything there, but there is a small squiggle by his name.

A flower?

I grip the back of the chair and picture Ava sitting here as she made up her mind to invite us all to dinner after ten years apart. Was that before or after she wrote a list of our deepest, darkest secrets? I sit down in her chair and put the paper aside in order to open the drawers. One by one, I rifle through them, but all I find are paperclips, envelopes, and pens. That's when I remember the tall filing cabinet by the wall.

Still sitting down, I spin around to face the closed door, then back again. This is in a completely different league from going through someone's bathroom cabinet. It's a clear step too far. Despite all that, I roll closer and open the top drawer, which is full of neat folders, each tab marked with one of our names.

I open the first of them, with Finn's name on it, and flick through the contents. Excerpts from his employment record, details of places he has lived, annual tax returns. There is also a copy of a divorce application dated two months ago. The past ten years of Finn's life, right here in my hands.

There must be a folder with my name on it too, I realize, setting Finn's down on the desk and leaning in to the drawer. At the very back, I find a slim record of my life. Registration documents from the period after William died, another covering the jobs I had during my studies and immediately afterward. On the bottom of the pile, I find a printout from a website I recognize all too well: the page profiling the employees of the radio station where I have been working for the past five years. There is a black and white photograph of each of us, along with our contact details. The picture of me in my glasses is at the bottom left, just above my name.

Sophie Lind.

That must be how she knew I'd changed my name, but how did she know where to look?

I dump the folder on top of Finn's and open the next drawer. There is only one thing inside: a thick stack of papers held together with a rubber band. A police case file. I pull it out and then roll back over to the desk with it in my lap. I set it down in front of me and then switch on the lamp, using my thumb to flick between sheets of paper containing statements and interviews. Documents I could have requested myself if I'd ever thought about it. There is no way I'll have time to go through everything before they start wondering where I am, so I scan through the sheets on top of the stack and quickly find an extract from the postmortem report. I pull the lamp closer and read the short text over and over again, unable to process what I'm seeing.

> *Traces of benzodiazepine. Blunt force trauma to the back of the skull.*

William didn't take drugs, and when was he supposed to have sustained a head injury?

> *Cause of death: drowning.*

I'm not prepared for the wave of disappointment that washes over me. So, he drowned after all. Alone in the bathroom.

A few pages beneath that, I find the interview transcripts from the night he died and the morning after. Seeing my own words in black and white, they feel completely alien to me. Did I really say that?

"He can't have done it, I just know it.

"Nothing happened, nothing was different.

"I wanted to leave early, but they wouldn't let me."

I would have said absolutely anything to get away from the station and forget all about that evening. This is the last thing I need right now, but I can't help but keep going, moving on to the others' statements. The lump in my throat grows as I read their words, general accusations thrown in all sorts of directions. At Jacob, who turned up without warning; Adrian, who was irritable and withdrawn; Tess, who was acting oddly. And then I start to sense a direction I hadn't expected.

Charlotte hints that I had seemed distant during dinner, as though there was something on my mind. Adrian comes straight out and says that it felt like I was hiding something from them and from William. Finn says I barely said a word at William's place that evening and asks whether anyone else will find out what he says during the interview. Tess says that she thinks I ran off before I'd even seen William's body.

The words Jacob said to me the first time we left the restaurant together ring truer than ever.

"It's obvious you're not part of the group."

When I'd asked him what he meant, he'd just shrugged. On the street that day, I just laughed it off, told him he didn't know what he was talking about. But I've never quite managed to shake the niggling feeling that he was right after all.

I roll over to the cabinet and try to open the bottom drawer, but it's locked. They'll be done with Ava's albums any minute now, and I know I should put everything back where I found it and leave the office before someone catches me red-handed, but I can't. Not before I know what's in the last drawer.

I get up and move over to the bookshelf, running a hand over the books and reaching in behind them. Where would Ava hide a key? I pause in the middle of the room, letting my eyes sweep over the shelves, the pictures on the walls, the bare window, and the desk chair.

The chair.

During high school, Ava had a big, beautiful desk that had to have been at least a hundred years old. It was made from mahogany, with curved legs and a number of small drawers on top. One of those small drawers had a lock, and though Ava never showed me what was inside, she did show me the key, black from years of use. The key she had fastened to the bottom of her chair with Blu Tack.

I drop to my knees beside the chair and crane my neck to look beneath the seat. Sure enough, there it is: a small silver key tucked into the join. I grab it before I have time to change my mind, then crawl over to the drawer, push it into the lock, and turn the key. Inside, there is a single white ring binder without any text on the cover. My heart starts pounding, and I know I shouldn't do it. Whatever Ava keeps locked in here is something she doesn't want anyone else to see. The hallway outside is quiet, but I can hear Finn and Adrian's deep voices from the dining room. I reach into the drawer and lift the file out with both hands.

At the front of the folder, there is a binder index. Every section is dated, and notes have been added next to some of the years in pencil.

Sjöstugan, Klingberg Clinic.

The first section seems to be full of medical notes. An emergency assessment carried out at one AM a week after William's funeral. The day after I left. Ava had had her stomach pumped and been given a drip after being admitted overnight for observation.

Attempted overdose. Patient referred to psychiatry.

Had Ava tried to kill herself?

Beneath that excerpt from her records, there is a document from a psychiatric unit. Ava had been prescribed therapy and antidepressants. I also find a final assessment from her doctor following her last therapy session.

> *The patient has severe feelings of guilt following the death of a close friend and is convinced that she is responsible. She suffers delusions and clings to irrational thoughts around what happened. I recommend ongoing conversational therapy in outpatient care and suitable medication as necessary.*

I rifle through to the tab where *Klingberg Clinic* has been scribbled down, the year after William's death. It sounds like some sort of secure unit, and Ava was admitted in February 2010 and not discharged until the end of November. I hear soft footsteps in the hallway outside and keep rummaging, turning my attention to the tab with *Sjöstugan* on it. Again, this seems to be a treatment center. At the front of the section, there is a care plan dated one year ago.

> *The patient has made real progress in processing the event through art, specifically painting with acrylics and oil paints. By depicting her memories, she has let go of the delusion that she was responsible for a close friend's death. This is the same method she made use of following a previous trauma. The patient has been discharged, but regular return visits (twice weekly) are recommended.*

More footsteps, pausing only a few feet from where I'm sitting. I close the file and return it to the drawer, then get to my feet to gather up the other papers and the police investigation. Once the drawers are closed, the key back where I found it and the list of names on the desk, I back up toward the door, trying to remember how everything looked when I came in.

The lamp.

I dart over and switch it off, pushing it back to where it was earlier before turning toward the door and cracking it open. I listen for any noises, then slip out through the gap and pull the door shut behind me.

"What are you doing?"

CHAPTER 20

Three hours and twenty-five minutes before William's death

WILLIAM HAD COME over to Ava's place the evening before they all met at Christos. She'd sent him a message at twenty past six, but it was almost eleven before he was sitting on the shabby two-seater sofa that she'd bought secondhand for next to nothing. Adrian's cigarette smoke was still clinging to his clothes, and his eyes looked weary. Ava had promised him everything was fine, promised herself that she wouldn't call him, but then her mom had turned up without warning that afternoon, wanting her to eat dinner with them at the house.

Ava had such clear memories from when they'd first moved into that house, the most beautiful place she'd ever seen. She had spent her first few years living in an apartment in town, her grandfather's old home. Her dad had taken it over after her grandfather dropped dead of a heart attack and her grandmother wanted to move out. Two years later, her grandmother had died too, and her dad had inherited the fortune Grandpa had spent his life building.

When Ava turned twelve, her parents decided they'd had enough of raising a child in the city and bought the grand old villa on the coast. It had a yellow plastered facade and white pillars on the steps by the main entrance, with tall cypress trees straining upward along one wall. The place was a dream, with expanses of lawn stretching all the way down to the water and the jetty. But Ava could no longer see the house without being overcome by grief and hopelessness.

The house by the water had been a place of parties and glamour, somewhere her father had invited his associates to come and do business. Her mother would bring in food that she served from silver platters on tables draped with white linen. Then she'd stand there with a champagne glass in one hand and an uncomfortable smile on her face. The men brought their wives; and the wives, their children. One of those children was a fifteen-year-old boy who had taken a shine to Ava as she came down the stairs in the white dress her mother had bought her the day before. It was fitted in the chest, with thin shoulder straps that tied behind her neck.

Two hours later, that dress was covered in mud and grass stains, her tanned legs streaked with cuts from the thorny bushes and the blood that trickled down her thighs.

In that house by the water, Ava had learned that money could buy anything but happiness. It could save a boy from being reported to the police and buy silence about something that should have tarnished a family name. She learned that a signed contract could be worth more than justice for your daughter.

It simply hadn't happened.

Everyone acted as though it had never happened, but it was all Ava could think about, and that drove her crazy.

"You would never be able to cope if everyone knew what you'd been through"—that was what her mom had said. *"If everyone started gossiping about what that boy did to you."*

But how long would she be able to cope when no one she spoke to even understood that something was wrong?

* * *

When William turned up clutching a folder, five hours after her message, eyes scanning her apartment for sharp objects or empty blister packs, she told him that he didn't need to stay. But he stayed, the way he always did, sitting with her until she drifted off to sleep on the sofa sometime around dawn. He was gone by the time she woke, the apartment as empty as it had been before he came. No trace of him but the folder, which was still on the chest of drawers in the hall.

Ava had never expected him to be there for her, but he had been. Ever since she'd convinced her dad to let her transfer to the local high school, to avoid having to see the boy who had attacked her, in the corridors of the fancy private school. Ever since that party in the house by the water, when William had found her half conscious in the bathroom, an empty pack of pills in one hand. He'd told the others that she'd had too much to drink, and convinced them to head over to Finn's place. Then he'd called for an ambulance that had taken her straight to the hospital to have her stomach pumped.

That was the first time.

Her father still hadn't forgiven her for the fact that the neighbors had seen the ambulance, and even now the official explanation was that Ava had fallen down the stairs and sustained a concussion.

Ava didn't usually drink. Drinking opened the floodgates, making her dream. Dark dreams about sharp thorns and rough hands, barbs clawing at her legs. But she just hadn't been able to help herself that evening, because she'd known something was brewing; she could tell by the way he looked away whenever she tried to make eye contact.

William was sitting with his arm around Sophie's shoulders, and Ava wondered whether he had already told her everything.

It had all started with Sophie.

Sophie had walked into their classroom and stood by the board with her hands clasped, nail polish chipped, red blotches on her throat as she told them who she was, and Ava couldn't tear her eyes away. She wore a thin silver chain around her neck, and everything about her piqued Ava's interest, from her filthy sneakers, scuffed at the toes, to her gray jeans and the huge bruise on her forearm.

As they'd sat on the stone steps outside their Swedish class one day, Sophie had told her that she'd moved north because her mom was depressed and needed to start over, and Ava had immediately known she was lying. She'd fiddled with her lower lip, and her eyes had wandered, and then she'd started drumming her chewed pen on the books in her lap.

All the telltale signs.

Ava had started waiting for her in the corridor after class, running to catch up with her on the street outside. Little by little, she'd begun to unravel the tangled mess that was Sophie Arène, getting lost in the details she discovered: the father Sophie kept at arm's length, the mother she barely spoke to. It was so obvious that she was desperate for someone to love, and yet that was also what she feared most.

She could have chosen anyone, but she'd chosen William.

That was what hurt Ava.

* * *

"What do you think about Sophie?"

The words dragged Ava back to the present, and she turned to Charlotte, who had appeared by her side at the bar. It took her a moment to remember where she was. Ava straightened up and did what she always did: pretended. Pretended to be interested in Charlotte's fruitless attempts to break into the film industry, pretended that she had been studying hard all afternoon rather than just staring blankly at her books.

"Sophie?"

"Yeah, it feels like she's waiting for something. That skirt is new, isn't it?"

"I don't know. She doesn't usually wear skirts."

"My point exactly. Do you think she's going to meet someone after this? She keeps checking her phone."

Charlotte was right. Sophie had made more of an effort than she usually did for their dinners. She normally turned up in a pair of black jeans and a vest top, but this evening she had clearly spent time on her makeup. She'd been in a hurry, though. Her hair looked like it had dried naturally, loose waves rather than blow-dried straight. It suited her better.

"And Tess . . . she's blown her whole paycheck again, asked me for money. When is she going to start taking responsibility for herself?"

"What about William?" said Ava, tapping her glass against her front teeth before taking a sip. "He seems kind of anxious, don't you think?"

"Has he said anything?"

Charlotte seemed to have noticed too. That meant it must be true.

"No, he hasn't said anything, but I know William. He's got something on his mind. It feels like he's avoiding me too."

"Why would he do that?"

"That's what I want to know. Will you help me?"

"Me?"

"He always listens to you, Charlotte. Do some digging, ask him what's up. I just want to know if it's something to do with me."

"I don't think I'm really the right person to do that, to be honest."

"Why not?"

Charlotte smiled in William's direction.

"It just doesn't feel right this evening. I'll try next week—would that work?"

"But we won't be here next week."

"Then I'll call him one evening."

"Okay."

"Food's up!" Christos backed out through the swinging doors, with a plate in each hand, and made his way over to their table.

"Finally!" said Charlotte. "I thought it would never be ready. Are you coming?"

"In a minute. You go on ahead."

Charlotte grabbed her glass and headed over to the table where William and Jacob had started clearing the empty plates. Sophie glanced back at the bar and Ava, then got up and walked toward the bathroom with her cell phone in one hand. Her look sent a jolt through Ava, who swallowed hard at the thought of everything they had lost. The evenings they had shared at Ava's place, nights when they'd talked for hours. Sophie's warm body tangled up in the sheets beside her after Ava had convinced her it was too late to start walking home on her own.

She barely said a word to Ava now.

Ava sipped her wine and watched her friends moving around the table. After a moment or two, Jacob paused and took his phone out of his pocket. William came toward her with a stack of dirty plates, and he smiled when he saw her.

"Aren't you hungry? The food's on the table."

"No, not really. Can we talk?"

"Sure."

He left the stack on the bar and wiped his hands on his trousers before putting a hand on her shoulder.

"Is something wrong?"

"That's what I'm wondering. You seemed so absent last night. You didn't say goodbye before you left."

"You were asleep. I didn't want to wake you."

"That's never stopped you before. Does this have something to do with Sophie?"

William was quiet, and he pulled his hand back.

"It does, doesn't it? What has she said? Is it something to do with me?"

She shouldn't have told William how she felt about Sophie. Sophie deserved to hear it from Ava herself.

"She hasn't said anything, but there is something I haven't told you. I wasn't sure how to say it. This probably isn't the right time."

There it was. She had been hoping it was all in her mind, a misunderstanding.

"Just tell me, William. I can take it."

He met her eye and took a deep breath.

"I'm thinking about moving, about leaving Gävle. Me and Sophie."

Ava looked around, searching for Sophie, but there was no sign of her. Jacob had taken a seat, his phone still in one hand. The other hand was in his blond hair.

She laughed. "You can't be serious?"

"It's the best solution for us. We might move back here sometime, but right now we need to get away. Start over someplace new, just me and Sophie."

"Get away from what? Is this because of me? I haven't said anything to her, I haven't called her. I did exactly what you said."

"Stop, Ava. It's not because of you. I haven't mentioned what you told me."

So, she didn't even know. Sophie had no idea, and now she was going to leave.

"You left your folder at my place yesterday. It's in my bag," she said. "I was hoping it belonged to someone else. How soon? Have you already signed?"

"No. I don't know yet. I need to talk to Sophie first."

"So you haven't even asked her yet? Who am I meant to call when I have those thoughts? What am I meant to do when I can't sleep?"

In the period after the assault, Ava had fallen apart. Her father hadn't wanted to get the police involved, and an acquaintance of her mother's—a nurse—had come over to patch up her superficial injuries. As for the rest, the spiritual wounds, no one had even noticed them. Left to their own devices, they had grown and grown, eventually reaching a point where they started eating her from the inside. In a desperate attempt to forget what happened, the event that no one else even acknowledged, she'd begun painting. For several years, she'd painted the house and the shoreline, the jetty; she painted and painted, trying to cover over the painful memories that had dug their claws into her mind. Delicate brushstrokes, watercolors, bright and happy. But the darkness still seeped into her scenes. Heavy brown earth tones, lengthy shadows, the metallic smell of blood and rotten leaves. And then she would crumple the sheet of paper and push it to the very bottom of the trash can under her desk.

Once the paintings were no longer enough, all she wanted was to forget and to feel numb.

Without William here, there would be no one who knew.

Without William, it was as though it had never happened.

What would she have left?

"You can still call me," he said. "I'll always be there for you. You know that."

A lie, of course.

"No, because you won't be able to come. You won't be *here.*"

William sighed and took her hands.

"You can do it, Ava. You're strong."

But she wasn't. Ava was anything but strong, and without him here, there was nothing to stop her. Without Sophie . . . She laughed again and pulled her hands away, had plenty of practice.

Don't talk about it.

If you don't talk about it, it never happened.

It's not real.

"You know what? We can do this tomorrow. I don't think either of you have really thought this through. Let me talk to Sophie."

"It's decided, Ava. This is what's going to happen."

"That depends on Sophie, no?"

He smiled again, picking up the plates.

"Go and eat. The food will be getting cold."

With that, he disappeared into the kitchen, leaving her with a taste of the future without him. Sophie and William, both gone.

That couldn't happen.

CHAPTER 21

Now

THE VOICE COMES from somewhere by the floor, and when I look down, I see Tess slumped against the wall. Her legs are tucked beneath her, and her smart trousers are creased, her shirt crumpled. Her head rocks from side to side, her dull ponytail following the movement, brushing against her shoulder and folding in on itself beneath her jaw. My hand is still on the door handle, and I stare at it as I desperately try to come up with a credible excuse for what I was doing.

I opened the wrong door when I was looking for the bathroom.

But one look at Tess is all I need to realize that she doesn't expect an answer. Her chin is resting on her chest, and she grunts as her body begins to tip over. I crouch down and grip her thin arms.

"Jesus, Tess. How much wine have you had?"

She raises a hand and struggles with it for a moment before managing to hold up two fingers.

"*Two?* Does that mean two bottles?"

"It's fine, Sophie," she slurs. "Stop worrying so much all the fucking time. I admit . . . I was a bit upset."

Understatement of the century.

"But she gave me a pill and now everything's great. We're friends, I don't care. Here's to another ten years."

She grins, tipping her head back against the wall with a thud that makes her laugh and squeeze her eyes shut as she presses a hand to her scalp. Then she spots something, and she reaches out and touches my earlobe. Her fingers brush the black pearl in my ear.

"I can't get used to you not wearing the snowflakes," she says, pursing her thin lips.

The earrings.

The first time William kissed me was in the stairwell between the second and third floors at school. We were standing by the windows with a view of the auditorium, and on the other side of the glass huge snowflakes swirled through the air. I was upset because I'd failed my psychology exam, and I remember him trying in vain to catch my flailing arms. In the end, he just pressed his hands to my face and kissed me. It felt like the walls around us had fallen away. The window ledge was hard against my hip, but when I opened my eyes all I could see was his eyes and the snow outside.

A week or so later, he pulled me aside outside the cafeteria, and as my breaded fish got cold, he pressed a small box into my hand. A pair of silver earrings in the shape of snowflakes. "No two snowflakes are the same," he said. The fact that we—two people who were so similar—had found each other was unique. I wore them every single day after that. Right up until the day he died.

"No two snowflakes are the same."

"A pill?" I ask, irritably brushing her hand from my ear. "Who gave you a pill? Ava? Charlotte?"

Her heavy eyelids flutter over her pale eyes as she looks up at me and presses a finger to her lips.

"Shh!" she says, spraying me with saliva. "Isn't that what we do? We keep secrets."

"Come on, Tess—get up. You can't sit here."

She's heavier than she looks, and it takes a real effort to get her up. We take a few unsteady steps down the hallway, where I spot a third door. I drag her with me, using my elbow to turn the handle and pushing the door open with my foot. The room on the other side is a bedroom. A dark floor and sand-colored walls, a gray armchair and a lamp in one corner, a large single bed in the other. It's neatly made with a gray quilted bedspread, no sign of any decorative pillows and no rug. I notice an open book on the armrest of the chair, a rectangular box on the windowsill, but there are no plants and no curtains. Nothing but a built-in blind between the two panes of glass in the window. *This must be a guest room,* I think. Or maybe it's the room Ava's mom uses when she comes to stay.

Either way, it'll have to do for Tess until I can get hold of some coffee.

I pull her across the room and let her drop to the bed, where she slumps onto her side, then I turn on the reading lamp and get onto my knees beside her. Her hands are freezing, and I try to rub some warmth into them.

"What sort of pill have you taken, Tess? Were you lying to us earlier? Are you still using?"

The mix of alcohol and some unspecified pill doesn't sound great.

"No, *she* had it."

"Who did?"

"Who cares? Nothing we do matters any more, does it? We've already chosen which path we want to take, and it makes no difference how fast we run; we'll never be able to escape the people we've become. Don't you get it? I'm the exact same person I was back then. That's why I'm here. It's why we're all here."

I don't want to hear this, not from her. Not after everything William did to make sure she could be sitting here now in her smart shirt and her subtle makeup.

"What are you talking about? Why are you here?"

Tess's eyelids snap open, and for a split second she looks straight at me, her eyes clear.

"Because Ava offered me money to come."

I knew it. I knew there was something off about their body language earlier, about Tess choosing to come here when she seemed to find every minute so painful.

"How much?"

"Enough for me to move on with my life, to ignore all the mistakes I made before. Enough to stretch to the sheltered housing where I work too. It could save someone else."

"Was that why she gave you a pill? To stop you from saying anything?"

Tess smiles and rolls onto her back.

"Why did you come?" she asks. "Back to everyone who knows you so well that you must have realized there'd be questions."

I came because I was the one with questions, I think.

"You know one of us was responsible for William's death, right?" she says, rubbing her head where she knocked it earlier.

"No, I don't. Ava shouldn't have said that. You know how she gets when she's been brooding about something for too long. Do you remember the time she accused Finn of stealing her laptop? She was *convinced* he had it, and all because he was the last person to leave her apartment and because he had a backpack with him."

Tess laughs.

"Poor Finn," she says, taking a deep breath. "Ava didn't speak to him for a week, not until she next went to the library and the woman who always wore stripes asked whether she might have left it there."

"You see? William killed himself that night. It was his decision, whatever we might think about it."

"But you know better," she mumbles, closing her eyes. "I saw it on your face, especially when Ava said why we were all here."

"I was just surprised, like everyone else."

"But you've wondered too," she continues. "What Charlotte said to William outside the bathroom in the restaurant, who Adrian was on the phone with all evening, why Finn was late."

She's lying.

"And I suppose you have all the answers?"

"No, because no one would ever say. But maybe you should think about it."

"Enough, Tess. I need to talk to you about something else. I found something in Ava's bathroom, and I'm starting to get worried about her."

Tess has a sudden coughing fit, and she clutches her chest.

"Are you okay?"

She tries to sit up, coughing so hard that her face turns red.

"Hold on—I'll get you some water."

There is no one else in the hallway, but I can still hear their loud voices in the dining room. I pull the door gently shut behind me and turn toward the bathroom. There isn't a toothbrush glass on the side of the sink, so I check the cabinet, but there is nothing in there either. In the cupboard beneath the sink, I find a pack of cheap plastic cups. I weigh them in my hand. Strange thing to have in such a lavish bathroom, I think.

The water sloshes over my hand as I hurry back to the guest room with the cup and stop dead in the doorway. Tess is lying flat out on her back with her arms and legs outstretched. I leave the cup on the windowsill and hurry over to her, patting her cheek, checking for a pulse.

"Stop . . ."

She waves a hand in the air and rolls onto her side with her back to me.

"Get some sleep," I whisper, lifting her legs to pull the bedspread out from under them and drape it over her. "Tomorrow's another day, and you'll realize just how far you've come from where you were back then."

Was this how William used to tuck her up in bed when she pounded on his door at four in the morning? Was this how anxious he felt as he sat by her side for hours, trying to make sure she was going to be alright and that she wouldn't stop breathing during the night?

I back away from the bed and study her for a moment. When I turn around, I bump into the armchair and knock the book to the floor. I bend down to pick it up. A paperback copy of *The Little Paris Bookshop*. It looks like it has been well read, the spine broken and many of the pages folded in the corner. I've heard of this book, about a man who mends broken hearts using novels. Everyone's but his own. I flick through the pages, which are full of underlined sections and pencil scribbles in the margins. Is Ava the one reading it? I find myself thinking back to the odd collection of books on her shelves again, classics and romance novels, before I put it down on the windowsill. The book nudges the rectangular box I noticed earlier. Latex gloves, size L. Looking down, I spot a small trash can between the radiator and the armchair. It's full of used gloves and torn wrappers from disinfectant wipes, and my mind drifts to the red marks on Ava's arm.

Who really uses this room?

And what do they use it for?

CHAPTER

22

Now

I'M BACK IN the narrow hallway with the closed bedroom door behind my back. My shoulders are aching from the effort of moving Tess. To my left, the paintings have taken on a very different meaning now that I know more about how Ava has spent the past ten years. So, I think. They represent her memories.

I move closer to the living room, pausing in front of the yellow canvas again. They seem to be getting ready for dessert in the dining room. I can hear the sound of clinking china, and the aroma of coffee is heavy in the air. Their voices are lower now, more subdued than before. I need to talk to Jacob. I glance over to the balcony, but I can't see him out there, so I take another step toward the painting.

I find the two letters right away, the S and the C, and I use the nail on my index finger to pick at the paint. It flakes away in small chunks, and I keep going, unsure how much I dare scrape off without ruining her painting, but in the end a large piece comes away to reveal a neat row of letters. I was wrong, I realize. It isn't a C at all; it's an O. Followed by the rest of the letters in my name.

Sophie.

I take a step back and study the painting again, tilting my head one way and the other. Those soft waves, with hints of orange: it's hair. The sharp curve with a glowing orb in the middle is an eye. The dark section at the bottom of the canvas, something I took to be a meadow full of billowing grass earlier, is actually the shadow beneath a jawline.

Ava has painted me.

"This one is my favorite."

I move over to the green painting hanging alongside it and run my hands over the rough surface in search of more letters. The paint is too thick, so I turn back to the yellow painting. There is something on the very edge, I notice. A faint line disappearing beneath the frame. I gently lift one side of the painting from the wall and gasp when I realize what I'm looking at. The back of the canvas is covered in words. So many words. There must be hundreds of them, so densely written that they cross over one another.

Unfaithful, lying, dishonest.

There are dates, addresses, names. Expletives. I've just let go of the painting, which thuds against the wall as I clamp a hand to my mouth, when I hear the tone change in the dining room. Their voices have grown louder, sharper, and Charlotte's stands out among the murmur of lower octaves. My boots click against the floor as I stride across the living room into the dining room. Charlotte is in the kitchen doorway, Finn on the other side of the table, with his back to the window.

"I did not," she shouts, her cheeks a deep shade of red. "I think time might have left you a little confused, among other things."

Finn laughs. "You'd like that, wouldn't you? But I remember it all like it was yesterday, and I don't think anyone here would disagree."

"Why did you have to bring it up now?"

I move over to Adrian, who is still at the table, and I give his shoulder a squeeze.

"What's going on?" I whisper.

"Lovers' tiff. Maybe you should give them some advice?"

He grins at me, and I box his shoulder. Jacob is there, standing by the little table with the lamp on it, staring straight at me. Ava moves slowly away from the dining table, past him, pausing a few feet from Finn.

"What sparked this?" I ask.

"Ava got her photo albums out to look for pictures from our last few dinners, and there was one of William with an arm around Charlotte, kissing her. That was all it took."

"William and Charlotte?"

"Don't worry, this was during the first year of senior high. Before you came along."

Still.

William and *Charlotte*?

"Why would she bring this up now? William never told me anything about hooking up with Charlotte."

"There probably wasn't much to tell."

But it had happened. At one point in time, he'd had strong enough feelings for Charlotte to kiss her, yet he hadn't thought that was worth mentioning to me. She must have had feelings for him too.

Maybe she still had those feelings when William and I got together.

"Speaking of having much to tell," I say. "I saw your reaction when Charlotte mentioned your love life."

"Come off it. You know I'm a lone wolf."

I feel the muscles in his shoulder tense.

"Oh yeah? So you haven't met anyone worth holding on to? You wouldn't have to persuade anyone to stay."

He turns toward me, his eyes sharp.

"I didn't mean the money, Adrian. You're a handsome man, and you have a great sense of humor. And you can be nice too. At least when you make an effort."

He doesn't smile, just looks away. I slowly take my hand from his shoulder.

"Sometimes you have to make sacrifices, Sophie. Simple as that."

"That sounds pretty cynical. Because you're afraid someone will get too close?"

"Because I don't want anyone to get hurt."

Finn raises his voice, and we both turn our attention to the drama playing out in front of us.

"It'll be interesting to see what's in your box, my dear. If Sophie's had an engagement ring you've been hiding for the past ten years, then yours must have something *really* special in it."

He laughs again, swigging straight from his beer bottle. Charlotte moves toward the table.

Ava stands perfectly still, a slight smile on her lips, and I shudder at the thought that she is enjoying this.

"You think this is funny, do you?" Charlotte snaps. "What do you think is in your box, huh? What's the one thing you regret most?"

Finn's face hardens.

"What was it you confessed to me while we were in bed together? Pleading and begging me to convince you it was nothing to worry about?"

"Charlotte," I say, taking a step away from Adrian. "Maybe the two of you should have this conversation somewhere else? Some other time."

There has never been any point trying to argue with Charlotte when she's in this sort of mood. She always used to raise her voice and cut off everything I said, her face scarlet, to the point where I could only manage one word at a time.

My . . . no . . . stop . . . you're wrong.

Curtains.

The best strategy was always to let her spit out everything that had been building beneath the polished facade. Only then, once she had got it out of her system, was it possible to have a normal conversation.

Charlotte glares at me now.

"Why wait?" asks Finn. "This is about you too, Sophie."

I tear my eyes away from Charlotte and turn to Finn, who suddenly seems so dejected as he rounds the end of the table and approaches his wife.

"It's about you, William, and Charlotte," he continues, without looking at me and without pausing. "You must have noticed the way she used to look at him. The way she was always hovering around him. I thought it would stop once William died, but how are you supposed to compete with someone who can never make any mistakes? Someone who will forever be perfect?"

He comes to a halt right in front of Charlotte and strokes her cheek.

"You're wrong, Charlotte. My biggest mistake isn't the unforgivable thing I'll never get over, as you so kindly brought up. No, my biggest mistake is that I married you."

Charlotte's palm strikes his cheek with such force that his head snaps to one side. Keeping his chin low, he bites his lower lip and clenches his fist. Jacob gets up from his seat, moves over behind Finn and puts a hand on his shoulder. Out of sheer reflex, Finn swings his arm back in an attempt to shake him off, and his elbow hits Jacob square in the nose. Jacob doesn't say a word, just staggers back with his hands to his face and blood seeping out between his fingers.

"Oh fuck," Finn shouts. "Shit, man, I'm sorry. I didn't mean to hit you. You all right?"

"It's okay," Jacob mumbles.

"It's *not* okay," Charlotte hisses. "What the hell are you doing, Finn?"

"You're bleeding," he says to Jacob. And then to Charlotte: "I didn't see him; I was just trying to get away and—"

"Come on," says Charlotte, taking Jacob by the arm. She reaches for one of the thick linen napkins on the table and presses it to his nose. "We need to get some ice on this."

They disappear into the kitchen, and Finn turns to look at me and Adrian.

"I didn't mean it, I swear."

"We know," Adrian reassures him. "These things happen. Sit down, take a minute."

I find myself wondering just how common this sort of thing really is at a dinner party, and I feel the atmosphere shift. What else is going to happen before the evening is over?

Finn slumps down in Tess's seat and runs his hands through his hair before pressing them to his face.

"Maybe it's time for this," says Ava. She is now standing right by the table, and she holds out Finn's box to him.

"Now really isn't the right time," I say firmly, making her look up at me.

"What's wrong, Sophie? Don't you want to know what happened to William?"

"What *you've* decided happened to him, you mean? Can't we just stop this game? Why don't you just tell us what you think and get it over with?"

"It doesn't matter," says Finn, taking the box from her. "I might as well just do it."

He lifts the lid and takes out a folded sheet of paper. Moving slowly, he opens it out and reads it carefully. Adrian snatches it from him and leans back in his chair, gripping it with both hands.

"Where the hell did you get this?"

"I saw it poking out of Finn's pocket that evening at Christos, all dog-eared and crumpled. It fell to the floor when he climbed up onto the chair to help me reach some glasses from the cupboard at William's place."

"This information was meant for William's eyes only. How did you get hold of this, Finn?" Adrian asks.

"You used my computer to check your emails and then forgot to log out."

"So you printed out confidential information and kept a copy for yourself?"

"Confidential?" Finn snorts. "What—were the two of you setting up some sort of public agency?"

Charlotte and Jacob have reappeared from the kitchen and are now standing in the doorway. Adrian looks down at the paper again, then folds it up and puts it on the table.

"What were you planning to do with this information, Finn? What did you do?"

"Adrian . . . Let me explain."

"Explain what?"

"Adrian," I say. "What is it?"

He grabs the sheet of paper and scrunches it into a ball, then holds it above one of the candles until the flame catches.

"What are you doing?!"

I snatch at the crumpled ball, which drops to the table and burns a hole in the white tablecloth before Finn manages to tip Tess's glass of water over the charred remains. I have no idea what could be on the sheet of paper, but I have a sneaking suspicion it might explain why William suddenly wanted to leave town. To leave everything behind.

"It's nothing that anyone else had any use for. Right, Ava?"

She doesn't speak.

"Congratulations, Finn," says Charlotte, moving toward the living room.

"Adrian," I say, keeping my voice low. "What was it? What information did Finn have?"

"It doesn't matter anymore," he replies, getting up to leave the room.

I look down at the dark hole in Ava's tablecloth, then grab our glasses from the table and head after Charlotte. With her little black handbag on her shoulder, she totters over to the sunken seating area and takes a seat on the step down. I hesitate for a second, then join her.

"I brought you this."

"Thanks," she says, taking the glass with both hands and tipping her head back. "What he said in there . . ."

"It doesn't matter, Charlotte. It was all so long ago."

"For the shortest time, I had the best thing that had ever happened to me, but I was too young to realize it." She shakes her head and rubs her cheek. "Sorry. He was your fiancé. I don't even know what I'm talking about."

"We all lost William. So the two of you were together?"

She laughs and gazes out through the window.

"It was him who made the first move, if you can believe that. But you know what? It was just a bit of making out and fooling around, over before I even had time to work out what it was. I spent every single day after that trying to win him back, but it was you he wanted."

A weary smile plays on her lips.

"You were trying to win him back until the day he died?"

She looks at me with a blank face.

"Of course not. I would never have done anything to break the two of you up. But William had the ability to make people feel special, you know? And for me it was different." She takes a deep breath. "We grew up together. He was the only person who knew the real me, before all this."

She gestures to her face and upper body and smiles again, wider this time, then leans toward me and lifts her glass to her lips.

"What a bunch, huh?" she says with a sigh. "You look terrible, Sophie. Have you been crying?"

I rub the skin beneath my eye. "It was the snow, I got some in my eye while I was outside. It's windy and—"

"Stop, you're just making it worse."

Charlotte lowers her handbag to her lap and opens it. She takes out a small velvet makeup bag, lifts my glasses onto the top of my head and dabs something beneath my eyes before opening a powder compact and sweeping a soft brush over my skin. With my eyes closed, it's easier to ask the question that has been hanging over me for so long.

"Do you think William could have cheated on me?"

I feel the brush leave my skin, and when I open my eyes, I see that my words have had the desired effect. Charlotte is speechless, her hand frozen in the air.

"Why are you asking me?" she asks, turning her attention to the makeup bag.

"You knew him longer than I did, and he liked you."

I can see it written across her face, all the forbidden thoughts she'd had, the pent-up emotions now burning beneath the surface, spreading a pinky hue across her cheeks.

"I'm sure you'd know better than anyone. Wait," she says, holding up a finger before rummaging through the little bag and taking out a pencil and using it to draw a series of short strokes on my brows.

"There. I've always thought you have such pretty eyes. Now they're properly framed."

"I'm worried about Ava," I say as her face bobs in front of mine.

"Ava? Why? She seems like the calmest person here."

Charlotte fiddles with the pencil and the lid in her lap.

"All this," I reply irritably, waving my hand. "What is she up to? Why are we letting her do this?"

"It's probably her desperate way of reaching out to us. I bet she's just lonely. Honestly, this place gives me the creeps. Who'd want to be all alone here?"

"No, it's more than that. I found something, Charlotte. Something that tells me she's been planning this evening for a long time."

"You know what, Sophie? I'm going to go and find Finn and see whether he's calmed down yet."

She fumbles with her bags, dropping the power compact to the floor.

"We all know what he's like when he's stressed about something out of his control. Things have been really tense between him and his dad lately. I think that's probably why he's so tetchy. In his eyes, Finn has never been good enough. And you know what? Ava likes playing games; she's never been able to drop anything. Once she feels like she's got what she wants, we'll be able to leave. Just let her think she has. It's not a big deal, is it?"

"How is everything with you and . . . Finn? Are you good?"

Charlotte studies my face. "Of course we are. Why wouldn't we be? Finn was there for me after the funeral; he never gave up. When I looked at him, I caught a glimpse of the person I once was and everything I'd always dreamed of. Sometimes you just have to make a decision."

She gets up on her towering heels.

"Why did you come back, Sophie?"

"What do you mean?"

Charlotte climbs the step and leaves me alone. The canvas on the wall in front of me is bright red.

As red as her hair.

CHAPTER 23

Two hours and forty-three minutes before William's death

"YOU NEED TO *pick a path in life and stick to it."*

As long as it's the path I've marked out for you.

IT was the future. His dad's words kept echoing through his head, despite the fact that it had been months since they'd spoken. The last time they'd met had been at his grandparents' house, dinner to celebrate Granny's birthday. Finn's dad had sat quietly, staring out through the window and sighing to himself as his mom talked about everything and nothing and kept glancing back at him over her shoulder. As though she knew he was just waiting for her to shut up.

Finn was now on the balcony, with his feet on the railing and a bottle of Brooklyn Lager in his hand. In the yard down below, two families had gathered by the little barbecue area, and the smell of the marinated meat they were cooking was irritating his nose. He swigged straight from the bottle with his eyes shut and felt Milton, his Jack Russell, brush up against his hand. In his head, Finn just kept replaying the conversation he'd had a few hours earlier.

He had called the police before he left work that afternoon. The man who had picked up had insisted he come in that same evening, even though Finn kept telling him he would rather do it over the phone, that he had plans, that his friends would be waiting for him. It was almost closing time when he got to the station, and the place was practically deserted. The dark-haired man behind the counter had looked up the minute he opened the door.

"Finn?" he asked.

"Yeah," said Finn, immediately regretting having agreed to do this face-to-face.

"Christian is waiting for you in his office. I'll show you up."

On the balcony now, he drank more beer and banged the back of his head against the wall, listening to the kids' shrieking and laughter and trying to focus on the adults' conversation as they turned the sizzling meat and set out plates on the shabby picnic table on the grass. But his thoughts kept drifting back to Christian's office. To the overflowing shelves, where stacks of paper were piled high on top of the folders; to the blinds that were closed to block out the hot sun. In that office, it was the stench of old sweat that filled his nose.

"So what exactly are you saying?" Christian had asked. "Is he your friend or not?"

In a moment of frustration, the detective had tossed the printed screenshots onto his desk. It seemed to bother him that Finn didn't have any answers, or none that he was willing to share, anyway. But wasn't it the police's job to work out how everything fit together?

Not Finn's.

Christian had leaned back in his chair, which creaked under his weight, and clasped his hands behind his head. The room was unbearably hot despite the fan blowing on Finn's face.

"No. I mean, yeah, he's my friend, but I don't think he's done anything wrong."

"Might I remind you that it was *you* who reached out to us. You filled in our online form to give us a tip off about suspected money laundering, and you attached this document."

"I know."

"Then could you explain why you did that if you don't think your friend has done anything wrong?"

"I think I might have just got the wrong end of the stick."

"The wrong end of the stick?"

"I probably shouldn't have contacted you."

"Maybe not. And yet you did, and the case now has been passed over to the Financial Crimes Division for assessment."

"Have they spoken to the bank?"

"There'll be an investigation, with closer analysis of the various transactions and activity. We'll just have to hope your friend is able to answer their questions."

"What? They're going to call *him*?"

"That's how it works. Whenever suspicions like this are raised, the bank will investigate the transactions and follow the money. And if it doesn't seem to add up, they have an obligation to report it to Financial Crimes."

"But I want to take back my report. Surely they can't take it any further if I do that?"

"You haven't made a report. You provided us with a tip. It's up to the bank to determine whether to report anything. This has nothing to do with you; you aren't the possible victim of a crime here."

"But I'm not even sure there *was* a crime."

"Leave it with us. On the basis of the information you've given us, it definitely doesn't look good. You did the right thing."

"Can I go now?"

"Sure. Just give me a call if you think of anything else."

"I don't know anything else."

Finn had gotten to his feet. His pants were hot and damp from where they had been pressed against the seat, and with his hand on the door handle, he paused and turned back to the police officer.

"None of this is William's fault. It's all Adrian. Are you going to take a closer look at him?"

"We'll follow the money, Finn. We always do. That's where we find answers."

As he left the room and closed the door behind him, his palms had been clammy. It was already six o'clock, and he knew there was no way he would be able to look William in the eye.

It was now gone nine, and the sun had dipped behind the buildings. Dinner was probably as good as over, and Finn was onto his third beer. In his other hand, he was still clutching the printout he had saved, the screenshots of Adrian's documents that he'd supplied to the police. He was convinced it had been the right decision to try to keep William out of this, but now it was too late to save him, which meant all he could do was try to minimize the damage.

* * *

Finn put the empty beer bottle down beside the others and headed inside. It wasn't over yet. He peeled off his T-shirt and tossed it onto the sofa, then went through to his bedroom and dug out a fresh one from his wardrobe, pulling it over his head. Before he left, he went back out to the balcony to get the sheet of paper. He had found the email from Adrian on his computer, a message in which Adrian asked William to transfer a sum of money that had been paid into his private account to their joint investment account.

In another window, he had seen an invoice for a financial consultancy firm.

A firm whose organization number didn't exist.

The sum was a dizzying forty-six thousand dollars.

Maybe he'd misunderstood the whole thing, maybe he'd made a huge mistake, but he couldn't forget the conversation he'd had with Adrian at the restaurant late one night, long after the others had gone home. Adrian had been slumped over the table, the ceiling light overhead painting long shadows across his face.

"A front company," Adrian had practically whispered. "Do you know how easy it'd be to move someone's money for a fee, then use it to make a profit on the stock market before paying it back?"

He had laughed then, drained the last of his drink, and pulled his jacket over his shoulders.

Finn folded the sheet of paper and pushed it into the back pocket of his jeans before running down the stairs and out onto the street. The worst of the heat had broken, and the warm breeze caressed his skin. He lifted Milton into the basket of his bike and clipped the lead to hold him in place. Then he got on his bike and cycled down the narrow streets behind the parking garage and the hotel by the mall, rolling across Stortorget and waiting impatiently to cross the steady stream of cars by the town hall. When he got to Christos's place, he leaned the bike against the wall.

Maybe he should have just called instead, asked William to meet him for a coffee and a chat that would change everything they knew about both each other and Adrian. But he couldn't bear the thought of another night with this secret gnawing away at him.

He tore the door open before he had time to change his mind.

Finn could hear their voices the minute he stepped inside. The air in the restaurant was cool but heavy with the aroma of food, garlic, and something he couldn't quite put his finger on. The bar to his right was deserted, cluttered with empty bottles, so he made his way toward the seating area at the rear and found them all sitting at the oval table in the back corner.

Tess raised her glass in a toast. Jacob was there too, which must be driving Adrian crazy.

"Cheers!" she shouted, and the others did the same.

Milton darted beneath the long tablecloth, and Sophie bent down to see where he had gone. Finn felt like his legs might give way as he approached the table and cleared his throat.

"Finn?" Ava blurted out. "Where have you been? We missed you!"

He doubted they had even noticed he wasn't there. Ava was clutching a wineglass in one hand, and her eyes seemed oddly lifeless. She was sitting beside Charlotte, who had rosy cheeks and red lips.

Standing there, Finn suddenly remembered the first day of senior high school, when he entered the classroom and saw Charlotte by the window. A day he hadn't even been planning to turn up, because the whole thing was his father's dream, not his. She had been wearing a vest with thin straps, and the breeze from the open window had made her red hair blow back from her freckled shoulders.

Seeing them all together now, without him, he had a clear vision of the point of no return, the fine line between misery and freedom.

Between life and death.

Was he ready to risk never speaking to Charlotte again?

She cocked her head and gave him a wry smile. Finn smiled back, and for a split second he forgot why he had come.

"Sit down," said Adrian, patting the seat beside him. "There's space here."

There were dirty plates and empty dishes all over the table. Finn glanced over to William, who was sitting beside Sophie, with his back to him.

"There's probably enough left for you," said Charlotte, taking stock of the leftovers.

"I'm not hungry."

"Pass me that plate from the table by the wall, and I'll dish it up for you."

"Don't bother, I . . ." he began, but she was so determined that he didn't have the heart to say no. "Just a little bit, then."

Charlotte scraped the last of the moussaka onto his plate, added a dollop of tzatziki and two pieces of garlic bread, then held it out to him. She was wearing a dress he had never seen before.

"Now spill," she said with a grin.

"Spill?"

"Where you've been. Why are you so late?"

Everyone had turned to look at him, even William, and Finn was convinced they could all see it on his face.

"Something came up at work, that's all. Someone messed up, and I had to fix it. It was so late by the time I got out that I wasn't planning to come, but my apartment was so hot I . . . Anyway, here I am."

"We missed you," said Sophie, rubbing his back. "We need someone to keep us in line."

"Yeah? So you haven't been talking shit about me? Sighing with relief that I hadn't turned up?"

"Of course we have," Jacob said with a grin. "But now that you're here, we'll have more ammunition for the next time you're a no-show."

"I knew it," said Finn, pointing at him with his fork. "You're a bad influence."

The others laughed, and for a moment he really did manage to relax. Charlotte's laugh was, as ever, the most beautiful thing he had ever heard. Finn wanted to spend the rest of his life listening to that laugh. His hand shook as he reached for the jug of water and filled his glass, Adrian on one side of him and William on the other. Adrian seemed tense, with a guarded look on his face, and he kept drumming his fingers on the table and checking his watch. He stunk of cigarette smoke too. William was half slumped in his chair, one elbow on the table and his other hand on Sophie's leg. Without warning, he got up and stroked her hair.

"I'll be back in a sec."

Finn watched as he walked slowly over to the bar, massaging the back of his neck. When he turned his head, he noticed that Charlotte was doing the same. She would never get over William. In her eyes, he was perfect. How was Finn ever supposed to compete with that? The truth was that she had never meant anything to William. She was just one in a long line of people who had fallen for his messy curls and strong chin.

But she . . .

She had never looked at Finn the same way after that short week of impossible romance with William.

"You okay?" he asked, dragging her back to the present, a smile lingering on her lips.

"I'm good, Finn. You?" she asked, leaning forward so that her red hair brushed against the tablecloth.

He wondered if she knew the effect she had on him, whether it was deliberate. But more often than not, he just wished she would do it again.

And again.

If she would just pick him, then all would be forgiven.

"What've you got planned next week?" he asked. "Do you have any days off?"

She straightened up before she answered.

"Ugh, it's going to be crazy," she replied, looking away. "Work every day, plus I have to help one of my colleagues move house. I'm not going to have the energy to do anything but eat and sleep when I get home."

She really did try hard to make herself unattainable.

"Cool. I was just wondering," he said, getting up.

"Why? Did you need something, or . . .?"

"No, no, I'm going to be pretty busy too. Back in a minute."

William had disappeared behind the wall by the bar, and Finn took out the sheet of paper and walked straight into him as he swung around the corner.

"Shit, sorry."

William tried to drift straight past, but Finn stopped him with a hand on his arm.

"Wait, William."

He paused.

"What's up?"

Clutching the sheet of paper in his hand, Finn glanced back over to the table, to Adrian. Adrian gazed back at them as he chewed on a toothpick. If this came out at some point, his dad would immediately assume that Finn was involved. But if he stood up for what was right instead, he might earn himself a pat on the back and an approving nod. It might even change the way Charlotte felt about William.

"There's something I need to tell you. Something I should have told you a long time ago."

"Okay, now I'm curious."

"I . . ."

Finn swallowed hard and fiddled with the sheet of paper. He saw Adrian get up and come toward them and was just about to shove it back into his pocket when Adrian walked straight by, stealing a glance at the paper in Finn's hand before opening the door and disappearing outside.

"What is it, Finn?"

On the other side of the glass, Adrian paced back and forth with a cigarette in his hand, glaring in at them. Finn turned toward the table again and saw Charlotte leaning back in her seat with one arm on the backrest, following their every move. He carefully folded the sheet of paper and pushed it back into his pocket.

"You know what? We can do this later, right?"

"Yeah, no worries. Are you coming over to my place? Everyone else is."

"Sure, I'll come. We can do this then."

His father was right. Finn had been given a chance to choose a path where he stood up for what he believed in and supported those he loved, but as ever, he had allowed his fears of what other people would think to take over.

He already regretted his decision and was worried about what consequences it might have.

"Great," said William, giving him a thump on the back. "See you at the table."

On the sidewalk outside, Adrian was standing perfectly still. He blew a cloud of smoke toward the window and stared in at Finn.

CHAPTER

24

Now

Adrian is out on the balcony, blowing smoke toward the living room window. I can see him shivering, using his free hand to rub his other arm, and I wave for him to come back inside. Someone needs to take charge and stop this madness from spreading like a virus, and he is the only person I know who refuses to back down in a crisis. But he just glares at me and then turns his back to the window, a cloud of smoke hanging around his head.

I sigh and hug my knees to my chest, taking in the rest of the living room. I hate that this sofa is so clean and white, the polar opposite of the shabby couch Ava had ten years ago, with all its soft blankets and colorful pillows. I hate that the entire apartment is nothing but a sterile shell without a single trace of her personality. And in the middle of the perfect white expanse: the explosion of red on the wall.

Charlotte.

I take a hesitant step down onto the rug, afraid my boots might leave marks, then slowly make my way past the sofas and the coffee table, pausing to watch the glowing tip of Adrian's cigarette out on the balcony again. I glance over to the dining room before taking another couple of steps forward and looking up at the painting. The hair is wild. Thick brushstrokes sweeping along the edges of the canvas, curling around the bottom. The eyes are either closed or hidden behind all of that hair.

Maybe it isn't supposed to represent anything but Charlotte's tangled locks?

After another unsteady step, I reach out so that my fingers graze the bottom corner. I hook a finger beneath the frame and lift it away from the wall, then lean in close to peer in behind it. I should have steeled myself for what I might find there, because I can't help but gasp.

"What the . . ."

I pull it farther from the wall and read the words scrawled across the back of the painting. Exclamation points, block capitals, black marker, and pencil.

Obsessed, betrayal, vain, spiteful.

I let the canvas drop and lean back against the wall. I need to find Jacob's painting, to tell someone what I've found.

Now.

"Have any of you seen Sophie?" I hear Ava ask from the dining room. "And where's Tess?"

"Sophie was just in the living room," Charlotte replies. "I haven't seen her come back out."

"I'll go and check."

Her clicking heels draw closer, and I move around the smaller sofa, pushing between the armrest and the wall and rounding the corner to the hallway, where I run straight into Jacob.

"Hey, relax! What's the hurry? Have you changed your mind?"

"Come with me," I say, dragging him toward the bathroom.

"No thanks, I just came from there. I don't need to go again."

"We need to talk."

The door swings shut behind us, enveloping us in darkness. For one second, two. Three seconds. I can hear him breathing, note that he still wears the same aftershave he did ten years ago. Or maybe it's something else containing the same citrus notes. Then the light comes on, and we're standing an arm's length apart.

"So now you want to talk, huh?" he says with a grin.

"Ava is sick."

"Oh yeah? Is it infectious?"

"Jacob, I'm serious. She's mentally ill."

"Slow down a second. What makes you say that?"

"This whole thing is insane," I say, doing a loop of the bathroom, with my hands to my ears, before pausing in front of the sink and looking up at him. "She has serious problems, and she's been all alone here, planning this evening. For a *long* time."

His grin is gone now, and I see the muscles beneath his skin tense as his jaw tightens.

"You should probably tell me what you're talking about."

"I can do better than that. I'll show you."

I stamp on the little pedal on the trash can, and the lid flips open. But the bag inside is empty.

Empty.

"No, it can't be. It was right here."

"What was?"

I reach into the bag and search every crease and fold, but it really is empty.

"A medicine bottle. The same stuff your dad used to take at night."

"My dad?"

"Do you remember the pot of tiny pills he took in the evening? It was on the top shelf of the bathroom cabinet. He sometimes took them during the day too. You know better than me. Tess said her granny had been prescribed them for her aggression, and I think—"

"Sophie?"

Ava's voice is right outside. She knocks a couple of times. "Are you in there?"

Jacob looks me straight in the eye, shrugs, and then takes a step toward me. I press my index finger to my lips.

"Yeah, I'll be out in a sec."

"Is something wrong?"

He reaches out and jabs a finger into my side, just beneath my ribs. I jump and swat his hand away, and he can barely contain his laughter.

"No, everything's fine. I'll be right out."

I wait for the sound of her heels to fade away, but the hallway is quiet. With my ear pressed to the door, I can practically hear her breathing out there.

"Okay," she says after a moment. "Will you hurry?"

"I promise."

She clicks away across the hard floor, and I box Jacob's arm as hard as I can and then move away from him so that I can think.

"I'm serious," I say, keeping my voice low. "It's not just the pills. I was in her office, and she has a whole load of information about all of us. Private documents, extracts from the police investigation. This is so much worse than a few stupid little boxes on the table."

His smile falters. "What sort of documents?"

"I don't know. I didn't have time to go through all the files—just mine and Finn's. But she knows where I work, my address. I think she made an anonymous call to my radio show the day the invite arrived. I recognized her voice. I found medical records too. Ava has been a patient at a few different treatment centers. And the paintings!" I grab his arm out of pure exhilaration. "The paintings represent us."

"They don't represent anything. It's just a load of paint."

"I found my name beneath the paint on one of them, and on the back of the canvas . . . I need to show you. You won't believe me otherwise."

Jacob looks down at my hand, which is still gripping his arm. One by one, I force my fingers to relax and let go. They leave faint red marks on his skin. I lower my hand, but he catches and holds it, then moves slowly toward me.

"What really happened, Sophie?"

I try to pull my hand away, but his grip tightens.

"What happened that evening? Why didn't I hear from you? Did you even talk to William?"

We'd settled on the plan a week earlier. That Friday would be the day when I told William about Jacob and me. There wasn't meant to be a party at his place that evening; I shouldn't even have gone to dinner with them. I was supposed to meet William outside his office and then call or message Jacob. I felt sick as soon as I woke up that morning. I canceled my meeting with William at the last minute, decided to show up at Christos after all, and felt like I was drowning under texts from Jacob all evening.

But what was there to tell William?

How, on those evenings when William disappeared, I found myself standing outside Jacob's door? How, with my back up against the kitchen counter, I watched as his dad drifted around the room in search of something to eat, leaving a trail of cookie wrappers and empty cans behind him? Should I have told him about the relief on Jacob's face when Stefan eventually accepted my presence and asked me to play cards with him? We spent hours playing cards, whole nights sometimes, the three of us at the little round table beneath the kitchen light. That became my refuge, a place where I could take a step back from a world where I'd started to wonder if I had ever really belonged. I'd never seen someone as vulnerable as Jacob on those evenings when

I said good night to him in the hallway, though I often imagined that would be exactly how Mom looked if I'd ever told her what I knew. His palpable sadness and loneliness reverberated through me, and when he finally kissed me, I didn't do a thing to stop him.

Nothing at all.

Maybe I should have told William.

"Jacob," I plead with him now, "it's over. It doesn't matter anymore."

"It matters to me. I want to know. I didn't hear from you—that's why I came to the restaurant. I thought something must have gone wrong. But there you were, with William's arm around you, acting like nothing had happened. Like it was just any other day."

I can feel his breath on my face, hot and heavy. He puts his other hand on my hip, and I close my eyes. Every touch sends a jolt of guilt through me. I've spent every single day since regretting the fact that I let him believe we had a future together.

"I waited," he continues in a whisper. "I waited so long the next day, for you to call or come over. I waited outside the church after the funeral, outside your apartment, but you never came. And then you were gone. It was like I'd dreamed you."

I open my eyes, and his face is right in front of mine. If I tipped my head forward even slightly, our lips would meet, and I know exactly how he would taste. But instead, I back away from him. He didn't deserve it, but he was there. He *saw* me. And he became my way out of an impossible situation that I no longer had any control over.

"If you'll just let me show you the paintings, you'll see what I mean."

His hand brushes my arm and then drops to his side. He takes a step back, pushes his hand into the pocket of his jeans, and nods, not looking at me.

"Fine. Show me the paintings."

I want to get out of the bathroom, which suddenly feels cramped and claustrophobic, but I can't bring myself to move. I'm frozen to the spot, unable to tear my eyes away from Jacob's slumped shoulders and bowed head.

"I just don't think this is the right moment to talk about—"

"You're right, Sophie. None of it matters anymore. Show me the paintings."

It's Jacob who leaves the room first. He opens the door with no thought to who might see us together, and he walks away without looking back.

CHAPTER 25

Now

LOVE IS A kind of poison. You spend your entire life chasing it, and once you finally manage to get your hands on it, you have no clue what to actually do with it. Little by little, it seeps into your bloodstream, spreading around your body and clouding your judgment. I can feel the traces Jacob left behind stirring to life inside me now, my body remembering everything I tried to forget.

It wants more of the poison that ruined my life.

Jacob walks down the hallway ahead of me, so close that I could reach out and touch his back. He has a V-shaped scar on his left shoulder, a reminder of the evening when his father forgot they lived together and attacked him with a shoehorn as Jacob bent down to take off his shoes in the darkness. I drove him to the hospital in my old Polo, then sat among the coughing babies and bloody drunks in the waiting room as they gave him four stitches.

He pauses in front of the green painting and points at it.

"So is this one yours?"

"No, the yellow one."

He takes a step to the side, his fingers tracing the damage I did earlier, stroking my name beneath the paint. He then lifts the frame from the wall and squints at the back of it. Still holding it in one hand, he glances over to me.

"Do you understand now?" I ask.

Jacob looks up at the words on the back of the canvas, and the thought that he is reading everything Ava has written about me sends a rush of blood to my cheeks. Words that I've screamed at myself for years and years.

Egotistical, disloyal, unreliable.

He lowers the painting again and turns to the green canvas.

"So whose is this?"

"I'm not sure. I couldn't find a name. I'm pretty sure the red one behind the sofa is meant to be Charlotte, though."

"Makes sense."

He lifts the edge of the green painting and presses his cheek to the wall.

"Betrayal, jealousy, schadenfreude, sabotage," he reads aloud. "She doesn't have a very high opinion of us."

"Is she wrong?"

Jacob doesn't reply, just straightens the painting and turns his head toward the dining room, where Adrian has raised his voice. After glancing back at me, he starts moving. I hurry after him. Charlotte is back in her seat, her chin propped up on her palm. Adrian is sitting too, with a glass of whisky in front of him. Ava is standing by the door to the kitchen and it takes me a moment to spot Finn on the other side of the little table with the lamp.

"So where's your box?" Adrian asks Ava. "Why don't you have one?"

"I don't need one," she replies with a smile. "I don't have anything to hide."

Given everything I found in her office, it takes a real effort not to laugh.

"You've got to be kidding." Adrian snorts before taking a sip of his whisky.

His movements seem loose, his voice loud. He's never been able to hold his liquor, and from what I can see, there isn't much left in his glass.

"You don't have anything to hide?"

He leans back, turning his head toward the living room and looking straight at me, standing just behind Jacob.

"So Sophie knows, does she?"

"Adrian, enough." Charlotte has straightened up, and she fixes her eyes on him before glancing over to me. Ava's arms have dropped to her sides, and the stiff expression on her face makes her eyes look as big and round as marbles.

"Come here, Sophie."

Adrian beckons me over, waving his arm more and more wildly until I give in and walk toward him. He hooks an arm around my waist and pulls me so close that he can rest his head against my stomach.

"I've missed you, girl," he says, hugging me so tight that it makes my ribs ache.

"Careful, Adrian. I've missed you too," I say, trying to pry the glass from his hand.

"Nah, nah, nah—don't start now, Sophie, not when we're having so much fun. Look at Ava instead."

But I don't want to do that. Ava looks like she wants the ground to swallow her up. Instead, I turn to Finn, who has moved over to the hallway, without a sound, and is now staring down at his watch.

"Has Ava told you?"

"You really shouldn't drink." Charlotte sighs.

She's right. One glass is fine, maybe even two. But after three drinks, there's no stopping Adrian.

"Shut up, Charlotte. Ava, have you told Sophie?"

"Adrian," I say softly, stroking his arm until it loosens around my waist. "What are you talking about? What is Ava supposed to have told me?"

He looks up at me and smiles that big grin I've missed so much, though I can see something else in his eye. Something cold and dark.

"That she was in love with you."

I keep looking at him, don't dare do anything else, but from the corner of my eye, I can see Ava, a slim, light shape quivering at the edge of my field of vision. She wasn't in love with me. We were close—closer than I've ever been with anyone else. But it was just friendship. A deep, indescribable friendship that surpassed everything else, one that I've missed every day since William died.

Right?

"No, I didn't know that."

"Well, the rest of us did," he says with a low chuckle.

"You promised," says Charlotte. "We all made a promise to William not to say anything."

"William knew?" I ask, pulling away from Adrian.

Was Ava in love with *me*?

I can't bring myself to look in her direction. All those times when she called William, all those evenings when he got home late, tired and weary.

Was all that about me?

"Adrian," Jacob shouts, "can I bum a cigarette? I think I need something to take the edge off."

Adrian grins and gets up, searching his pockets for his cigarettes. He and Jacob head out onto the balcony. Ava takes a step into the kitchen, her hand lingering on the doorframe. She looks back over her shoulder.

"I'm just going to check on the coffee," she says, disappearing with flushed cheeks.

"What a great evening," Charlotte mutters, bending down to rummage for something in her bag.

The opening into the hallway is empty. Finn is gone.

"I need to get something from my coat pocket," I say, striding past the little table lamp and taking care not to glance into the kitchen as I pass.

Finn is standing with his back to me. There is a leather bag on the floor by his feet, and whatever he is holding is emitting a cold, dim light, illuminating his face. I slowly move closer and peer over his shoulder. It's an iPad.

"You've got an iPad?"

Finn wheels around and I tear it out of his hands. On the screen, I see that he has started a message to someone called Veronica.

"What are you doing? Give it to me."

He tries to snatch it back, but I turn away and hold it out of reach.

"Why didn't you say anything, Finn? We could have used this to contact someone and get them to open the door."

"Give it to me!" he practically screams. I don't think I've ever seen him so agitated before. "The battery's going to die any second now."

"Even more reason to do something useful with it."

I duck beneath his arm and move over to the corner, by the hidden coat cupboard. Gripping the iPad in both hands, I read his message.

Going to be late, you shouldn't come tonight. Charlotte's thinking about coming back to the hotel with me, so don't go there.

Finn grabs the iPad from me just as the screen goes dark.

"Fuck!"

He hits the cupboard door and turns away from me. Leaning against the wall, I breathe in the tense air between us and study the curly hair at the nape of his neck. He looks as dejected as he always did back then, when the evening came to an end and we all went our separate ways. Even though he always drank the least and shouldn't have had anything to worry about.

"So, who's Veronica?"

"You wouldn't understand."

"Try me."

"We were classmates at university. There was a reunion in Gävle last year, and I saw her for the first time since I moved to Stockholm. We've been seeing each other ever since, either here or in Stockholm. I can't go on like this, Sophie. Charlotte was supposed to be at her parents' place tonight, but I've got a hotel room. She's pissed at me for reasons I don't even understand, but now she's suddenly decided that she's going to join me at the hotel, so if I can't get a hold of Veronica . . ."

"Charlotte doesn't know? I mean, surely it's no secret that you're getting divorced?"

Finn turns to me. "Did Charlotte tell you that? What did she say?"

He takes a step closer, and if I weren't already pressed up against the wall, I would try to move back, away from his animal desperation.

"No, she didn't say anything, and I didn't ask."

"So who told you we're getting a divorce?"

"Ava," I lie. "She knows."

Finn sighs and turns away. "Of course she does. Nothing gets past Ava."

"It's not the end of the world. There are probably more divorces today than happy marriages. Nine years isn't nothing."

"It's just that Charlotte doesn't want to. I've had to file a petition, which means there's a six-month consideration period, even though we don't have kids. My parents have taken her side, and if they found out about Veronica . . . Sophie, you have to swear you won't tell her."

"Of course. It's none of my business."

He slumps back against the door with a sigh. "I can't take much more of this farce. Do you think Ava will get bored and unlock the door soon?"

"Why didn't you use the iPad to get out earlier?"

Finn bangs his head against the door and closes his eyes.

"Because I wanted to know. I wanted to know what was in Charlotte's box. She knows everything about me. I thought if I could just find out something about her that she'd rather keep to herself, she might let me go."

"And now Adrian knows what was in yours. You don't have a charger, do you?"

"No, I don't."

I think about who I would have contacted if I'd had the chance. Malika, possibly, though there's a risk that she will be in a crowded bar somewhere, with a glass of wine in one hand and some guy's mouth a few inches from her ear. She wouldn't notice a text message come through in the inside pocket of her expensive handbag. Other than her, my mom is the only person who comes to mind. Just a short drive away, she could come over and take the elevator up here, demand that the guy unlock the door.

No, it would have been Malika.

"Finn, wait," I say, putting a hand on his arm as he moves away. "That evening, at Christos. You were so late. What kept you? You were usually always first."

"I wasn't always first," he argues, pulling away from me.

"Fine, but I can't remember a single time you turned up after me—other than that evening. What happened? Was it because you didn't want to see someone?"

He snorts and turns away, slowly taking a few steps back and shaking his head, but I can see that I'm onto something here.

"It was ten years ago." He laughs. "How am I supposed to remember? Maybe I just needed to take the dog for a walk."

"Was it Adrian?" I ask.

He stops dead.

We hear raised voices from the dining room, the sound of chair legs scraping.

"We should probably get back," he says, shoving the iPad into his bag.

I nod and we make our way through to the dining room, where Ava has backed up against the dark windows. Adrian is standing in front of her, and I can see his twisted face in the glass. Ava's wide eyes meet mine over his shoulder.

"William made a mistake by trusting you, didn't he?" says Adrian, taking a step forward and forcing Ava to bump against the window. "This whole evening is just your way of offloading the guilt that it was *you* who drove him to it, isn't it? That it was your betrayal that made him drown himself while you were on the other side of the door?"

It's frightening how close Adrian is to the truth, and all I want is for him to stop talking, but I can't manage a single word.

"That's enough, Adrian," says Finn. I'm standing so close to him that I can feel him trembling in frustration.

Jacob is sitting at the table, and I gesture to ask why he isn't doing anything to stop Adrian, but he just shrugs. Charlotte is standing in front of the painting by the window, her arms folded over her chest.

"Adrian is right," she says without looking at Finn. "You've made such an effort with all of this, Ava. Dug up our grubbiest secrets to play out your little fantasy that one of us killed William. What exactly are you trying to hide? Sophie, tell us what you found. Why you were worried about Ava."

"What?"

My eyes dart from Ava to Charlotte, and Adrian looks back at me over his shoulder.

"Whatever you started telling me earlier. What did you find?"

The blood drains from my face, and on the other side of Adrian, I see Ava slump, as though she's already given up. She takes a deep breath and smiles at me. The same way she smiled at me when she was twenty-two, when she told me that her grandmother—the only constant in her life—had died. After that, she had locked herself in her apartment and didn't speak to any of us for two weeks.

I've betrayed her.

"This isn't the right moment, Charlotte," I say.

"None of us ever thought William would kill himself. We thought it'd be you, if anyone," says Adrian, turning to Ava with a cold laugh.

"Stop it."

The voice comes from the opening between the dining room and the living room. Tess is unsteady on her feet, her eyes barely open.

"Leave her alone," she says. "Don't touch her."

She does her best to straighten up and stand tall, with her feet a hip's width apart, but she has to take a step backward to regain her balance. I move forward to support her elbow, and she lifts her head and flashes me a look of gratitude, tendrils of fair hair hanging loose over her forehead.

"Stay out of this," Charlotte snaps at Tess. "You've had a shitty attitude toward the rest of us since the minute we got here. Enough."

Moving surprisingly fast, in a straighter line than I thought possible, Tess strides over to Adrian and starts hitting his shoulders. Charlotte grabs her arm and tries to pull her away, but Tess shakes her off and aims for his head instead, her fists now clenched.

"You didn't tell William everything," she roars, swinging her spaghetti arms toward him. "Don't you dare blame what happened on Ava!"

Adrian tries to stop Tess's arms and hands, but she clings to his back. In one fluid motion, he straightens up and throws her off, sending her sprawling to the floor, where her head hits the corner of the china cabinet.

CHAPTER

26

One hour and twenty-three minutes before William's death

THERE WAS A clear reluctance among the wealthy to do business when the temperature was hot enough to make a person's blood boil and the streets were full of bare legs and sunglasses—especially if it was Friday. Adrian found that out the hard way as he took a cold shower at six o'clock that morning, pulled on his black trousers and a fresh shirt, downed a cup of microwaved coffee and started his computer. Despite that, he had managed to organize two meetings and a couple of jolting phone calls at the very last minute. One was in a dark, empty bar, with a bitter gin and tonic in hand. Another was in a borrowed conference room at William's office, with William reluctantly shepherding them in while the rest of the team was in the weekly meeting. He had checked in on them through the window onto the corridor and showed them out just as they heard voices at the other end of that corridor.

Adrian's head was aching, the muscles in his face tired after a long day of having to consider every dazzling smile and pay close attention to the slightest of hand movements, palms clammy and back straight. Happy and positive, strong and driven: that was the image he desperately wanted to give off. Adrian had weighed every word, consciously speaking slowly and clearly in order to be able to change track if it didn't produce the desired response. He'd noticed when people's eyes had glazed over and begun to wander. But he was so close now. The line had been cast, and the big fish were on the verge of taking the bait. One had already spat it out, but two were still circling at a safe distance, snapping their greedy little mouths.

Adrian clapped his hands to his flushed face and gritted his teeth at the thought of all the decisions he'd made too soon. Stupid, eager decisions that gave away just how inexperienced he was. The made-to-measure couch clad in gray velvet that would fill the living room in his new apartment; the built-in floor-to-ceiling bookshelves with the recessed lighting. If he didn't manage to pull this off, he would never be able to pay the bill, and when he called that afternoon to cancel his order, he had ended up swearing and hanging up on the poor woman on the other end. Apparently it simply wasn't possible to cancel bespoke furniture that was already in production.

His order remained in progress.

* * *

His father had left Chile in the early 1980s, before Adrian was even planned. As a political asylum seeker, he had endured a few months in a refugee center before laying the foundations of a new life. He had knocked on his Swedish neighbors' doors and offered them fresh empanadas in exchange for them letting him watch soccer on their TVs. A year or so later, Adrian's mom had arrived, right before the authorities began sending Chilean refugees straight back upon arrival at Arlanda. And just a year after that, Adrian had been born.

His mom had never really come to terms with the move. Sweden was too cold for her; its people too. And now Adrian was about to ruin everything.

He tugged at the collar of his shirt. He already had more buttons undone than was really acceptable for a twenty-four-year-old man trying to make it in the world of finance, but he just couldn't stand it any longer. His smooth chest was visible in the gap, slick with sweat, and he was already starting to feel light-headed from the beer. Ten hours' work and nothing but a gin and tonic for lunch tended to have that effect, no matter how much greasy Greek food you wolfed down in the evening.

It made him irritable.

On the other side of the table, Jacob was glaring at him. Blond hair standing on end, the sun shining in through the window behind him like some sort of halo around his head, a five o'clock shadow, and an expression that promised there would be consequences. Adrian glared back, gripping his beer bottle and picking at the label with his thumbnail. The bruise on his cheek had faded, but he still felt the dull ache in his bones every time he saw Jacob. Once everyone else had gotten up from the table earlier, Jacob had come over and said they needed to talk. "She's never going to pick you," Adrian had hissed back, watching as the color drained from Jacob's thin face. That had made him back off.

Adrian had been repressing the problem for a long time now. Keeping himself busy with transactions and purchases, reading up on the market and reassuring William that everything was going to plan. If his father could talk his way into an apprenticeship with a construction company during his first few months in Sweden—unable to speak the language—then surely Adrian could keep track of a bunch of numbers. But the truth had caught up with him. The phone calls that woke him in the middle of the night and led him to pace back and forth in his stuffy apartment had made it clear that his future was hanging by a thread. He should have known better than to put his faith in quick fixes to big problems, and now someone was onto him. He could feel their hot, sour breath on the back of his neck, and he knew it was someone other than the usual bloodhounds snapping at his heels.

Someone who had sniffed out something that wasn't meant for them.

It could have been Jacob. Their conversation in the crowded living room at Adrian's place had really convinced him it was for a while. The taunts, the jibes. Jacob clearly thought he knew something, but the truth was that he didn't know shit—that had quickly become obvious. Still, the fact that he *thought* he knew, that he had noticed something wasn't right . . . That was enough to put everything at risk if he started talking.

As a result, Adrian had kept quiet about why Jacob had punched him in the face.

He had kept quiet about the thing he himself had brought up with Jacob, saliva spraying from his mouth: threatening to share what he knew about Sophie and Jacob with William. It was amazing that no one else had noticed the looks they gave each other, the way Jacob always left the restaurant immediately after she did. If he said anything, that would mean breaking Sophie's trust, and she would never forgive him for that.

But the way Jacob was staring at him now made it feel like the entire evening was doomed to end in disaster, and Adrian was starting to think that he was right. For the past hour, he had been following William's every move, glancing over to Adrian with a grin.

Why did he come?

Adrian couldn't just sit there, fiddling with the stained tablecloth. He leaped up from his chair and made his way to the door, reaching into his pocket for the crumpled pack of cigarettes. As he walked, he thought about all of the phone calls he could have made if he hadn't been stuck in the restaurant all evening. He shoved the door open and stepped out into the hot air. If he closed his eyes, he could imagine he was somewhere else, in another country on the far side of the Atlantic.

Chile.

After his father ditched them to go off in search of happiness in Stockholm when Adrian was eight, his mother would sit, with her arms wrapped around him on the balcony, and look out at Styrmansgatan down below. In smooth, velvety Spanish, she told him all about the harbor in San Antonio, full of fishing boats and other ships. She closed her eyes as she described el Paseo Bellamar, the promenade along the strip of coastline, lowering her voice to a whisper as she remembered the crowded streets lighting up in the evening. The warm breeze, the hum of voices at the market.

They had never gone back. Adrian had never seen the country where his parents had been born and shaped. Instead, he took on all his mother's memories of a place that formed a huge part of him without him being a part of it. He could only imagine the void it must have left in her.

* * *

Behind Adrian, the door creaked open again just as it was about to click shut. He shook a cigarette out of the box and took a first, dizzying drag on it before turning around.

William was standing, with his hands in his pockets, right outside the door. He had tipped his head back against the wall, raising his dimpled chin high in the air. Adrian paced back and forth along the sidewalk with the cigarette in his hand. It didn't matter how many times he puffed on it; it did nothing for his trembling nerves. Getting William involved had been a huge mistake. He would never be able to explain the choices he'd made, and was no longer sure he could actually trust William when push came to shove.

"Can you believe Jacob showed up? After what he did," he said before William had time to speak. Adrian cast a quick glance at his friend before turning around and trudging away from the door, with his back to him.

"What were the two of you talking about?" William asked quietly.

"When? Before or after he slugged me in the face?"

"Today. When Christos came out with the food. Jacob got up to help, but you stopped him. What did you say?"

Adrian snorted. "I don't even remember. I probably told him to keep his fists in his pockets."

"I got the sense he came here to speak to me," said William.

"Hey." Adrian paused right in front of William and came close to jabbing a finger into his chest. "You should stay away from that guy, you hear me? Nothing he says is worth listening to, believe me."

With that, he tore the door open and headed back inside without waiting for William. Adrian moved through the restaurant, painfully aware of William's presence behind him and of the phone buzzing stubbornly in his pocket.

"Bathroom!" he shouted as he bumped into Sophie, who hooked an arm around his waist and pulled him close.

"Always in such a rush," she said with a laugh. "Come and sit with me. I feel like I've hardly spoken to you all evening. I do actually have something I need to ask you, if you have a minute."

"Soon, soon. I promise."

He half-heartedly squeezed her shoulder and saw the disappointment in her eyes as he pulled away from her. A few seconds later, he disappeared through the ivy-clad archway into the bathroom. Adrian slumped down onto the toilet lid and buried his face in his hands. He ran his fingers through his sweaty hair and got back onto his feet. Everything was about to go to shit. He was *so* close.

Everything he'd ever dreamed of was finally within reach, but it could be torn away from him in the blink of an eye. Adrian had spent his life being told he would never amount to anything. He remembered staring down at the books in school and seeing the letters dance on the page in front of him. The shame of feeling so much dumber than everyone else had made him tear them up and bunk off class, and all so he would never have to admit defeat. If it hadn't been for his mom's iron will, he never would have made it through senior high. She had been determined that they wouldn't both be left empty-handed, with no prospects for the future. And now that he was on the right track for the first time in his life, he had to pay her back. The sense of being able to take nothing and make it grow into something—that was magical.

But he had failed.

The next few days would decide how life panned out for him going forward, and the most important thing was to keep William's name out of it if everything went to hell. Adrian couldn't stop thinking about the phone call from the bank. They wanted to meet him, and he knew what that meant.

Someone had said something.

Someone had found something.

But the bank was the least of his problems.

He had started looking for shortcuts before he'd even graduated from senior high, working off the books, cash in hand. During the nightshift at a club one evening, he'd heard a few of the men talking, and that was when the idea came to him: moving a sum of money in exchange for a fee.

He took his phone out and stared down at the number that kept chasing him, day and night. They wanted their money. Money he had been given to look after until they expected it back. Money he had decided to make a hefty profit on while he was borrowing it.

Money he no longer had.

The whole thing had seemed so simple. A vague acquaintance who called late one evening and asked if he'd be interested in earning a bit of dough by helping a friend of a friend. How could he say no? The compensation and returns would be enough to give his mom the life she'd always dreamed of: a little house in Chile. He'd thought he knew what he was doing, whom he was dealing with.

But he had been wrong on every front.

Adrian slammed his palm into the wall and swallowed an expletive, then splashed his face and throat with cold water. Hunched over the sink, he studied himself in the mirror. His eyes were bloodshot. It was written plainly on his face:

You're a loser.

He dried his face with a paper towel and took a deep breath before unlocking the door. William was standing in the archway outside, leaning back against the wall. No matter where he turned, William was always there with his nerves and his never-ending questions and his goddamn conscience, which would drag them both down.

"Can we keep talking?" asked William.

"We've been talking all evening." Adrian laughed and boxed him on the arm before pushing past William to join the others.

"Finn! Are you coming over to William's later?"

Finn's face lit up, as though he had been waiting for Adrian to talk to him. His little white and brown mongrel ran over, and Adrian picked him up and scratched him behind the ear.

"Yeah, definitely. William already asked."

"Great! You see?" he said, turning to William. "After-party at your place with everyone you love. We can fill the tub with cold water and ice, and buy as much beer as Christos will sell us."

Adrian winked at him and lowered the dog to the floor before making his way over to the bar with a growing sense of panic in his chest and white fur clinging to his black shirt. He heard heavy footsteps behind him, and he squeezed his eyes shut before bringing his hand down on the counter.

"An IPA, Christos. Cold as hell."

Christos opened the bottle and set it down in front of him as William reached the bar.

"Why are you avoiding me?"

"I'm not."

"I've been trying to talk to you all evening, but you keep talking to someone else or walking away."

"What's so important that you need to talk about it right this second?"

"The investment. The company."

Adrian held his tongue.

"I called my contact earlier, and—"

Adrian grabbed William's arm and dragged him over to the wall by the door into the kitchen.

"Why did you do that? We're not talking about this here."

"What's going on, Adrian? The bank wants to talk to me about something, but they wouldn't say what it was over the phone. It's got something to do with the money that was paid into my account. Where did it come from?"

"Nothing's going on. Everything's going according to plan."

"Don't lie to me."

Adrian raised the bottle to his lips and took a couple of deep swigs of beer. He then lowered it to his chest and leaned back against the wall with a sigh.

"All right, I'm going to be straight with you."

"I hope so."

"The money we invested isn't where I said it was."

William stared at him. "So where is it?"

"Just let me handle this. You don't need to worry."

"What do you mean the money isn't where you said it was?"

"These things happen when you're dealing with stocks. You take risks, you have to make quick decisions. I've made an adjustment that will be more profitable in the long run, but I don't want you to start digging into this. Just let me handle it, like we agreed."

"But the money was meant to go into our company. I quit my job, Adrian. Fuck, that was all the money I had. You can't tell me not to worry about where it is. That money could have gone toward a deposit for a house. Why didn't you say anything yesterday?"

"There's no need to get worked up, William. I said I would make an investment that would make the money grow, and I have. You can relax—everything will be fine now that you've transferred the money that went into your account."

"I haven't transferred it, and I still want out. I want my investment back."

William's face was pale, his eyes wide. He pressed his hands to his temples and took a couple of deep breaths. Adrian grabbed one of his wrists and hissed in his ear.

"Pull yourself together, for fuck's sake. You can trust me, okay? I've got something in the works—a loan. Everything will be just fine, and you'll get your money back several times over, but you need to transfer the deposit to the company account."

And I'll be in debt indefinitely.

William shook him off and backed away.

"William. Don't do anything stupid now."

"I know what I need to do. I have to make a few calls."

"William, just let me handle this. I've got it under control."

William turned around and walked away with his phone in his hand. Adrian's own cell phone started ringing in his pocket. Long, stubborn vibrations followed by one last buzz. A message. He hesitated for a moment, then dug it out and looked down at the screen.

You've got until tomorrow.

CHAPTER

27

Now

All the details I found beautiful earlier feel different now. Looking around the apartment, all I can see are the hard lines and sharp edges. The cold expanses of glass, metal, and stone.

The cage we're trapped in.

Tess is on the floor with her knees pulled in to her chest and her neck at a worrying angle, her white shirt the only bright spot on the otherwise dark floor. For the few long seconds before she tentatively reaches up to touch the back of her head, I completely forget to breathe. Adrian takes a couple of steps away from her slim body and holds out both hands in her direction.

"She attacked me! You all saw that, right?"

In different circumstances, involving a different person, we would have protested. We would have pushed him aside and taken control of the situation.

But this is Adrian.

And it isn't the first time we've seen him like this.

"Could everyone just calm down?" Finn begs us, adrenaline making his voice shake.

Ava is still standing with her back to the glass. Her eyes are fixed on Tess, her face surprisingly calm. She has a smile on her lips as she slowly lifts her chin and looks straight at Adrian, and as though he can feel her looking at him, he turns back around and points a finger at her.

"This is your fault," he says through gritted teeth. "All this is because of you and your fucking conspiracy theories."

"I think we've all had a bit much to drink," Finn continues. "Why don't we sit down? Maybe that's enough for one evening, before something we really regret happens."

All it takes is one glance from Adrian, and Finn stops speaking. His eyes are filled with the same bottomless darkness as the evening that ended with raised voices and Jacob's clenched fist striking his cheek. Jacob, the new guy no one had quite managed to figure out yet. The one who saw straight through all our lies and bullshit. Adrian, who we'd all known since the time when a perfect Saturday meant a shared capricciosa at the pizza place by Vasa School.

How do you beat that?

Scattered around the room now, all frozen to the spot, the gulf between us has never been clearer.

Never deeper.

Charlotte fiddles with her dress and chews on her bottom lip. Finn runs his fingers through his hair. Adrian is breathing heavily through his nose, and Ava slips away from the wall of glass behind him without a sound, leaving it as dark as the night outside. For the first time all evening, we're seeing each other for who we really are, who we've always been. What Adrian has just done means we can no longer turn a blind eye to the question we've been ignoring for so long.

How far would we be prepared to go to protect ourselves?

How far was someone prepared to go ten years ago?

I leave Finn by the doorway to the kitchen and position myself between Adrian and Tess.

"Calm down," I whisper to him. "Is this what you meant by someone else getting hurt? Is this what happens when you drink?"

I press a finger to his collarbone, where the bruise is now hidden beneath his buttoned shirt, and I see him flinch before I drop to my knees beside Tess.

"Are you all right? Have you hurt your neck?"

"Head," Tess replies, rolling over onto her stomach in order to get onto all fours.

A few locks of hair have come loose from her neat ponytail, and her mascara is smudged beneath her eyes.

"Hold on—you might have hurt your neck too. You should lie still for a minute."

"I need to get out of here," she mumbles, on the verge of tears. "Away from him."

She scrambles up onto her hands and knees and reaches for the handle of the china cabinet, and I sigh and grip her elbow to help her to her feet. Charlotte is still leaning back against the wall in front of us, right by the painting.

"I wish I could say I'm surprised," she says, "but some things never change."

"Stop, Charlotte," I say, though she's right.

Just not in the way she thinks.

Tess is unsteady on her feet, and she turns toward the living room.

"I need to lie down. My head is spinning."

I lead her through the archway into the living room and down the step to the sofa. She slumps onto her side on the soft cushions, twisting and pulling a face before rolling over onto her back. I grab the two decorative pillows from the corner and tuck them under her head, then I push her shoulder down and place her hand on her stomach, squeezing it until it relaxes. As I tuck her wild locks back behind her ears, it's hard to remember how she looked when I arrived. The neatly pressed pants, the bright eyes, the sleek ponytail.

The pride I felt that she'd moved on and got her life in order has been replaced by a deep sorrow that she's now lying on the sofa in this state.

She didn't even want to be here this evening.

"Just take it easy, Tess. Try to lie still and get some rest. I'll find a way for us to get out of here."

She nods and closes her eyes, and I slowly get up. As I turn around, she has already tipped her face toward the back rest.

In the dining room, Adrian, Charlotte, and Finn are huddled together by the table, talking in low voices. Just behind them, Jacob is still sitting where he was earlier, watching them. His words are forever etched into my mind, and it suddenly seems so clear that he has always been right.

"You're not part of the group."

"We need to get Tess to the hospital," I say. "I think she could have a concussion."

They turn to look at me, and they consider my words in silence for a moment before splitting up to start opening cupboards and drawers.

"Did you hear what I said? We need to take her to the emergency room. What are you doing?"

"We're taking charge of the situation," Adrian replies, marching toward the kitchen. "Someone has to if we're ever going to get out of here."

He's right, of course. We should try to find our cell phones, a key for the door. And yet I can't quite shake the feeling that he's looking for something else in the kitchen as he starts opening drawers that I already know contain no sharpened knives. Finn seems to feel the same way, and he mouths something to me, stopping abruptly as Charlotte approaches.

"Can I help?" I ask her.

"Do whatever you want."

Painfully aware of each other, we move around in the dim light of the candles, searching Ava's home, constantly glancing back over our shoulders. Charlotte pauses by the table and starts gathering up the unopened boxes.

"Leave those," I say.

There are three of them left. Tess, Finn, and I have all opened ours, but we still have no idea what could be in Charlotte and Adrian's. Or Jacob's.

"We don't need them anymore." She hesitates and looks all around. "Where's Ava?"

Adrian slams a cupboard door and pops his head out from the kitchen.

"Good question," he says. "Probably somewhere she doesn't want us to be."

At that, Charlotte dumps the boxes in a heap on the table. They bounce, making the lids come off. She gasps quietly and reaches for one of them, then goes to meet Adrian by the kitchen. They both peer in the direction of the hallway, listening carefully, then turn their heads toward the living room. Adrian starts walking, and Charlotte is right behind him.

"Come on, Finn," she shouts.

Finn shoots me a guilty look before hurrying out and leaving me alone with Jacob.

"This is a disaster," I say.

He still hasn't gotten up from the table, and I move closer to tidy up the mess Charlotte left behind.

"Did you really expect anything else?"

Oddly enough, I had. I'd expected a civilized dinner full of smiling faces as we reminisced over the good times we'd once shared, but I realize now that was asking far too much. My fingers brush the objects that have fallen out onto the table. A photograph of William taken somewhere I don't recognize. He's smiling at the camera, at whoever took the picture, and at first I assume it must be from before we met, but then I notice his engagement ring. I pick it up and study it closely. It looks like it was taken inside someone's house. There is a chest of drawers behind him, and a window with a pair of heavy curtains and a green plant on the sill to his right. It makes my heart ache to look into his eyes.

As I tuck the photograph into the back pocket of my jeans, I notice something catch the light beneath the jumble of boxes and lids. I carefully push them aside and immediately know what it is. The little silver snowflake glitters as though it were new. The last time I spoke to William, as I uttered the last ever words he would hear from me, I dropped those earrings into the pocket of his jeans.

Whose box was it in?

"What is it?" I hear Jacob ask, and I realize I've been staring down at the table as though paralyzed.

He is on his feet now, standing across from me with his hand on the back of one of the chairs.

"Ava is right," I whisper.

He doesn't look at me right away. His face is lowered to the table and my clenched hand. He slowly raises his head, and I know I shouldn't say it, not out loud. Not to him. But this is the reason I said yes to this dinner, what I've been waiting for all these years.

Now that I have the truth in my hand, I regret coming.

"What do you mean?"

"She was right all along."

"What makes you say that?"

With shaking fingers, I pick up the tiny snowflake and hold it out to him. I can't breathe as I wait for him to make the connection, for him to react. But he doesn't seem to understand, so I lift it to my ear.

"I gave this to him just a few minutes before he was found dead. It was in one of the boxes on the table."

Jacob takes the earring from my hand and studies it.

"Are you sure it's the same one? It could just be from a similar pair."

"I'm sure," I say, taking it back.

"Whose box was it in?"

Ava's voice cuts through the silence of the apartment, and I hear a door slam against a wall. I shove the earring into my pocket and follow the sound of her voice, not bothering to wait for Jacob. There is no sign of anyone in the narrow hallway, but when I reach the door to Ava's office, I see them all inside. She is huddled up in the corner, beside the row of bookshelves. Finn is standing in front of her, his eyes darting between Ava and what is going on at the desk. The desk where Adrian is slumped in the chair, Charlotte just behind him. There are documents and folders scattered across the surface in front of them, illuminated by the lamp.

"Jesus Christ, Ava," Adrian mutters.

"What is it?" Finn moves away from her.

"This is crazy," says Charlotte, closing a folder and tossing it onto the desk. "Totally crazy."

Adrian spins around in his chair until he is facing the filing cabinet. Every drawer but the bottom one is wide open, and he leans forward and pulls the handle of the last, locked drawer, which opens without any resistance.

Over in the corner, Ava gasps and meets my eye.

I locked it.

I did, didn't I?

I locked it once I was done, and then I put the key back beneath the chair. Only, I'm no longer sure of any of that. I feel the blood rush to my cheeks and see Ava slump back against the bookshelves, disappointment written across her face.

She knows.

She knows it was me who found the key and opened the drawer.

"Fuck me," Adrian mutters, the stack of Ava's journals in his hands. "I knew it."

Charlotte leans in over his shoulder as he flicks through them, her red hair spilling down his back in a stark contrast to his navy shirt.

"What should we do?" she whispers.

"That's enough now."

Adrian drops everything back into the drawer, with a thud, and then gets up and leaves the room. Charlotte shifts her weight from one foot to the other and moves a few papers on the desk before following him out. The minute she has tottered away, Ava slaps down Finn's hand, which he had raised to keep her in the corner, and he backs up as she pushes past him to get to the desk. Moving unsteadily, she gathers everything into a pile and drops it into the bottom drawer, on top of her medical notes, then slams it shut. The sound echoes through the room.

As she gets onto her knees to reach for the key beneath the desk chair, she turns to look at me.

"Ava, I—"

"No, I don't want to hear it."

She locks the drawer and grips the key in her clenched fist, then leaves the room without a single glance back.

Jacob is waiting in the hallway outside, and he grabs my arm as I come out.

"Just let it go, Sophie. Nothing we do now can change what happened. Let's just get out of here and never come back."

I stare at him, can't understand what he's talking about. It would change everything. It would justify all those sleepless nights after I woke up screaming in the darkness; it would banish the demons that have been crowding my head for the past ten years. Surely he knows that.

I yank my arm out of his grip and hurry after Ava, who has paused in the opening between the dining room and the living area. I see her face in profile when she notices the open boxes on the dining table; her shoulders practically tremble with every shallow breath she takes as she clenches her other fist and turns into the living room. Charlotte is over by the balcony door, with her back to the room. Her fingers drum her arms as she stares out toward Brynäs, her hair gathered over one shoulder. When she hears us, her long nails dig into the soft flesh beneath her dress. Adrian is by the blood-red armchairs in front of the bookshelf.

"Are you worried, Adrian?" Ava asks him. "Scared someone else might have had time to read your file?"

His face breaks into a grin as he sits down and leans back in one of the chairs. I don't dare take my eyes off him, searching for clues as to what could be going through his head. What could be scaring him as much now as it did back then.

What he is planning.

"No more than you should be."

"Tell us about the money, Adrian. Tell us about the money you lost."

His face pales against the red fabric, becoming tense and troubled. He opens his mouth as though he is about to reply, then closes it again and grits his teeth.

"You lost it all, didn't you? All the money William put into your project went up in smoke."

I feel the blood drain from my cheeks, and I sway.

Was William's money gone?

"What is she talking about?" I ask Adrian, but he refuses to meet my eye.

Ava slowly moves closer.

"William had a hunch something was wrong, and he wanted to pull out. But you kept reassuring him that everything was alright. He knew it was a lie. He knew it the evening we found him dead in the bath."

"I had nothing to do with that," Adrian snaps, sitting up straight.

"You avoided him all evening at the restaurant, and when we got to his place, both of you were agitated. I saw you go into William's bedroom together, and when you came back out you were alone. Not long after that, he was dead. Problem solved."

"No," Adrian protests. "It was just a setback. I took a shortcut to earn us some decent start-up capital, and it went wrong. But I was going to fix it—William knew that."

"You were the last one who saw him alive. What did you say to him? Did you follow him into the bathroom? Were you waiting for him there?"

Adrian leans forward in his seat and blinks a couple of times. *Now* he is looking at me, and I wish the floor would swallow me up.

"That's not true," he says. "I wasn't the last person to see him."

Ava seems speechless, glancing from Finn to Charlotte, who has moved closer with a frown.

"What do you mean?" Charlotte asks.

"Didn't you know? I couldn't get him to listen, so I left him alone in the bedroom. And once I left, Sophie went in."

CHAPTER

28

The last few hours with William

WHEN I GOT to the restaurant and wove my way between the tables, I had no idea what shape the rest of my life might take. I should have had a vision of William and me living in a small house in a quiet area, with a stroller by the front door and toys scattered across the lawn. I should have been looking forward to spending the rest of my life with him and seeing the first gray hairs start to creep into his thick, dark hair.

But I wasn't.

Because I knew that evening would turn everything upside down and that nothing would ever be the same again. When I really thought about it, I realized I'd probably never had that vision for us. I've spent my entire life waiting for everything I love to be snatched away from me.

It had been a long time since I got sick of waiting for him to come home. Instead, I started following him when he left the apartment. I would wait beneath the cherry trees on the little scrap of grass opposite his office, and then I would blend in with the other people on the street as he walked toward the center of town, taking the backstreets behind the library to get to the buildings behind Söderhielmska Gården.

The buildings on Brunnsgatan, where Ava lived.

* * *

I'd eaten every last bite of crème brûlée and pushed the bowl away from the seat where I'd been slumped for most of the evening, but I couldn't help but trail a finger around the rim and pop it into my mouth. There were conversations I wasn't a part of going on all around me, and inside a storm was raging. One that threatened to tear me to pieces. No matter what I did, I knew someone would be heartbroken by the end of the night. No matter what decision I made, I would be a wreck. I could sense William behind me again, and when I turned my head I saw him with his phone to his ear. He had barely sat still all evening. Whenever I took a deep breath and tried to say something that would break the ice between us, he kept leaping up to follow Adrian or look for Ava.

William ended his call and I reached out for him, but he slipped away before my fingers managed to find him. Over to Ava, who was standing by the window. He whispered something in her ear, and she wrapped her arms around him. It was an embrace that made me look away, but the image of the two of them was seared into my retinas.

"She's got a nerve, doing that in front of you." Charlotte was sitting across from me with a glass of wine in her hand. Her cheeks were flushed from the heat.

"They're friends. I don't care."

"I would."

I couldn't help but glance back over to them as she said that. They were talking, huddled together. William shook his head a few times, but Ava reached into the pocket of her shorts and pressed something into his hand. He looked down at whatever it was, then shoved it into his own pocket and kissed her on the cheek. I turned back to Charlotte, who was smiling, barely able to hide the schadenfreude in her eyes. A moment later, I felt William's warm hands on my shoulders, his strong thumbs digging into my tense muscles, his beer-tinged breath on my cheek as he leaned in and whispered that I should stay at his place tonight.

"Shall we go, then?" he asked, though his usual cheeriness seemed to have been replaced by a low, weary tone.

Hand in hand, we walked along the empty sidewalk to his apartment, a few blocks from the restaurant. The mild breeze had blown away the last of the heat, and though neither of us said a word, though our eyes didn't meet, the knowledge that something was about to happen hung like a deadweight between us. Behind us, the rest of the group all seemed to be deep in thought, spread out across the paving slabs. Adrian was smoking cigarette after cigarette and kept kicking the pebbles on the sidewalk. I had been trying to get him alone all evening so that we could talk, so I could ask what was bothering William, but he was avoiding me, and I saw something in his eye that I'd never noticed before.

Contempt.

Finn brought up the rear, pushing his bike in one hand and holding Milton's leash in the other.

With every step toward William's place, my heart started pounding harder and harder in my chest.

There was no sign of the cooler evening air in William's apartment, and a day's worth of heat hit us as he opened the door. He went from room to room, opening every window as wide as it would go, but it didn't make any difference. A barefoot Tess swirled into his living room and rummaged through his CD collection, eventually putting on something by Alicia Keys. She started dancing with her eyes closed in the middle of the floor, arms raised to the ceiling.

"Let's make cocktails!" said Ava. "Frozen berries and juice."

She dragged Finn off to the kitchen, and I heard them opening the fridge and freezer in search of ingredients. Behind them, Charlotte was hovering like an ominous shadow, looming over all of us with her sharp glances and harsh words.

Jacob.

Jacob was last to come in, and he hesitated for a moment before kicking off his shoes and making his way through to the living room. He sat down on the chair by William's desk and stared at me without saying a word.

He didn't need to say anything. His body language already told me everything I needed to know, and that was the moment when I made the decision that would change my life forever.

All I wanted was to talk to William one-on-one, but from the moment we got to his place, it was like he and Adrian had been drawn to each other, talking in low voices with their heads together. They filled the tub with cold water and dropped the beers into it, along with what little ice William had in the freezer, muttering short sentences without ever really looking at each other. Before long, they both disappeared into William's bedroom and closed the door behind them.

I slumped down onto a footstool by the coffee table, with my bag on the floor by my feet. And that's where I stayed, counting the seconds and minutes. Charlotte came into the room and leaned back against the bookshelves. She watched Tess dancing for a moment, then her eyes drifted down to me and over to Jacob. It was obvious she had started to put two and two together. I heard raised voices from the bedroom, and I got up and slowly moved closer, trying to make out what was being said. Right then, the door flew open, and Adrian came stomping out.

Charlotte hurried after him, and Tess turned up the music and disappeared into the kitchen. From his seat at the desk, Jacob was still staring at me.

And so I made my way into the bedroom and closed the door behind me.

William was on his bed. He had a glass of water in one hand, and in the other he was holding something that he shoved into the pocket of his jeans. I had never seen his tall, straight back so crooked before, his posture so deflated. And as I moved toward him over the rug, he lifted his chin and looked up at me with watery red eyes.

He drank most of the water in his glass and put it down on the nightstand before holding both hands out to me.

"Sophie."

His hands were shaking.

I took a step forward so that he could wrap his arms around my waist, and with his forehead against my stomach, he sighed and slowly stood up. His hands moved up my arms to the back of my neck, and he leaned in to kiss me on the lips before pulling me close and holding me to his chest.

"Let's get out of here," he mumbled into my hair. "Away from Gävle. Let's move someplace else and start over. I don't care about any of this anymore. It's over. All that matters is that we're together, that I've got you. Fuck, I love you more than anything else. I've been thinking about this all week, and I've told Adrian to give me my money back, but he . . ."

I pulled away from him and took a step back.

"Sophie?"

A numbing chill spread through me as I searched for something to say, but my mind was empty. Completely blank. I realized that I had started shaking my head. Words are just words; that was what Dad had shown me when he'd betrayed Mom. When he'd betrayed me. Our family. Actions speak louder than words, and promises could always be broken. William was standing in front of me, the hands that had just caressed my skin so gently now hanging in the air. Skin that other hands had touched, without his knowledge.

"What's wrong?" he asked.

"I can't, William. I'm sorry."

"Can't what?"

"Is there something going on between you and Ava?"

"Ava?" He studied me with a creased brow. "Why would there be anything going on between us?"

I tried to laugh, but I felt the tears spill down my cheeks.

"Stop it. I know you've been with her. I've seen you together. Those nights when you didn't come home . . . I know you were with her."

"Sophie, it's not—"

"Not what I think?"

He was quiet.

"So what is it, then? Tell me. I know you were there, even those times you said you were at Adrian's."

William sank down onto the edge of the mattress and ran his hands through his hair.

"I can't tell you, but you're wrong. You have to believe me."

"Then I can't do this anymore."

My fingers had swollen in the heat, and it took me a moment of tugging to get the diamond ring over my knuckle. It eventually came off and fell to the floor, and I bent down and combed the thick rug for it. When I found it and straightened back up, William was standing in front of me with his hands over his face.

"What are you doing?" he asked, slowly lowering them.

"It doesn't matter," I said, putting the ring down beside his glass. "This wouldn't have worked. You've lied to me and I've lied to you."

"What do you mean?"

"No one can promise to love someone forever. Sooner or later, someone always ends up getting hurt."

"Stop it, Sophie. Whatever this is, we can get through it."

"There's someone else."

I couldn't look him in the eye as I said it, but I heard him gasp.

"Who?"

"That isn't important. It doesn't mean anything, and it's over. I need to be on my own."

I turned away from him, but he grabbed my arm.

"Don't just walk away from this. We can talk about it tomorrow, without the others."

"So are you planning to tell me the truth about Ava?"

He didn't reply, and that told me all I needed to know. I reached up to my ears and took out the little silver snowflakes, then shoved them into one of his pockets.

"Maybe you were wrong," I said. "We're not so similar after all; this was impossible from the very start. I'm sorry, William. I'm just not meant to be with anyone. You'll be better off without me."

I left the room without looking back, pulling the door shut behind me. As I crossed the living room, I heard Jacob get up from his chair.

"Sophie? How'd it go?"

I couldn't bring myself to look at him either. The only right thing was to leave it all behind, so I started walking toward the front door and the freedom of the cool night outside, but Ava was in the hallway.

"Stop right there. Where are you going?"

"Home."

"I don't think so—not yet. You can stay at my place. I've got something to tell you, and it needs to be tonight."

Her gentle fingers gripped my wrist, making the blood surge through me, her words snaking through my consciousness. She pulled me back into the kitchen and pushed me down onto the chair behind the table. One part of me wanted to shout and scream until she let me go, but another wanted to make sure that William was okay after all. Just one last time before I left. I wanted to see him come out through the doorway and into the same room as Ava.

And so I stayed.

CHAPTER

29

Now

Five blank faces stare at me from around the room. For the past ten years, I've lived with a pleasantly selective memory full of black holes. Blurry gaps that emerged through hazy dreams from which I've woken, sweaty and confused, with a feeling of grief lingering in me. As though one part of me is still in the dream, even though my mind doesn't remember it. But the whole truth is now hanging over the room, and I've moved over to the sofas. Every image that surges through my head hits me like a blunt knife to the heart.

William with his arms around my waist and his mouth on my throat; William on the edge of the bed when I came into the room, head bowed and one hand gripping the sheets. The rush of happiness that made my body tingle when we went to the open house together; the unbearable pain in my chest when I saw him with Ava.

Again and again and again.

Ava is over by the bookshelf, and I see her shake her head dejectedly. Her eyes are wide—terrified, almost—and she is breathing heavily. I turn away, because I know what she's thinking. I know what they're all thinking right now. A sudden warmth spreads across my shoulders and down my arms, and I realize that Jacob has his hands on me. Now that I'm quiet, I feel them slowly move away and the heat fades. Finn is by the doorway to the kitchen, Adrian leaning against the wall by the hallway where the two paintings are hanging. Charlotte has taken a seat on the step again, and she pulls off her heels.

"These have been killing my feet all evening. I'm not used to wearing heels anymore," she mumbles, dropping them to the rug.

"*I* killed him," I whisper, though the words seem to echo between the walls and my head. "I'm the reason he's dead, right? That's what you're all thinking."

My vision is hazy, my eyes burning, and I want to scream that they're wrong. What would have happened if I'd managed to talk to Adrian? If I'd stayed with William?

"Stop," I hear Jacob say behind me. "You didn't kill him."

"All he wanted was for me to move away from Gävle with him, but I left him all alone. I made the wrong decision, and if I hadn't done that, then William would still be alive today."

"How could you have known?" Charlotte asks. "He could have said something to you."

I nod, though if anyone should have known what was coming, it was me.

"He didn't say anything about the money. He kept me on the outside. Why didn't he say anything?"

"I guess he wanted to protect you," says Finn, who has moved closer.

"But he lied to me. He disappeared pretty much every night, and he lied about where he was."

"He was with me," says Ava.

William and Ava, together in her apartment. William with Ava, Ava with William. I can't decide which feels worst.

"I know he was. I saw your texts, I saw you together. I could smell you on him when he got home."

Her sugary scent permeated his clothes so deeply that I used to dream about her when I finally managed to drift off to sleep. Ava in the glow of a flickering candle; Ava sprawled on the jetty by her fancy house, her bare feet in the dark water.

Ava, Ava, Ava.

"It's not what you—"

"Think? No. That's what William said too."

"He was with me because he was worried I'd hurt myself."

Her words make me tense. I shudder at the memory of Ava holding the shard of glass up to the light earlier, pressing her finger to the sharp edge. The journals documenting her suicide attempts.

"Why would you have hurt yourself?" Charlotte asks.

"Because I'd tried earlier, before I met any of you. And after."

No one speaks. We're probably all thinking the same thing: how close we had come to losing two friends, utterly preoccupied by our own problems.

"So he killed himself, then," Finn says drily. "Surely there's no doubt now?"

I slump down onto the sofa beside Tess and tip my head back against the cushions.

"No," says Ava. "I spoke to him at the restaurant. He didn't kill himself."

"But it would make sense," says Adrian. "No job, no money, dumped by the woman he wanted to marry."

"The earring," I say, reaching into my pocket and holding it up for everyone to see. "Where did you get this, Ava?"

"It was on the floor in the stairwell when I went out to meet the paramedics."

That can't be possible. The last thing I did was shove the earrings into his pocket. I hold my tongue and turn my head slowly. My hand is touching Tess's foot.

Tess's surprisingly cold foot.

I immediately leap up and grab one of her legs, start shaking it.

"What's wrong?" Charlotte asks, getting up from the step.

I work my way up her body until I reach Tess's face, but I quickly back away again with my hands to my mouth. One of her hands is resting above her head, the other hanging down to the carpet on the floor. Her face is still turned toward the backrest, but I can see lumps of vomit clinging to her pale cheeks beneath her glazed eyes.

"Tess," I pant. "Tess is dead."

Everything William did for her, all his efforts, only for her to die right in front of us just like he did. And yet again, I've just stood idly by. I feel myself sway.

"What? She can't be. Move."

Two hands shove me out of the way, and Charlotte moves over to the sofa. She gently lifts Tess's limp hand from the floor and presses two fingers to her wrist. Like so many times before, she leans over Tess, her red hair brushing her pale skin as she pats her cheek, stroking Tess's matted hair back from her face.

"Tess, can you hear me? It could just be low blood pressure—that can make the heart rate drop," she says, not taking her eyes off Tess.

Charlotte was always so good at this sort of thing. With a hair elastic around her wrist, ready to tie up her hair when the evening's drinks made a reappearance; with a bottle of water she'd had the foresight to pack. Seeing her standing in front of Tess now, I find myself hoping I'm wrong. Maybe all Tess needs is for Charlotte to fuss over her a little, and then she'll cough and sit up, feeling sorry for herself.

"We just need to help her up," Charlotte continues, and I hear her voice break. "Or lift her feet to get more blood to her head."

I feel my own blood drain from my cheeks as she speaks, leaving my face ice cold. Charlotte puts an ear to Tess's chest and then drops her hand, which thuds to the floor.

"What are you doing, Charlotte?"

Adrian is on the step, and I back away as he moves toward me.

"We have to do something! Mom was a nurse, she taught me what to do. If we can just—"

"It's the booze," he says. "She shouldn't have drunk so much. God knows what else she might have taken."

"What should we do?" I ask.

With two fingers beneath Tess's pointy chin, Charlotte turns her face toward us. The rest of us gasp in union when we see her wide eyes staring blankly ahead. The muscles in her jaw have started to stiffen, making her mouth gape open.

"Sophie's right," Charlotte mumbles with a sniff. "She's dead."

"Tess is dead?" The disbelief in Finn's voice cuts right through me.

Why did I leave her there on the sofa?

Tess is dead.

The words echo through me.

Charlotte is still standing by the sofa, and she lifts Tess's limp hand onto her stomach. Adrian is just in front of me, and I can hear Jacob's heavy breathing behind my back. At the top of the step, Finn is pacing back and forth, rubbing his forehead.

"We need to call an ambulance," I say. "We need to get her out of here, to the hospital."

"If she's already dead," Adrian says coldly, "then what difference does it make? There's no rush."

"But that's not up to us," I protest. "She needs to get out of here."

"Not yet."

Ava's voice is right behind me, and I spin around.

"What are you talking about? This isn't funny any-more—open the door."

"Not yet," she repeats without looking at me. "We can't just leave things like this. Not again."

"Leave it how?" Charlotte asks, turning her back to the sofa. She brushes her hands together, shakes them, as though she wants to get rid of any trace of dead skin.

"Our friend has died, even though we were all right here."

"Or because of it," I mutter, though I immediately regret it when I see the cold look Charlotte shoots me with her bloodshot eyes.

"Ava is right. We need to think this through," says Adrian. "Work out what we're going to say."

Charlotte slumps down onto the other end of the sofa and stares at her hands.

"That's not quite what I meant," says Ava.

"Jesus Christ, how are we supposed to explain a dead body on the sofa?" Charlotte blurts out.

"How much did she have to drink this evening?" Jacob has moved over to my side. "From what I saw, she didn't have anywhere near enough to cause something like this. It can't be the only reason."

"You know what she's like," Adrian snaps. "Once she starts, she can't stop. It was only a matter of time before something like this happened."

"She shouldn't have had anything at all," Charlotte agrees, looking down at Tess.

That's when it hits me, and my body reacts by sending my heart rate through the roof.

Don't say it.

"But it's not just alcohol, is it," I say.

Finn pauses by the balcony doors.

"What do you mean? She'd quit the drugs, hadn't she?"

"Tess had, yeah. But that doesn't mean someone else didn't have something."

"Who?"

I hesitate.

"Are you saying someone else had something, and she took it?" asks Adrian.

The look on Ava's face crushes me, and I know what she's thinking.

"I'm saying that someone gave her something," I explain, turning to the sofa where Charlotte is sitting uncomfortably.

"Charlotte?" Finn speaks up.

"Oh, come on," Charlotte snaps. "It was nothing, just something to calm her nerves. Thanks so much for sharing, Sophie."

"I thought you wanted me to be honest," I say. "That could be it. The pill combined with the alcohol."

"What did you give her?" asks Jacob.

"It was just a Valium—hardly the end of the world."

"And you thought that was a good idea, did you? After all that wine?"

"No worse than leaving her on her back on the sofa," Charlotte replies, fixing her eyes on me.

"And then there's her head," I add. "She hit her head when Adrian shoved her. Hit it really hard."

"I didn't shove her."

"We saw you do it," says Finn. "You practically threw her to the floor."

"She attacked me!"

"I can see why you would be scared, Adrian. How much does she weigh? About a hundred and ten pounds?" I say, reluctantly moving over to the sofa to turn Tess's face back toward the cushions; I don't want to have to look at her lifeless eyes.

Her skin feels cold as I put a palm on her chin and another on her forehead to gently push her head to the side. On the cushion beneath her, I notice a red stain.

"There's blood here," I mumble, reaching out to touch the mark. "I didn't see any blood when I helped her over earlier. I don't understand . . . I never would have left her if I'd known she—"

"So," Ava speaks up, cutting me off, "just to summarize: Charlotte gave Tess a controlled substance despite the fact that she'd been drinking, and Adrian threw her to the floor hard enough to give her a head injury. Does that sound about right?"

"She *fell*," says Adrian. "What do we do now? She can't stay here."

"Let's move her," says Charlotte. "To another room. And then we can call for an ambulance or the cops or whatever. We can say she got drunk and went to lie down, and by the time we found her it was too late."

"You can't be serious?"

I stare at her in shock. Is that all Tess was to her? A problem to be solved?

"It was an accident, Sophie. Or do you want to explain why you didn't help your friend as she choked on her own vomit a few yards away? Just like back then, when you ran away as William was killing himself. Do *any* of you feel like explaining to the cops why we're in this situation again?"

"Charlotte is right," says Adrian. "No one here wanted to hurt Tess."

I don't believe him. They've all been looking askance at her since they got here.

"If we tell the truth, it'll only cause problems for us."

"And you don't think they'll wonder either way?" I ask.

"What about her head?" Finn speaks up. "How do we explain that and the blood on the sofa?"

"She was drunk," says Charlotte. "They'll see that when they test her blood. We can say she fell earlier in the evening but that she wouldn't let anyone see her head."

"And you don't think that same blood test will show your pills in her blood?"

Charlotte glares back at him.

"We can tear off a few from the strip and put them in her pocket. Hang on."

Charlotte strides through to the dining room and lifts her handbag onto the table. She finds a hair elastic and gathers her long hair in a messy bun on top of her head before deftly tearing the blister pack of pills in two. Now that her thick hair is tied up, I can see that she has a tattoo on the back of her neck.

"This is serious, Charlotte. Do you realize what you're suggesting?"

"It has to be obvious that she's taken them."

She pops out a few of the pills into her makeup bag and drops the other half of the pack into her bag before coming back over and pausing with the now-empty blister pack in her hand.

"What would you suggest, Sophie? Do you want another investigation? To sit in an interview room again? Wasn't what we went through ten years ago enough? We're all equally guilty here, and that includes you."

I shake my head.

"No, this is your fault. Yours and Adrian's."

"Oh yeah?" She gives me a weak smile, looking down at my fingertips. The blood from Tess's hair has seeped in beneath one of my nails, forming a dark half-moon.

"I'm not doing it," I say, holding my hands up in the air. "I refuse to be a part of this."

"Finn!" Adrian shouts. "Come and help us."

They push past me to the sofa and grab Tess's limbs, lifting her up with a jolt.

"Where can we put her, Ava?"

Ava backs away without a sound, her lips pressed tightly together.

"Try the hallway," says Charlotte. "There must be a bedroom somewhere."

Adrian wraps his arms around Tess's upper body, and Finn grips her ankles. Her pale, lifeless hands trail on the floor. Charlotte saunters after them in her bare feet, telling Adrian which way to go.

Would their reaction be the same if it were her they were carrying?

If it were me?

From where she is leaning back against the wall, I notice Ava staring at me. If the truth really came out, if the others knew . . . I would never be able to control the inferno that unleashed.

"We need to get out of here," I whisper to Jacob.

His fingers graze mine, but I can't stop picturing another face on the body being bundled away.

"Just do as they say. We'll be out of here soon."

With my cheek to his chest, I let him wrap his arms around me and hold me close. His heart is pounding beneath my ear, so powerful and strong.

So warm and full of life.

CHAPTER

30

Now

THE PLATES HAVE been cleared from the dining table, and the candles have almost burned right down. Everyone is back in their seat—everyone but Tess—and I can't help but glance over to the empty chair beside me, at the red wine stains on the tablecloth where her glass was earlier. Outside, the snow is now coming down heavily. The basket of cell phones is in the middle of the table, but no one has even tried to reach it. Jacob's eyes are locked onto me from the other side, and I see his mouth forming words: "It's going to be okay."

But is it, really?

"Who's going to make the call?"

All heads turn toward the husky voice, toward Finn, who is slouched back in his chair. Silence settles over the room once more.

"I'll do it," says Adrian. Everyone looks up in tense anticipation, shoulders slumping in relief.

Despite his words, he doesn't move right away. He hesitates for a moment or two, then leans forward and rummages through the box of phones until he finds his black

Samsung. Exhaling deeply between his lips, he unlocks it and dials the short number, then listens to the bright voice on the other end of the line.

"Yes, hello. There's been an accident. My friend . . ." He hesitates and looks up, and Charlotte nods. "I think she's dead."

It's done now. No going back.

"No," Adrian continues. "We're in an apartment where my friends and I have been having dinner. We found her in a bedroom. Yes, alcohol. Maybe something else—she has a history of drug abuse. Yes, we've tried. No pulse, and her jaw has started to lock. She must've been dead almost an hour. Andra Magasinsgatan Five. I understand, thanks."

He ends the call and lowers his phone to the table, in the same place a plate of grilled saganaki stood only a few hours ago.

"They're sending an ambulance."

"So what do we tell them?" Charlotte asks, her red nails clawing at the tablecloth.

"Exactly what we agreed," Finn replies, earning a nod from Adrian. "She got drunk and fell over, then she went to lie down. By the time we found her in the bedroom, it was already too late."

"So we're going to lie, in other words?" I say. "Is that really what we want to do?"

"We don't have to lie," Adrian tells me. "We just don't have to give them the whole truth. If this comes out, I'm screwed. You know that, right? There'll be a trial. Involuntary manslaughter—maybe even voluntary manslaughter. I'd lose everything."

"I thought you said she fell," I mumble, trying to avoid his eye.

"I already have a police interview on Monday," Adrian continues, ignoring me. "Old sins. Money laundering. We've struck a deal in exchange for information about . . .

others. I'd really like to avoid adding a sudden death to the charges."

"What are you talking about?" I ask.

"Ten years of blackmail. A bad decision I've been paying for ever since. The money that was meant to fix everything disappeared with William, and keeping secrets is expensive. Really expensive."

The bruise on his collarbone.

He notices my eye and adjusts his collar.

"Why haven't you spoken to them before now?"

"Because I've always valued my mom's life above all else, and you don't want to know what they threatened to do to her. You don't want to know just how much detail they went into when they described how they'd mess up the face of the German model who was living with me. Emblyn," he mumbles, closing his eyes.

I swallow hard and look down at the table. So, this is why he has chosen a life of solitude. All that money, and he can't even enjoy it.

"She had no idea what was going on when I forced her out and told her we could never see each other again three months later. I managed to ship Mom off to Chile a few years ago—bought her a house in her sister's name—and I haven't seen her since. They gave me three years, Sophie. Three years to build something that could earn back the money I'd lost. And when that surpassed expectations, they decided they had bigger plans for me."

"*You* might not have anything to lose," Charlotte speaks up, looking at me. "You could go back to your little job at the radio tomorrow, and no one would care. But I'm *this* close to getting a foot in the door on TV."

She holds up her fingers to show just how close she is.

"Don't you already work in TV?"

"I'm in *makeup*. I'm a makeup artist and a stylist. I'm the one who makes sure everyone looks good before they walk out onto the show I want to host. But I have my contacts, and if I can just . . . This can't come out. It's as simple as that. What do you think will happen if someone hears I was mixed up in a death?"

"But you *are*. Two, if we're really being honest."

Charlotte's nostrils flare as she breathes in and out.

"It's not going to be a problem," Finn says quietly, not looking at anyone in particular. "What happened was a long series of unfortunate coincidences. No one deliberately hurt Tess. We loved her, didn't we?"

His words are followed by another uncomfortable silence.

"The main thing is that we all give the same version of events," Adrian clarifies.

He turns to look at me.

They all do.

"Fine," I say.

"Sure?"

"I'll stick to your story."

"If ever there was a good time to unlock the door, this is probably it, Ava," says Adrian.

Ava has been sitting quietly at one end of the table, but she lifts her head and nods up at the ceiling. A moment later, I hear the lock click out in the hallway. Everyone immediately gets to their feet. Everyone but Ava and me. Charlotte snatches up her handbag and tosses her phone into it before rummaging around in the pocket inside.

"Where's . . .? The rest of the pills, I put them back in my bag. Did someone take my pills?"

"Come on!" Finn shouts from the hallway.

She gives me one last look before walking away. A shiver passes down my spine as the others leave the room, one after another.

How did Ava give the sign to unlock the door?

How did the man outside know to open it right then?

With a sigh, Ava leans back in her chair and reaches up to loosen her hair. It tumbles down over her shoulders in soft waves. She then unclasps her wristwatch and shakes it off onto the table. Without the others around us, it almost feels like it used to: Ava and I alone at the table after dinner, with the candles burned out and the dark night outside. Nights I didn't want to end.

"Why did you invite us here tonight?" I ask her.

"The same reason you said yes. To force out everything that was never said. The truth about what really happened to William."

William.

What would have happened if William had never come between us?

What might have happened between Ava and me?

"And did it work?"

"Well, I know what happened to William," she says with a soft smile.

Ava sighs again and rubs her face, then looks down at her watch on the table and pushes her untouched coffee away. She is so pale and fragile that I just want to wrap my arms around her and hold her tight.

"Aren't you going to drink your coffee?"

"I'm saving it for later."

"The earring," I say. "You didn't find it in the stairwell, did you?"

I remember just how deep into William's pocket I reached that night. There's no way it could have fallen out when they wheeled him away on the gurney.

"Did you take it from him?"

She shakes her head and sighs for a third time.

"There's so much you don't see, Sophie. That you've never seen."

She's wrong, of course. I've seen far more than she realizes, I just haven't wanted to admit it to myself.

"Why don't you tell me, then?"

"Where are you sleeping tonight?" she asks me instead.

"I'll head back to the hotel."

"Don't do that. Stay here. I can make up the sofa for you."

She sees me recoil at the thought of the sofa where Tess's dead body was just lying.

"The other one," she clarifies.

The prospect of spending the night here makes my heart race. Just me and Ava, together again.

"I don't think that's a good idea."

"It's no problem."

"No, I'll go to the hotel."

"Okay, stay at your hotel, but don't walk back there. Promise me that. Call for a cab, and let me know once you arrive."

"Sure."

It's touching to see that she still cares despite everything we've been through. Despite the fact that I abandoned her.

"I guess we'll all leave here today with a heavy new burden to carry, rather than answers," I mumble, thinking about how I have spent the past ten years being tortured by the belief that I drove William to death. "How are we supposed to live with this lie?"

"We don't have to," Ava replies. "I told you, there's a lot you don't see."

She looks up and points to the corner of the ceiling.

"There's a camera right there. Do you see the little black circle? I've got two in the living room, one in the bathroom and another in the bedroom. There's one in the kitchen too. Above the island."

"What about the office?"

She smiles again, fingering her earlobe.

"You're wondering whether I'll be able to watch you finding the key under the chair and opening the drawer, aren't you? But the answer is no. Your secret is safe."

The blood drains from my cheeks. "I just wanted to know—"

"It doesn't matter. I just wish you'd locked it again once you were done."

"So you have a recording of everything that's happened this evening?"

"More or less. I didn't want to miss a single word."

In my head, I replay the evening from the very beginning. I see myself snooping in her bathroom cabinet, talking to Jacob, tucking Tess into her bed.

"What are you going to do with the footage?"

"Hello?"

A deep voice calls out from the hallway, and a man in dark glasses appears around the corner. He is wearing a black leather jacket and is carrying a bag in one hand. In the other, he is gripping a heavy key ring that jingles with every step.

"Oh, sorry. Am I too early? I thought everyone had gone."

Ava gets up and welcomes him with a hug.

"No, don't worry. This is Sophie, one of my best friends."

"Sophie, right. I've heard a lot about you."

"Is this your . . .?" I begin, hoping she will fill in the blank.

"Mattias works for my parents."

"I'll just put my things down," he says, heading off toward the bedroom.

"What does he do?" I ask once he is out of earshot.

"He's a nurse. He takes care of my medication and stays here with me at night."

"Because . . .?"

"Because that's the only way I could get my parents to agree not to lock me up somewhere. There have been times when I've . . . wandered at night."

"Wandered?"

"I suppose they're scared I'll fall from the balcony or walk out in front of a car."

"You sleepwalk?"

Ava smiles softly, but she doesn't speak.

"What about during the day?"

"During the day they keep an eye on me, as you might imagine," she says, gesturing up in the direction of the camera again.

"So this Mattias guy just sits here all night, watching over you?"

"I like having him here. He reads to me."

"So those books *are* yours? All the romance novels? I thought they must be your mom's."

Ava laughs. "Tess was right about literature. Sometimes we just need an escape from reality."

Tess, who will never curl up under a blanket with a dog-eared book again.

"How does it work during the day? Are you allowed to come and go as you like, or do they keep you locked up here the way we've been locked up this evening?"

"As Adrian pointed out, it's not exactly legal to keep someone locked up—not unless you run some sort of care facility. There's an electronic system that tracks everyone coming in and out. The minute I leave, they know about it."

"This is crazy, Ava."

"It's not as bad as being stuck on a secure ward. Believe me, it could be worse. It can always be worse."

The whole thing feels awful. I hear heavy footsteps approaching, and Mattias reappears with wild eyes, his black glasses now in his hand.

"Jesus Christ, Ava. Who is that in your bed? She's dead."

His face is deathly pale, his brow clammy.

"That's Tess, she—"

But before Ava has time to go on, we hear a knock at the door, and two paramedics come in with a gurney.

"There was an accident," Ava tells Mattias, turning to the paramedics to show them the way.

"I'm going to head off now," I say.

Ava catches my wrist and holds it in her slim fingers. "Are you sure? Can't you stay?"

"I'm sure. I need to go."

Her fingers tighten around my wrist, and I feel a sudden weariness in my arms and legs.

"It wasn't your fault," she whispers. "What happened to William. You know that, don't you?"

"I know," I reply with a weak smile, though my thoughts immediately turn to the row of photographs of him in my apartment. All carefully chosen to remind me of what I allowed to happen and to make sure it never happens again. I don't know what I want—never have—and that indecision has hurt so many people over the years.

"Don't be afraid to let someone love you," she continues.

I laugh and try to pull away, but she clings on.

"I mean it, Sophie. Don't punish yourself."

Her hand lets go, and I take a few steps back before turning around and walking toward the hallway on unsteady legs. Toward freedom. I want to look back, to stay and tell her just how incredibly lonely the past ten years have been.

But I keep walking.

"I'll have to call your parents," I hear Mattias say. "They need to know about this."

"Not yet," Ava begs him. "I saved you a little coffee; it was too hot. Help yourself—sit down. Wait until the paramedics are done. For me?"

I pause and watch as he reluctantly takes a seat at the dining table and sips from her cup. Ava looks up, and the knuckles on her hand turn white as she grips the back of his chair.

"Do you promise you'll take a cab straight back to the hotel?" she asks me.

I give her a half smile and leave the apartment.

CHAPTER

31

Now

THE ELEVATOR DOORS seem to take forever to open, and I can't get out of the claustrophobic mirrored box quickly enough. As I cross the polished floor and fumble to call for a cab, I can make out the shape of the ambulance on the street outside. The lobby felt so elegant earlier, but it now stirs up completely different emotions, and I feel the sense of panic rising inside me as I struggle with the heavy door. Finn, Adrian, Charlotte, and Jacob are huddled together by the wall of the building, and both Adrian and Charlotte are smoking. Charlotte shifts impatiently from foot to foot, now wearing a pair of lined boots, her heels in her hand. They beckon me over, but I stay where I am, with my arms hanging limply by my sides, snowflakes melting on the sliver of bare skin beneath my open coat.

A hand grabs my arm and gently pulls me away from the door, and I give in to it, though my eyes are still on the ambulance.

"Sophie."

"What?"

I turn my head and come face-to-face with Jacob. His eyes look anxious, and there are tiny snowflakes clinging to his stubble. A bruise has already begun to bloom on the bridge of his nose, where Finn's elbow hit him earlier. He leans down so that our faces are level, and all I can do is meet his eye.

"Are you okay?"

I just stare at him, blinking away the snow that lands on my eyelashes, then shake my head. I can't manage a single word. The street is deserted, the entire world muffled by a thin layer of snow. Jacob wraps his arms around me, and I sigh. I love that he smells so familiar despite the fact that it's been ten years since I was last this close to him.

"I wish there was something I could do," he whispers. "I wish you hadn't pulled away back then. Please don't do it again."

I step back, far enough to be able to meet his blue eyes, but just as I'm about to reply I hear a car pull up by the curb. Two doors slam, and I don't need to turn around to know that the police have arrived. That's what they do when someone reports a dead body.

"Adrian?" one of them asks, a man with short, fair hair.

The others are standing with their arms wrapped around themselves against the cold. Charlotte tugs at her green dress, trying to cover as much of her legs as she can. Finn has done up his black jacket and turned up the collar over his mouth and nose.

"Yes," Adrian replies, raising his hand and taking a drag on his cigarette, making the tip glow.

"We're here following a report of a sudden death. We'll need to speak to each of you separately."

"I understand," he says.

We all do. We've been through this before.

"Is this everyone who was present in the apartment?"

"Us three and those two over there."

The two officers glance over at Jacob and me. Jacob nods to them, and I start to raise my hand in greeting, only to let it drop to my side.

"And Ava, who is still up there. It's her apartment."

"We're going to need backup," the blond officer says into the radio clipped to his shoulder, nodding to his partner. "Andra Magasinsgatan. Yeah, my colleague here is going to ask you a few questions about the events leading up to the death, just to rule out foul play and to get an idea of what happened this evening. In the meantime, could you all take out your ID?"

He turns and heads inside, leaving the older officer to start talking to Adrian.

It feels like an eternity passes before I notice, from the corner of one eye, a movement in the bright lobby. The door opens, and the paramedics wheel the gurney back out. Everyone stands quietly, staring down at the eerily still body, wrapped in a couple of bobbled hospital blankets. I can't tear my eyes away. I can make out the shape of her hips and face, and can almost imagine a cloud of white breath rising up through the fabric covering her mouth.

Tess.

The paramedics pause, and the police officer with the furrowed face goes over to talk to them. Their voices are so low that I can't hear a word they're saying, so I move closer, but I still only catch fragments.

District medical officer. Too late in the day. Death certificate.

Before I know it, I'm standing right by the gurney, and I reach out to where I imagine Tess's cold hand must be.

"What are you doing?"

I flinch and pull my hand back, then look up at the paramedic by Tess's feet.

"I just wanted to . . . Where are you taking her?"

"To the hospital, so the medical examiner can do an autopsy and establish the cause of death. That's standard procedure following an unexplained death."

Unexplained death.

They grip the gurney and push it over to the back of the ambulance. Within the space of just a few seconds, they've managed to load it inside and close the doors, and then they get back into the front and pull away without any sirens. I suppose they don't need them; it's already too late for Tess.

My eyes drift up the side of the building, and I see a pale figure in the window on the top floor. Ava slowly raises a hand and presses it to the glass, then turns suddenly and disappears. There is no sign of Mattias.

"What's your name?"

The police officer is standing right in front of me, studying me closely. He has a strong chin and watery gray eyes.

"Sophie. Sophie Arène. I mean *Lind*. Sophie Lind."

I open my bag and take out my wallet and driver's license, and he jots down my name with his blotchy red fingers.

"Could you take me through what happened this evening?"

"Sophie is pretty shaken and exhausted." Jacob is by my side, and I feel his hand on the base of my spine. "We all are. Look, it's late, and we're all in shock. Could we come to the station to give our statements in the morning instead? You could talk to the others in the meantime. We were together all evening—they'll corroborate that."

Jacob holds out his driver's license, and the officer listens to him, but his eyes are on me the whole time. He peers back over his shoulder to the others, and I guess he is about as keen to be stuck out here in the cold as I am, because he jots down Jacob's details and closes his notepad.

"Sorry," he says. "We need to talk to everyone this evening. Separately."

He gives Jacob a knowing look, and Jacob glances at me before turning back to the officer.

"Well, surely I can stay with her, at the very least?"

Another police car has arrived, pulling up behind the first. When the passenger-side door opens, the officer with the gray eyes waves to his colleagues and then turns back to Jacob.

"You stay here," he tells him, guiding me a little farther down the sidewalk with a hand on my shoulder.

"Can't we do this inside, in the apartment?"

"No one can go in there while it's a possible crime scene."

His words hit me hard, like a dead weight in my gut.

"Are you going to talk to Ava this evening?" I ask.

"Ava?" He looks up from his notepad.

"It was her dinner party."

"My colleague is already up there. He'll talk to her."

I nod. "Good."

Behind me, Jacob is talking to a woman with short hair, but his eyes haven't left me for a second. The police officer's questions are short and to the point, but I barely remember any of my answers. Over by the door, I can hear Adrian laughing and shouting. He's drunk. Two of the other officers lean in to discuss something among themselves, then one of them tries to calm him down with a hand on his arm.

"This is probably as far as we're going to get this evening," says the gruff-faced officer in front of me. "You'll be called in for a more in-depth interview tomorrow."

Jacob is standing by the second police car, with his hands in his pockets, and I feel a wave of relief wash over me. As I approach, he comes toward me and puts an arm around my shoulders.

"How are you holding up?"

His arm presses against my back, pushing me forward, and we walk away from the others without saying goodbye.

Away from Ava. Why had William told her we were planning to leave Gävle? The first I'd heard of it was in his bedroom, right before everything fell apart, so why did Ava know before me?

And what about the earring?

"I know what happened to William."

I try to look back, but Jacob keeps pushing me, speeding up. He doesn't slow down until we've turned the corner, walking on with my hand in his. It's warm and dry, the same as ever.

"What are you doing?" I ask.

"Taking you home. The way I used to."

His eyes are fixed on a point at the end of the street, but then he turns to me with a crooked smile.

"I'm staying in a hotel," I say. "It's on the other side—"

He stops. "I'm not leaving you alone tonight, Sophie. Not this time."

He squeezes my hand, and I know he is afraid I'll disappear again the minute he lets go. He's probably right, and I'm glad he is keeping me here, stopping me from changing my mind. Our breath rises into the air between us in a billowing cloud.

"Okay."

We walk slowly, quietly, between the deserted warehouses, but I can't quite shake the feeling that I've left something unfinished behind. When I strain against his firm grip and turn my head to look back over my shoulder, I'm convinced that all the unanswered questions are slinking somewhere behind us in the soft snow.

But the street is deserted.

CHAPTER

32

Now

HAND IN HAND, we walk along Andra Magasinsgatan, which is glowing white in the light of the streetlamps. When we reach the old fire station with its arched doorways, we cross the street and make our way down into the tunnel beneath the railway tracks, a route I never would have taken if I were alone. We continue along Drottninggatan, and I can make out groups of people wearing far too little up ahead, glowing cigarettes in their hands, standing by the brightly lit entrances of bars. The music from a balcony reverberates through me, pounding in time with my racing heart. I turn around and think I catch a glimpse of a pale figure outside Central Station. Someone standing at a distance, alone.

Watching.

"Maybe we should go back," I say, breaking the silence.

"Go back?"

The moment when Charlotte started desperately searching her bag for the remaining pills has etched itself into my memory, Ava slowly looking up from the table and meeting my eye. Too much remains unsaid.

"Maybe it would have been better to tell the police more. They should know what I found in Ava's office."

I'm no longer sure I'm doing the right thing. As ever, I'm convinced that it is my destiny to make the wrong decision at every crucial moment.

"They were there because of Tess, Sophie. They wouldn't have listened if you'd started bringing up our old problems."

"If it had a bearing on what happened this evening, they would."

He doesn't speak, nor does he slow down.

"We should have tried, at the very least," I continue. "We know so much more now than we did ten years ago."

"Do we? Really?"

Jacob stops walking and looks straight at me. He seems exhausted.

"Didn't we already know that Adrian would do anything for money? That Finn could never let an injustice go; and that Charlotte had set her heart on someone she would never be with? Is it really a surprise to you that Tess is impulsive, that she seizes an opportunity whenever it suits her?"

It hurts to hear him say Tess's name.

Jacob starts walking again, striding along the pavement.

"Ava could easily have had something to do with his death. Have you ever considered that? You'll get a chance to talk to them tomorrow. I can give you a ride to the station, if you want. All that matters now is getting away from there, and that this isn't just a repeat of what happened ten years ago."

He stops suddenly and turns to me.

"Please tell me this isn't going to end the same way it did then."

His chest is heaving, his hand still gripping mine. I squeeze it, and he squeezes it back. We're at the crossing with Hattmakargatan, my hotel just a short walk down to the left. I could pull away from him, thank him for keeping me company, and lock myself in my room.

"No," I say. He blinks, and I smile. For the first time in my life, I feel sure about something. "It's not going to end the same way, I swear."

Jacob turns right, and we follow the street north. We cut across Nygatan and pass Roma Pizzeria before he comes to a halt outside number thirteen. It isn't the same door I remember from our nightly walks to his dad's apartment, but it does feel welcoming. Like I was destined to end up here this evening. Like I was always meant to end up here, and if I'd just played by the rules, then none of the things that shaped my life would ever have happened.

We stand side by side, as though we're both afraid of losing the sliver of physical contact between us. Jacob puts an arm around my shoulders and tips his head toward mine.

The longing for strong arms and warm skin is unbearable with him by my side. He slowly turns his head and looks at me through half-closed eyes. Eyes that are studying me the same way they have so many times before. Over the table at the restaurant, behind my back on the way to William's. Eyes I couldn't bear to see before the church doors closed behind me as we buried William and everything we'd had.

"Are you coming in?"

I gaze upward, taking in the facade and the dark windows. I miss Alex's warm smile from the other side of the counter at Kwang Garden, the greasy duck and peanut sauce. I miss Malika and the magnolia scent of her perfume. I wonder what Luna is up to and whether the mountain of biscuits I left in her bowl will be enough to last the weekend. I know I should turn around and head back to the hotel. Curl up under the duvet in my hot room and shut out the world.

But instead I nod, because this is all I've ever wanted.

A second chance to put things right.

Jacob leads me over to the doorway, where he starts searching his pockets for his keys, his face rosy from the cold air. I hear something behind me. A soft muffled sound, like footsteps in the snow. When I turn around, I see a shadow flutter past at the corner of one eye, but the street is empty. As empty as all the other streets I've left behind me over the years, but I can't quite shake the feeling that something is going to ruin everything that's finally within reach. I squint down at the snow in search of footprints, but ours are the only ones there. Over by the corner of the building on the other side of the street, something catches my attention.

"Are you coming?"

Jacob is already halfway inside. With my hands in my pockets, I try to ignore the feeling of being followed, brushing the snow from my shoulders and hair before following him in. He starts slowly making his way up the stairs, with one hand on the railing, and I hover by the door until I hear the lock click; then I set off after him.

Two floors up, Jacob pauses by the first of three doors and pushes his key into the lock. The door swings open with a soft creak.

"Is the door to the street always locked?"

He hesitates for a moment before replying, reaching inside to flick the switch on the wall. Light fills the narrow hallway.

"Yeah, why?"

I take a step away from the stairs, toward Jacob.

"I thought I heard something."

"I can't hear anything," he says, peeling off his jacket and hanging it on a hook.

There is a large black rug on the floor in the hallway, a full-length mirror with a black frame on one wall. Standing in the doorway, I meet my own dark eyes behind my glasses.

"It was probably nothing."

"Come in. You look like you're frozen solid. We could probably both do with a hot drink after that walk; I'll boil some water."

"Anything other than red wine."

I unbutton my coat before I have time to change my mind, then step forward into the hallway. Jacob closes the door after me. Conscious of his movements behind my back, I bend over and tug down the zips, kicking off my sweaty boots at long last.

Jacob disappears down the hallway, and I slowly make my way after him with my bag on my shoulder. I linger in front of the tall bookshelves covering one wall, trailing a hand over the creased spines and glossy dust jackets. One of the shelves has been given over to his collection of whisky, rum, and gin, and beside the bottles beneath the bright spotlight, there are a couple of heavy-bottomed glasses. My fingers brush the rough label on one of the bottles: Diplomático. I grab it and turn around to take in the living room. There is a pale three-seater sofa with a chaise longue section, and a round coffee table with a stone top. On the walls, I can see two large black and white photographs of misty mountaintops.

No dirty shirts on the floor, no indentation on the sofa from a middle-aged man who spends his days watching TV.

"Do you want honey?" he shouts through from the kitchen.

I pause in the doorway, my eyes scanning the kitchen table. It's so different from the one we used to play cards at with his father.

"Your dad . . ." I say.

It takes my eyes a moment to adjust to the room, where the only light is from the streetlamp outside and the bulb above the stove. He has a stainless steel bread bin on the counter, a pestle and mortar, and a box of herbs. At the other end of the room, there is a small dining table with two chairs.

"Died four years ago. Spent the last few years in a care home."

Four years. Wasn't that when Jacob said he had given up his job to travel the world?

"Could we have a little rum in it? Like we used to."

Jacob looks down at the bottle in my hand and then takes it from me with an amused smile. I move over to the window and peer down at the street below. From where I'm standing, I have a clear view of our footsteps, a neat trail leading from the street corner to the doorway, mine doing a small pirouette where I turned around. But my eyes are drawn to the footsteps from the other direction. Footsteps that weren't there when we came inside. They start over by the corner of the brown building on the other side of the street.

Jacob puts a hand on my shoulder, making me jump and yelp.

"Sorry," he whispers, laughing as he kisses the back of my neck. "I didn't mean to scare you. Why are you so tense?"

I feel him wrap his arms around my waist, but I can't tear my eyes away from the street.

"I saw someone," I say.

He immediately lets go of me and moves over to the window to look out.

"Where?"

"By the corner. And by the door."

"It could be the newspaper delivery guy. I guess it's closer to morning than night. Can you keep an eye on the water? I should have peed before we left Ava's place."

He kisses me on the cheek and then peels away from me, to leave the room. With my back to the window, I turn my attention to the stove, where the pot of water is illuminated by the light on the extractor fan. Jacob has set out two large cups on the counter, plus a bottle of honey in the shape of a bear, beside the bottle of rum.

I smile when I notice that, because it's the exact same honey his father used to have in the kitchen. The pot of water is nowhere near boiling, so I leave that and slowly make my way through the living room, taking in the person Jacob has become. The window sills are bare, the windows themselves hidden behind thin privacy curtains. On either side of those, there are heavy blackout curtains made from pale gray velvet. At the far end of the room, beside the sofa, there are a couple of large green plants, and I rub one of the leaves between my fingers to check whether they are real. They are, of course. I remember Jacob growing chilies and peppers in the kitchen window, but I couldn't even manage to keep my ZZ plant alive.

His bedroom door is open, and I can't resist having a look inside once I've dumped my bag on the sofa. The floor is carpeted in here, the large bed neatly made. I run a hand over the bedspread and feel butterflies at the thought of what could happen here this evening if only I'd let it. One of Jacob's tops has been draped over the back of a chair, and I pick it up and smell it, put it down on the low chest of drawers, and turn on the little lamp. After casting a quick glance back at the door, I open the top drawer and smile at his folded white boxers and balled-up socks.

Everything is different, but it's as though nothing has changed. As though we've picked up right where we left off, and I can't get enough of all the memories that brings back, no matter how much they hurt. I slowly open the second drawer and frown. I had expected to see neat rows of T-shirts and sweaters, but what I find is something else entirely. The drawer is practically empty, containing nothing but a few books from Jacob's student days and a messy pile of photographs. Photographs that are all too familiar: from Ava's jetty, William's cottage, Charlotte's kitchen.

I also find a box.

A black velvet box, just big enough to hold a ring. The kind of box you'd have in your hand when you dropped to your knees to propose to the woman you love.

I slump down onto the foot of the bed and press a hand to my mouth. I must have hurt him so much more than I ever imagined. Jacob had believed in me. He had taken my silence to mean that I was going to leave William for him, that we had a future together. And then I'd dumped him when he needed me most.

I reach for the box and cup it in my hands, remember how I felt when William held out a similar box to me. The happiness, the excitement.

The lid flips open with a click, and my blood runs cold. Without thinking, I reach up to touch my earlobe, rubbing it as my other thumb strokes the tiny glittering snowflake in the box.

A snowflake that is bent out of shape after being used to turn the lock on a bathroom door.

CHAPTER

33

William's death

William spent a long time sitting on the edge of the bed with the ring in his hand. He turned it over and watched as the soft light from the window bounced off the polished diamond. The pain in Sophie's eyes had been so clear, and he had shared it. He knew it was his fault she had turned away from him. He hadn't been present, hadn't looked at her the same way he used to. He had neglected her and what they had, and she deserved better.

But he could be better. She didn't need someone else.

He put the ring down on his bedside table, tucking it behind the pen so that he wouldn't accidentally knock it to the floor and lose it. It would be back on her finger before long—he was sure of it. This wasn't the first time they had argued, that she had threatened to leave him. The first time had been over something as stupid as where they should live. Sophie had wanted William to move in with her, but William had thought it was better for them to keep separate apartments. She hadn't spoken to him for a week after that.

The second time had been because he had thrown himself into his new job. William knew that was one of his biggest weaknesses: the desire to make everyone happy. He hadn't hesitated to take on new projects despite the fact that he was already snowed under. He had started going to the office earlier and earlier, staying long after the others went home. That had meant it was always late by the time he got to Sophie's apartment and reheated the plate of food she had saved for him. She was often asleep when he arrived, sometimes didn't even notice he was there. Frequently, she was clutching her phone too, and he imagined her repeatedly checking the time and wondering when he might turn up.

No, he hadn't been the world's best fiancé, and now he was on the verge of paying the price for that.

All the pressure he had been under lately was starting to take its toll. He was sleeping badly, felt the anxiety in his chest almost all day long. Right there and then, it didn't matter how much money he had lost. Nothing else mattered if he didn't have Sophie in his life.

He hesitated for a moment, then reached into his pocket and took out the pill Ava had given him. He didn't like taking them, didn't like the way they made him feel. Numb, hazy. But he needed that this evening: to forget everything for a while, to make his brain stop whirring.

To be able to think clearly in the morning.

William paper-clipped a label to the folder Ava had given him when they got back to his apartment. He wrote a few quick lines and put it down on the nightstand, then got up and left the room, closing the door behind him. Given the loud music, he had expected to find the others in the living room, but Tess was the only one sprawled on the sofa, Jacob doing something on his phone at the desk in the corner. There was a cool breeze blowing in through the French doors.

William noticed movement in the doorway to the kitchen and felt a sudden urge to be with the others. He hoped Sophie hadn't left yet. He wouldn't push her this evening; he would leave her to calm down. But he would make sure she knew he was there.

That he would always be there for her.

* * *

William left the living room and made his way out into the narrow hallway. Before he joined the others in the kitchen, he needed to use the bathroom. Not just to ease the pressure on his bladder after an hour of heavy conversation, but to calm his nerves.

He closed the door behind him, turned on the light, and met his own bloodshot eyes in the mirror. William chuckled to himself and lowered his head to splash cold water onto his flushed cheeks. When he looked up again, Jacob was standing right behind him. He gasped and ran his damp hands through his hair, pulling it back from his forehead.

"Shit, man, you scared me. Where'd you come from?"

"Sorry. I saw you come out of the bedroom. You were in there so long; I've been waiting for you."

"Yeah, I had a thing or two that needed sorting out."

William dried his hands and face, hung the towel back on the hook, and turned around.

"Did you need something?"

Jacob backed away and leaned against the wall. "You spoke to Sophie."

William furrowed his brow, and his mind started racing again. "Yeah . . ."

"What did she say?"

"I mean . . . that's between us, don't you think?"

Jacob studied him for a moment. "It depends on what she said."

William felt something in the pit of his stomach, something cold and heavy that kept getting bigger, making him reach back to support himself against the sink behind him.

"What are you trying to say?" he asked. He was starting to feel light-headed and hot, and it was getting increasingly difficult to focus on Jacob's cold eyes.

"She wasn't wearing her ring when she came out."

The pill had started to take effect, and his legs were like jelly. William dropped down onto the toilet lid and shook his head with his hands to his cheeks.

"Don't say it . . ." he begged Jacob, closing his eyes.

"Sophie always struggles to make big decisions. Sometimes she just needs a nudge in the right direction."

"You?" William asked, his face twisted into a pained grimace. "Are you the one she's been seeing?"

Jacob just stood there with a stony expression.

"She's moved on," he said after a moment.

William stood up, shook his head.

"No. You're wrong. She's been feeling lost, and I haven't been there for her, but that's going to change. I'll show her. I've done it before. This isn't the end. I'm going to talk to her. She'll understand once I tell her the truth. I should've done that from the very start."

"It doesn't matter anymore, William."

"I'm going to take her away from here, Jacob."

"What do you mean?"

"We're moving. I've got it all planned out. We're leaving as soon as we can."

"Hang on, you don't understand . . . Sophie can't leave Gävle."

William attempted to reach the door, but Jacob grabbed his arm and pulled him back, making him fall down onto the toilet again. The back of his head hit the towel rail, and he groaned and slumped forward. With his head between his legs, he reached up and pressed a hand to the back of his skull.

"What the . . . What're you doing?"

"I didn't mean to, I just wanted to stop you from leaving. I—"

William jumped up again, unsteady on his feet. Jacob pushed him farther away from the door.

"Just hold on a second . . ." Jacob pleaded with him. "I need to explain."

"Let me out. I want to talk to Sophie."

"Calm down, William. Why don't you and I talk first?"

William tried to push past Jacob, but his weak arms had little effect. Instead, Jacob shoved him, and he staggered back against the bathtub and stumbled over the edge. The water came up to his waist. The ice had long since melted, but there were two lukewarm bottles of beer bobbing beside him, clinking against the enamel.

"Leave her be," Jacob said quietly. "What she and I have . . ."

"Why would I do that? We're *engaged*. I love her and I'm going to tell her just how much I love her as soon as I get out of here."

Jacob's hands hit him square in the chest, pushing him under the surface. William kicked and lashed out, but he felt the hands holding him down against the bottom of the tub. The pressure began to build in his chest, his lungs crying out for oxygen. He tried desperately to pull himself up with his weak arms, to hit Jacob's head, but he didn't have the energy and couldn't reach anything but thin air.

After one last glance at the wall, which looked blurry and warped through the water, he closed his eyes and thought about Sophie. He thought about Sophie the first time he saw her at the front of the classroom, red blotches all over her throat, and he thought about her the first time she lay in his arms, with her dark hair fanned out across his skin.

He thought about the day when he realized he didn't want to live his life without her. How bright the sun had been, how strong all the scents had seemed.

He thought about the way Sophie's eyes narrowed whenever she smiled that warm smile of hers, and then he gave in to the water, which flooded into his throat and lungs.

CHAPTER

34

Now

"SOPHIE?"

The little velvet box practically jumps out of my hands as I close the lid and throw it back into the drawer. I push the drawer shut as quickly as I can, and the screech it makes feels so loud that I'm convinced the people across the street must have heard it stick. Jacob leaves the kitchen, and I leap up and rush past the doorway to the other end of the room, looking around in panic for something that can save me.

His footsteps draw closer, pausing just outside the bedroom. I can hear him breathing behind me as I stare down at the little desk to the right of the bed, and at the very last second, I pick up one of the framed photographs and turn around.

"Where did you take this?"

Jacob looks down at my hands and then glances over to the chest of drawers before moving closer and taking the frame from me. His mouth curls into a soft smile, and he brushes the glass as though he were wiping off some invisible flecks of dust. Without the frame to grip, my hand starts shaking, and I hide it behind my back.

"Can't you tell?" he asks.

For a split second, I forget what I just found in his drawer and study the photograph I've barely even looked at. The image is a close-up of water. A shimmering expanse, bursting with light where the sun hits the surface. In the foreground, a heavy branch is hanging down toward the water, and I can make out something that doesn't quite seem to fit with the rest of the scene in the background. Dark blue, sharp edges, at odds with the lush greenery.

"Is that . . .?"

Jacob nods without looking up at me.

"The bench is right here," he says, pointing to an area out of shot. "And here . . ."

His finger lands on the blue shape.

"The concert hall," I say.

We spent hours on that bench the night we didn't go home. That bench was where I shared thoughts and feelings that now make me blush. And then I listened to him tell me about his mother, who had left when he was a child; about his father's dementia, which had come creeping up on him with angry outbursts. Jacob moves over to the desk and sets the frame back down, and I find myself wondering what the other images are of.

But before I have time to look, he interrupts my thoughts.

"You forgot the water. The tea's steeping now."

"You know how it is, a watched pot and all that."

It sounds unconvincing, even to me.

Jacob walks back over to the doorway, and I follow him. Just before he reaches it, he pauses, his head swiveling. He stands still for what feels like a long time, then picks up the top I left on the chest of drawers. He quickly tosses it back onto the chair where I found it earlier and then heads through to the living room.

I can barely move, but I force myself to keep going. One step at a time. This is Jacob, I tell myself.

And he has your earring, the voice in my head reminds me.

He has dimmed the lights and lit two candles in smoky-gray handblown holders on the coffee table.

"I know what happened to William."

Ava's words echo through me.

"I think I should call Ava," I say.

"Ava?"

"Just to make sure she's okay. She seemed pretty shaken up when I left. Maybe I should have stayed there tonight."

Jacob studies me for a moment and then nods. "Yeah, maybe it would be good to give her a call, just to let her know you're thinking of her. Sit down."

I reluctantly take a seat on the sofa, my hand shaking as I rummage through my bag for my cell phone. With eager fingers, I bring up Ava's number and listen to it ring and ring. When I look up, I'm surprised to see that Jacob is now on the sofa too, between me and the hallway. What am I going to say if she answers while he's sitting right beside me?

The signal blares in my ear, over and over again.

But she doesn't pick up, and then her voicemail kicks in.

"No answer," I say with a breezy smile.

"I'm sure she's fine. Ava is strong. She can handle more than you think."

He stretches an arm along the backrest, tips his head to one side, and smiles. I clutch my phone, closing apps and swiping through the home screen, wondering whether I should call her again. Leave a message.

"I can't believe you're actually here," he says. "With me."

"Yeah, who would've thought it?" I mumble.

"I've never stopped hoping, Sophie. Never."

I stop swiping, and after one last tap of the screen, I put the phone down beside my bag and meet his eye.

"Jacob," I begin, already regretting what I'm about to say next, "there's something I need to ask you. Something I've been thinking about for the past ten years, and which only raises more questions after this evening. The reason I'm here now."

His smile fades slightly, and he straightens up. "Okay, shoot."

"Where did you go that evening?"

His silence is like a ton weight, and he lifts his arm from the sofa and rubs his neck.

"Where did I go?"

"When I went in to talk to William, you were at the desk in the corner, and when I came out, I saw that you were still there."

"Yes, so?"

"But when I left the kitchen"—my heart is pounding so hard that I can't hear anything else—"I bumped into Adrian in the hallway; he was on his way out for a cigarette. And Tess was the only one in the living room. Why did you leave?"

"Why would I have stayed?"

My cheeks grow hot. We're arguing the way we used to, throwing words back and forth between us. Tiptoeing around the thing neither of us dares actually say out loud. Me begging and pleading for him to move his dad into a care home so that he could live his own life; him accusing me of being shut off from my emotions.

"Did you speak to William that evening?" I spit out.

Jacob studies my face in silence, then turns away and looks at something behind my back. After a moment, he leans forward with his elbows on his thighs.

"Sophie," he says, his voice soft, "what were you doing in my bedroom before I came in?"

"I was having a look around, I . . ."

He sighs and leans back again, with his hands to his face. We both know what that means.

"I loved William," he says through his fingers, and the tears make my eyes burn. "He made me see that life was still worth living, forced me to challenge myself and my vision of how the rest of my life might look. But you can't open the door to the world and then close it again. He would never have let you go, Sophie. Never . . ."

He sighs again and tucks a lock of hair behind my ear.

"You were the first person I ever let in. The only one who I brought back to the apartment, to Dad. I'd forgotten how it felt to share the burden with someone else, to let my guard down and be myself. If I'd known how it was going to end, I would have done things differently. But you meant everything to me. You were the reason I got out of bed in the morning. So the idea that you would . . ." He turns away. "I had to talk to him."

"When did you talk to him, Jacob? What happened?"

He looks me straight in the eye and shakes his head.

"Right after you left him in the bedroom. I just wanted to talk. He didn't lock the bathroom door, and I . . ."

He trails off, and the sad smile on his lips makes me feel sick.

"Why are you asking me about this, Sophie? Surely I don't need to tell you any of this?"

I grit my teeth and force myself to hold his eye.

"You already knew, didn't you? You've known all along, haven't you?" he says in a whisper. "That's why you left Gävle."

I get up from the sofa and move over to the window. I can no longer bear to look at him because what he is saying is true.

I've always been convinced it was Jacob who killed William.

CHAPTER

35

Now

WITH MY ARMS wrapped around myself, I look down at the street and the untouched snow now covering all trace of the evening. Ava isn't going to come and stop me. She has probably already taken her medication and curled up in bed, with Mattias in his armchair. He'll be reading aloud to her, stories about broken hearts being mended. Stories that make her forget everything she lost.

No one is coming. It's just me. Me and Jacob.

Exactly how I want it.

"Am I right?" he asks my tense back, and I stretch my weary neck before slowly turning around.

"I didn't want to believe it," I say. "I spent a week lying awake at night, going over and over everything, trying to square the image I had with something else. Adrian leaving the bedroom, Tess on the sofa. But I just couldn't ignore it. I was sitting in the corner of the kitchen that evening. All I could see was the hallway."

My throat tightens at the memory of the heat in the apartment, the clinking of glasses as Finn and Ava made cocktails echoing through me, the shape of Jacob coming out of the bathroom and crossing the hallway before opening the door and disappearing into the night. Just before he left, as he passed the doorway into the kitchen, I saw him shove something into the pocket of his jeans. The skin on his arms was glistening with what I assumed must be sweat, and there were dark patches on his chest.

Splashes of water.

I got up and followed Charlotte into the living room only a few minutes later, watched as she searched for William and knew with every fiber of my being that it was already over.

It was really over.

"That's why I came this evening. I was hoping I'd missed something, that there was another explanation."

"So what happens now?" he asks.

Ten years ago, I sat with a cup of cold, tasteless coffee in my hands, sweating under the pressure of the police officers' questions at the station. I was surprised by just how naturally the lies came out, right up until their last question.

"Did you see anything unusual around the time of William's death? Anyone in the vicinity of the bathroom?"

You've got a terrible poker face, that was what Jacob always used to tell me when I lost at cards. Well, if only he knew.

"Now we talk," I say.

I glance down at my bag and phone and then leave him on the sofa to go through to the kitchen. The steam is still rising from the two mugs on the bench, each with its own tea strainer, the scent of chocolate and cinnamon. My hands are shaking slightly. Maybe it's the winter chill, or maybe it's something else.

He killed William.

He really did kill William.

Instinct tells me to grab my bag and run, but I carefully shake the water from the two strainers instead, carry them over to the sink, add a good squeeze of honey, and lace both mugs with a swig of rum, focusing as much as my confused mind will allow. Things clatter against the worktop. All I want is for this evening to be over, but I take my time, making sure everything is right.

"What are you doing in there?" Jacob shouts from the living room. "Do you need any help?"

"No, no. Stay there—I'm coming."

With a mug in each hand, I go back through to join him, and take a seat on the sofa. He crinkles his nose as I hand him his tea.

"Jesus, how much rum did you put in here?" he asks.

"It's your favorite."

He takes a sip, a couple of deep mouthfuls, and I lean back, nursing my own mug. We sit quietly, doing nothing but drinking. For five minutes, ten. The hot liquid burns on the way down, loosening my tense muscles. At the other end of the sofa, I see Jacob slump slightly.

"Will you come with me to the station tomorrow, like you promised?" I ask him.

He slurps down more tea instead of answering.

"Will you tell them the truth?" I ask.

"About what?"

"About what happened to William."

He laughs and lowers his mug to the coffee table.

"Come on, don't be stupid."

"If you won't, I will."

"And say what, Sophie?"

"I've got the earring you must have used to lock the toilet door from the outside. The earring I put in William's pocket less than half an hour before he died."

"A crooked old earring doesn't prove anything."

"At least let me know what happened to him."

Jacob's hand shakes as he reaches for his tea and drinks the last few mouthfuls.

"Stop it now, Sophie."

"Just let me hear that it wasn't me that drove him to it. You owe me that much after all these years."

My voice breaks, and I see the muscles in his jaw twitching. Jacob hesitates, considers his words.

"He was so sure of you," he says with a laugh, his eyes welling up. "So sure he knew exactly where he had you and that he would never lose you. And I believed him. I knew he was right. I'd spent all evening telling myself that you were the answer to everything I'd been looking for, but once I got into the bathroom with William, I realized he was right. I was wrong."

"So you killed him?"

His eyes darken.

"It wasn't like that. He was going to come and find you, make you change your mind. He just would've had to put an arm around you and flash that brilliant smile of his, with that damn dimple in his chin, and you would've forgotten everything you said to me. So I held him back, just to make him stay. He hit his head on the towel rail. I didn't mean for it to happen."

Jacob looks up at a spot on the ceiling, and I can see that his eyes are losing their focus.

"What happened after he hit his head?"

"Huh?"

His head tilts as he turns to look at me. He blinks firmly a few times and rubs his forehead.

"He just wouldn't stop, but he was dizzy. I shoved him again, not hard at all, and he fell over the edge of the bath."

He reaches for the neck of his top and tugs at it, his face suddenly pale and clammy.

"Because he'd hit his head? Or because of the drugs in his system?"

"He wouldn't have given in, Sophie. I knew he wouldn't give in. I just wanted to keep him there, to make him stay. Stop. But the water . . . He . . ."

Jacob's breathing is heavy, and his eyelids droop.

"What did you do, Jacob?"

"I . . . I held him under the water. I just wanted to keep him there."

I'd already worked this out, have thought about it every day for ten years, and yet his words break my heart, and I have to take a deep breath. Fighting for air, just like William must have done in those final moments of his life.

"And the earrings? How did you know where they were? Why did you take them?"

Jacob takes a deep breath of his own and shakes his head.

"I didn't. I just thought it wouldn't be so surprising if he'd taken his own life; he'd been so stressed lately. But that meant the door had to be locked. I couldn't find anything to use in the bathroom cabinet, so I tried his pockets. I must have dropped one of them, and the other . . . It was the only thing I had left of you."

"Thank you, Jacob," I whisper, moving my phone to the table.

He looks down at it for what feels like a long time, at the bright screen and the timer counting the seconds in the voice memo app.

"You know I'm not going to stay here, don't you?" he slurs, pulling back from me with a look of disgust on his face. "I've spent years on the move, traveling wherever . . . my job has taken me. There's nothing keeping me here. I can be gone within a day. I could take your phone and delete that recording right now, no problem."

His hand shoots out and knocks his cup over. My eyes sting as I reach up and stroke his cheek. I feel an ache in my chest as he angrily pulls back from me, and my mouth curls into a sad smile at the thought of just how wrong he is.

"I know," I say, though my voice barely holds. "You and I have always been alike in that sense. We run whenever things get too hard, don't we? Either by putting up a facade or by disappearing. That's why I'm not going to let you run this time, the way I did back then."

I reach behind me and pull Charlotte's pills from my back pocket, then set them down on the table beside my phone. He stares down at the empty pockets in the blister pack and attempts to get up, but his legs give way and he slumps to the floor. His eyes dart from me to the mug.

"How many have you given me?"

"I'm not sure. Enough. Though it might have been a few too many—I was in a hurry."

He starts crawling toward the front door on all fours, moving jerkily, his dark jeans collecting dust. After a moment or two, he stops and collapses onto his stomach. With one last burst of effort, he manages to roll over onto his side, his breathing now shallow, one palm on the floor. I slowly get up from the sofa, hang my bag over my shoulder and drop my phone into my pocket. When I reach his side, I crouch down and toy with the thought of just leaving him here. Opening the door and walking away without calling for help. Would I be able to live with myself?

He'd managed it.

Would it dull my guilty conscience?

I hook my fingers beneath his chin and lift his head so that our eyes meet.

"Bye, Jacob. I'm sorry."

CHAPTER

36

Now

DELICATE SNOWFLAKES SWIRL through the air around me, landing on my shoulders and in my hair. I close my eyes and raise my face to the sky, waiting for the emptiness to fill me. Instead, it feels like there is a fire raging inside my chest, eating its way outward. Inward.

Jacob's motionless body on a gurney.

His pale cheeks in the bluish light inside the ambulance.

Farther down the dark street, I see a set of headlights approaching from Staketgatan. I get up from the cycle rack and brush the snow from my pants as it swings into the curb in front of me and comes to an abrupt halt. The Golf looks so small in the ambulance's tire tracks. The paramedics had said that they needed to pump his stomach within the next fifteen minutes, and were gone before I even had time to process what was happening. If Jacob had been conscious, they could have just induced vomiting, but I must have gotten a little carried away when I crushed the pills and added them to his tea.

Mom gets out of the car. Her fair hair is gathered in a messy low bun. She is wearing a pair of thin polka-dot pajama bottoms and a thick down coat.

The minute I see her, I realize it was a mistake to call her. In just a few seconds, I've been dragged back to my teens. Mom picking me up from Folkparken after the end of term at school, drunk and giggly on a park bench, with a police officer by my side; Mom hurrying into the grocery store by the school after the cashier locked me in the storeroom with all the chocolate I'd stolen in my pockets. But before I have time to think about how I should behave now, seeing her for the first time in over a year, she has wrapped her arms around me.

"Sophie, are you hurt?"

Her hands cup my face, grip my upper arms. Searching for cuts and bruises.

"Why didn't you tell me you were here?" she asks, inhaling the scent of my hair, her hot breath making my scalp burn.

"I didn't think I'd have time to see you."

"Nonsense," she says, holding me at arm's length so that she can get a good look at me. "Do you hear that? Nonsense."

She smiles and shakes her head, as though I were twelve and had stayed out too late.

"Come on—let's go home. You can tell me what happened in the car."

Home.

I shudder as I get into the warm passenger seat. The radio is on at a low volume, an old Céline Dion track that gets under my skin and makes me break out in a sweat. Between the seats, I can see Mom's pink floral thermos cup, the one she lugs around between classes and seminars.

How long does it take to drive to the hospital?

What will happen to Jacob if they don't get there in time?

"So, this Jacob," Mom says, looking both ways before slowly pulling out toward Central Station, "is he another of your friends from school? I don't recognize the name."

"No." My answer comes out far too quickly. "He was . . . He and William met at university."

"Ah, so he was one of William's friends?"

"No!" From the corner of my eye, I see her flinch and turn to look at me. "He wasn't William's friend, he was . . ."

The tears hit me without warning, spilling down my cheeks and digging their claws into my chest. Mom's hand finds mine and squeezes it tight for the rest of the drive. With an arm around my shoulders, she leads me from the parking lot to the house, illuminated by fairy lights that have probably been hanging in the cherry tree since last winter. She goes in ahead of me, and I pause in the doorway. Beside her flat black boots, a pair of Dad's shoes are still on the rack.

"Aren't you coming in?" she asks with a laugh.

I nod and step inside onto the doormat.

"Careful you don't trip over the paint."

We squeeze between a mountain of paint cans and masking paper. Mom struggles out of her coat and hangs it up before making her way through to the kitchen. The whole house smells just like her: warm and spicy, with a hint of fresh paint. On one of the open shelves in the kitchen, I can see the large wineglasses she and Dad used to sip from as they sat in the hammock in the garden, and all I can think is that I want to get away.

"I would have done a bit of tidying if I'd known you were coming. Or at least bought something to eat. Would you like some tea?"

"No, thank you. I just want to go to bed. I have to check out of the hotel in the morning."

I start moving toward my old room, but I pause when I reach the doorway and see that there is nothing but a desk and a wall of built-in cupboards in there. Mom leans against the doorframe behind me.

"There's no way I'm letting you go to bed in this state. Cognac it is. That'll help settle your nerves."

"Have you been renovating?"

"I needed an office. I did try to bring it up with you a week or two ago."

Her texts.

"You can sleep on the sofa bed in the living room."

She turns away, and I slowly make my way through there, reluctantly stepping into everything I left behind.

"Grab one of the blankets from the sofa—you must be freezing," Mom shouts from the kitchen.

The blanket on the sofa looks like someone just threw it there, and there is a single cup and a plate with crumbs on it on the coffee table. The gray sideboard by the wall is cluttered with framed photographs from school graduations and confirmations and Mom and Dad's wedding photo. His black and white shots from his parents' farm in France are still hanging on one wall. There are traces of him everywhere, a version of him that will never be erased and that doesn't square with the one in my head. Standing with my back to the room, I wrap my arms around myself just as Mom reappears with a glass of cognac in each hand.

"You know what?" I say. "This was a bad idea; I shouldn't have woken you. I'll just go to sleep and call for a cab in the morning."

The amber liquid sloshes over the rim of the glass as she steps in front of me to block my way.

"Sit down," she says.

"I have to go to the police station too—I told them I would. They have the audio file of Jacob's confession, and they want to ask a few more questions about Tess. I should probably call for a cab now."

I move around her, trying to pass her on the other side, but her shoulder hits my arm with such force that I lose my balance.

"Sit down on the sofa, Sophie."

Her tone of voice makes me freeze, and I turn around to do as she says.

"Thank you," she hisses, pressing the glass into my hand.

She starts pacing around the room in her creased pajama bottoms, sipping her cognac whenever she isn't pulling on her hair or sighing loudly. Her fine-knit white sweater has slipped down from one shoulder, and I notice that the sleeves are too long.

"Why won't you let me be a part of your life?" she asks. "Why aren't I allowed to be there for you, to share it with you?"

My heart is now pounding harder than ever. Exactly which part of my life does she want to share? Not the one that has a room to come back to here, clearly. Nor the one that has been carrying lies and betrayal for the past ten years.

"Mom . . ."

"No, this stops right now, today. You've spent your entire life running away from your problems. I'll admit it was your father's fault the first time, when he decided the solution was to move up here," she says with a shrug. "But not the time after that, after William died."

She takes a deep breath and points at me, and I can see a number of angry red blotches on her pale throat.

"You left everything. Everything and *everyone*. Please, Sophie. Just tell me what I did wrong."

"It wasn't about you, Mom."

"So what was it about? Come on? Because I can't cope with this distance any longer. And I don't mean the five hundred miles you chose to put between us."

"Dad!"

She stops her pacing and stares at me. I take a couple of deep breaths and swig from my glass of cognac, which makes my throat burn.

"Dad and William."

Mom sits down beside me on the sofa, and I realize just how tired I am. Tired of running, of lying. Of hiding from the world.

Hiding from *life*.

Mom is right that it has to end today. I no longer need to run because after tonight there won't be anyone chasing me.

"Tell me."

"Dad cheated on you. He brought other women home. I caught him at it."

"When?"

"Junior high. I was thirteen or fourteen. He made me promise not to say anything, told me it would be my fault if you found out. I couldn't stand being anywhere near him, and I haven't been able to look you in the eye since."

I lean back against the cushions and drain the rest of my glass before daring to look up at her. Mom clutches her chest, tears glistening in her eyes.

"And this is the reason I didn't say anything," I add, burrowing my head deeper into the backrest and gesturing to the room around us.

Mom grips my wrist and takes the glass from my hand.

"I had my suspicions," she says quietly. "He wasn't very good at hiding it. I convinced myself it didn't mean anything, that what we had as a family was more important than a few silly missteps. But if I'd known he . . . that I would lose you because of it . . . I just wanted you to have a family that stayed together. He should never have put you in that position."

She pulls me toward her so that my head is in her lap and gently strokes my hair. With her free hand, she pulls the blanket over me, and I feel her shudder.

"And William?" she asks.

"William was everything to me, just like Dad was when I was little. So I was constantly expecting him to hurt me the way Dad had, finding fault in everything he did. I thought he would betray me the way Dad betrayed you, and when he didn't, I hurt him instead. And now he's gone."

"Sophie . . ." Her fingertips dig deeper into my scalp, and I close my eyes. "Who is Jacob?"

I squeeze my eyelids as tightly shut as I can and try to forget the sight of Jacob on the floor. Crawling away from me with a body that gave up. I need to call the hospital. I need to know where he was admitted and how he is doing. A soporific warmth spreads through me beneath the blanket, making my eyelids heavy. Mom squeezes my shoulder and strokes my cheek, but I can't help but glance over to the photograph of William and me from our graduation ball.

"Jacob was the only person I didn't betray, even if he didn't realize that himself."

CHAPTER

37

Now

I WAS SEVENTEEN WHEN Dad decided he'd had enough of my contempt and uprooted us right across the country. It turns out it's pretty impractical to have a daughter who knows all about your affairs with other women. It's also risky when that same daughter feels like she no longer has anything left to lose.

I suppose his plan was to give me something to live for.

Something to lose.

As a result, I suddenly found myself standing at the front of a class full of students in a school I barely knew the name of, introducing myself with a shaky voice and scarlet cheeks. The first person I noticed was the thin girl in the front row, the girl with the blond hair and the icy-blue eyes.

There was no missing her intense gaze or her perfect posture. Eyes that revealed layer upon layer of secrets and painful experiences she had refused to allow to break her. My first thought as I took my seat at the back of the room was that I wished I were like her.

Strong.

Confident.

So aware of my strengths that nothing else mattered.

* * *

I must have walked past the little café several times before I finally noticed the recessed door between the entrance to an apartment building and an archway to a courtyard. Two small display windows full of ratty old books, flowers, and cupcakes. Ava is sitting by the window onto the inner courtyard, with the sun on her face. She called me yesterday evening and asked me to meet her here. When I first came in, she was facing the window, her eyes hidden behind a pair of large dark sunglasses. They are now on the table by her coffee, and with her eyes closed, she lifts her face to the bright sunlight and wraps her hands around her hot cup. Her lower lip trembles slightly as she breathes in, purses her lips, and fixes her eyes on me.

"So, here we are," she says with a weary smile.

With her hair gathered in a simple bun and her face bare of makeup, it's obvious just how thin she has become. It's impossible to ignore just how delicate she is too. Everything that happened just a few days ago still feels like some sort of fever dream.

Ava barely touches the cardamom bun on the table in front of her, just breaks off a tiny piece from time to time and pops it into her mouth, chewing slowly as she gazes out through the window. Like a caged bird, longing for freedom on the other side of the glass.

"Yup, just us," I reply, wishing I had managed to find her sooner during my frantic searches online.

I suspect that would have been good for both of us.

"I have such a clear memory of how you looked the day you joined our class," Ava says suddenly. "Your dark hair was cut short, and you always wore ripped jeans and pale T-shirts that made you look tanned. I was so jealous of how tanned you got."

She chuckles to herself.

"I could tell right away that you had something special. There was something about you that caught my eye, a kind of depth when you listened. Like you really took in everything you heard. I couldn't stop thinking about you and found it so hard to tear myself away from you during class. Sadly, William got in there first."

My cheeks grow hot as I realize what she is saying, and I turn to look at the children playing outside without a care in the world.

"You don't have to let them treat you like this, you know."

Ava smiles at me, her chin resting in her palm.

"It was necessary. Their ultimatum. This life or one in a secure facility somewhere. Did you know that my parents blamed me for what happened to William?"

"You?"

"They said I'd put too much pressure on him, been too clingy. They made me think it was my fault that he died, that he couldn't cope any longer. All those late-night calls, all the times he stayed with me when I couldn't sleep. And I believed them. Then there was the pill too. He was really stressed that evening, so I gave him a pill. I thought that was why . . ."

"Ava . . ."

"If you're told you're crazy often enough, you start to believe it. Therapy helped. It made me open my eyes to what was going on outside our little love triangle. But they didn't believe me. They just saw it as proof of relapse, of my mental weakness; they called it delusions. I had to show them. To show myself. And you."

"So what happens now?"

"Mom has agreed to let me go away for the weekend. She's booked me into a spa in Dalarna—her reward for being such a good girl. Or maybe it's to show me that other people have been bad. Healthy food and all sorts of relaxing treatments."

"Sounds nice."

"It does, doesn't it. Mattias is ready to give me a ride down there once we're done here. Having him come along is one of the conditions, obviously. I can't be trusted, as you might understand."

She winks at me and then nods to the other end of the café, where a man with dark hair and sunglasses is sitting at a table by the wall. Mattias. I hadn't even noticed him, but he has clearly been keeping an eye on us.

"What's going to happen to you now?" asks Ava.

"As soon as the police are done with me, I'll head home. I'm staying with my mom until then. You could come and visit me in Malmö once I'm back. Stay a while. It'd be fun."

"Maybe."

"What will happen to Adrian? Or Charlotte?"

Ava shrugs. "I don't know. I doubt they'll be able to avoid an investigation. As far as Adrian is concerned, it doesn't look great—not with the video evidence. But they deserve it. You know that, don't you? I found your earring outside the door when I let the paramedics into William's apartment. Adrian and Jacob were the only ones who'd left. That was all I knew."

The memory of everything that has happened over the past few days washes over me, and I realize just how close I would have come to being a suspect in William's death if Ava hadn't stopped me from leaving the apartment ten years ago.

"You don't have anything to worry about, Sophie. It's obvious from the tapes that you did everything you could to help Tess."

"There was an article about Adrian in the paper today," I say. "Huge pictures of him leaving his apartment. They've been hounding him. I think he's going to lose his company."

"I'm sure he will. Have you spoken to Jacob yet?"

I've had several missed calls from an unknown number, which I assume must be Jacob, calling me from prison.

"I can't. Not yet." I might never be able to speak to him again.

Ava turns away, gazing out across the café with a glazed look in her eyes.

"I want to stay in touch once all this is over," I say, leaning forward so I can put my hand on hers. "I'll come and visit again. I can bring food from one of your favorite restaurants. I promise. And we can talk on the phone as soon as you get back. It can be just like . . ."

I trail off.

"Like before," Ava says with a grin.

She turns her hand over so that I can squeeze it, though after a moment she pulls it back and lowers it to her lap.

"You know what?" she says, getting to her feet. "I need to use the bathroom before we head off."

She drapes her coat over her arm and, with her back to me, reaches for something in her bag before hanging it over the same arm. She then puts on her huge sunglasses, covering half her face. At the far end of the room, Mattias stands up, but she raises her hand and gestures to the bathroom. He nods and sits down again.

"I never thought it was you, Sophie. I hope you know that. It was never your fault."

I nod mutely.

"I just wanted you to know that it wasn't me either. And I wanted you to have something you should have had a long time ago. Closure. Ciao for now," she says, blowing me a kiss before heading off toward the bathrooms.

I remain where I am, drinking the rest of my cold coffee. Ava didn't tuck her chair back beneath the table, and I notice there is something on the seat. Mattias is still sitting at the other end of the café, and he doesn't notice me get up to reach for whatever it is.

A folder. The kind real estate agents give out.

My heart starts racing as I open it and see a printout of an email conversation. A message from William to an agent in Sigtuna. The agent says that they can arrange to meet and sign the contract as soon as William has solved the problem with his deposit.

I lift the flyer out of the folder and stare down at the color image of a gray villa in bright sunshine. The garden has a simple white fence, and there is a large terrace with an awning. On the other side, there are images from inside: three bedrooms and a large kitchen with an island. Everything I've ever dreamed of in a house.

What *we* dreamed of.

I close the folder and touch the little handwritten note paper-clipped to the front. The minute I recognize the handwriting, I clap a hand to my mouth and try to blink back the tears.

> *Sophie! Keep hold of the ring for now. Everything will be okay, I promise. You'll see. William.*

My fingers trace the ink on the paper, the last thing he ever wrote. William never gave up. Even on the darkest day of our lives together, he had bright hopes for the future. It's painful to hold the life that never materialized in my hands, but I also feel a rush of warmth at the thought that I hadn't managed to pull away from him, no matter how hard I'd tried.

At the table by the far wall, Mattias is on his feet, his eyes darting nervously from me to the other end of the café before he sets off after Ava. She has been in there for a while now. His anxiety rubs off on me, and I get up from my chair. After just a few minutes, he reappears with his phone to his ear.

"She's gone," I hear him say to whoever is on the other end of the line, grabbing his jacket and hurrying outside.

I stare in the direction of the bathroom and see an older woman come out. Then I step sideways and look out into the courtyard, where the snow-covered furniture is all untouched. The door is ajar, and a small trail of snow has blown inside.

She's gone.

I grab my coat, wrap my scarf around my neck and pause when I notice something beneath Ava's chair. Something small that must have been hidden beneath the folder and fallen to the floor when I grabbed it. I crouch down and pick up the postcard. The image on the front is of a village at the foot of a lush green mountain, clear blue water glittering in the sunlight. On the back, my first name has been written in the address box, nothing else. And in the space for a message, there are two short lines in Ava's sweeping handwriting.

Ciao, bella! Until we meet again.

I'm powerless to hold back the laugh that makes the other cafegoers turn and stare. I push the postcard into my pocket and then walk through the murmur to the front door, out into the biting cold. When I reach the sidewalk, I pause and look in both directions. I raise my face to the sun, which makes my eyes sting, then lower my head and peer over toward the archway into the courtyard, where a set of footsteps leads out to the edge of the curb and disappears. I turn right and smile at the people I pass as I walk down the street, though at the same time I can feel the lump in my stomach growing bigger and bigger.

For some reason, I'm sure that was the last time I'll ever speak to Ava.

ACKNOWLEDGMENTS

Thanks

I'D LIKE TO start by giving a huge thank you to Piratförlaget, for putting your faith in me, and to my publisher, Anna Hirvi Sigurdsson, for believing in me and my story. It has been so much fun to see this book take shape in working with you. Thank you to my incredible editor, Emma Karhunen, for polishing my linguistic mistakes and making me think about what I *really* mean. A special thank you to my agent Josephine Oxelheim at Salomonsson Agency and everyone at Crooked Lane Books for making my dreams come true and allowing my story to reach the English-speaking world.

Writing a book is a long process, and it requires a lot of help along the way to get the pieces to fall into place. Thank you to Katarina Persson and Ellen van Lokhorst for always being there, for reading early drafts and giving me invaluable feedback. Thank you to Johanna Wistedt too, for reading one of the later versions and sharing such insightful thoughts.

I'm so lucky to have had a number of experts to turn to for guidance in the areas where I lack knowledge. Thank you to Pia Manderhjelm for answering all my medical questions, Charlotte Andersson for your help in understanding how police investigations work, and to Martina Thun for explaining what happens in a radio studio. Special thanks also go to Karin Stjärnborg for taking me on a tour of my old hometown, Gävle, to rediscover the areas depicted in the book.

Last but not least: a huge thank you to my family, friends, and colleagues for your untiring support and encouragement during the writing process. You know who you are. It's thanks to you that I have the energy to keep going when things get tough.